Grave Consequences

by

DEBRA DUPREE WILLIAMS

FIREFLY
SOUTHERN FICTION
LIGHTHOUSE PUBLISHING OF THE CAROLINAS

GRAVE CONSEQUENCES BY DEBRA DUPREE WILLIAMS
Firefly Southern Fiction is an imprint of LPCBooks
a division of Iron Stream Media
100 Missionary Ridge, Birmingham, AL 35242

ISBN: 978-1-64526-267-1
Copyright © 2020 by Debra DuPree Williams
Cover design by Elaina Lee
Interior design by Karthick Srinivasan

Available in print from your local bookstore, online, or from the publisher at:
ShopLPC.com

For more information on this book and the author visit: debradupreewilliams.
blogspot.com/

Brought to you by the creative team at LPCBooks: Eva Marie Everson, Jennifer
Leo, Brenda Kay Coulter. Author's photograph by Hannah Robles Rossiter/Robles
Reflections

Library of Congress Cataloging-in-Publication Data
Williams, Debra DuPree
Grave Consequences / Debra DuPree Williams 1st ed.

Printed in the United States of America

PRAISE FOR *GRAVE CONSEQUENCES*

Set in the 1960s, *Grave Consequences* is pure Southern with all its culture, crazy relatives, and foibles. And it's all wrapped up in a delightful mystery. Debut author Debra DuPree Williams writes with a Southern storyteller's voice that drew me into the story and captivated me until the final page. I highly recommend it.

~**Ane Mulligan**
Bestselling author of
The *Chapel Springs* series

Debra DuPree Williams writes with charm, humor, and passion. Her characters are well drawn and sweep you right under their southern spell. *Grave Consequences* is a delightful read that will make you want to curl up on a front porch and flip the pages until you reach "The End." This one needs to go on your keeper shelf.

~**Lynette Eason**
Best-selling, award-winning author
The Blue Justice Series

Debra DuPree Williams blends the right ingredients of southern charm, cozy mystery, and humor to keep the reader turning pages.

~**DiAnn Mills**
Bestselling author
Airborne

Grave Consequences by Debra DuPree Williams delivers colorful characters from the South. Packed full of unexpected discoveries, genealogy, and relationships that weren't what they seemed, you'll want to trek along with Charlotte Graves as she tracks down a murderer and uncovers long-hidden mysteries in her town. You'll enjoy this fresh new voice in fiction.

~**Michelle Cox**
Bestselling author of the *When God Calls the Heart*
and *Just 18 Summers*

Debut author Debra DuPree Williams knocks it out of the park with her southern mystery, *Grave Consequences*. The story, set in the 60s, immediately pulled me in and the characters were so well written I forgot I was reading a book. This is definitely an author I put on my TBR list. I can't wait for her next book!

~**Edie Melson**
Author and Director of the
Blue Ridge Mountains Christian Writers Conference

The southern sleuth, Charlotte Graves (bless her heart) got my attention from the very first sentence. By the end of the first scene, she had me totally hooked. Every instinct told me this would be a terrifically entertaining, fast-moving, delightful, intriguing story and I was not disappointed at any point, especially with all those twists and turns. Debra DuPree Williams has a winner with *Grave Consequences*, and although I'm still savoring the memory of this one, I'm already anticipating Charlotte's next adventure.

~**Yvonne Lehman**
Editor, *Divine Moments* series
Author of 59 novels including
Hearts that Survive—A Novel of the Titanic

Author Debra DuPree Williams has delivered a story with all the feels! The excitement, intrigue, sass and sweetness in *Grave Consequences* had me turning page after page until I finished! If I hadn't known better, I would've thought I was watching a movie. Her descriptions invited me right into the scene.

~ **Tammy Karasek**
Writer, President of the Word Weavers Upstate SC Chapter

DEDICATION

To the One who placed a song within my heart and Who gave
me a voice with which to sing Your praises, thank you for the gift of
a second voice. May my words always bring honor and praise to Your
holy name. Soli Deo Gloria.

ACKNOWLEDGMENTS

Writing and publishing a book isn't a solitary undertaking. It takes many people to make that happen. I was blessed to have a lot of praying people alongside me. Heartfelt thanks go to the following people:

Sally Apokedak and Michelle Medlock Adams who, at my first conference, said unforgettable words—*you are a writer*. For your words of encouragement and the opportunities you've extended to me, I'm forever grateful.

Eddie Jones and the team at Firefly Southern Fiction/Iron Stream Media: thank you for taking a chance on me. Being a part of ISM is like coming home.

Yvonne Lehman: I thought you were kidding when you invited me to join Blue Ridge Writers. I'm so thankful you were serious as there is nothing like learning from the best. To you and all our group, my deepest thanks. I love you.

Eva Marie Everson, my editor, writing coach, mentor, and my friend: from the bottom of my heart, thank you for believing in me. Thank you for showing me what my work could be. This book wouldn't exist if not for you. I love you, dearly. And to Jessica Everson, thank you for being there alongside your mama. Y'all are a dynamic duo.

Edie Melson, social media coach extraordinaire, marketing guru, teacher, mentor, friend: you have blessed me in ways that go beyond the writing realm. We've proven grandmas can learn new tricks. You know I love you.

Word Weavers, Page 11 and Upstate SC: without you and your input, this book wouldn't be what it has become. You saw things I missed and offered ideas with love and grace that made it so much better. I love and appreciate each of you.

My ancestors whose stories were told and lived out long before I was here: as your blood flows through my veins and your stories take shape within my heart, may my words always bring honor to you.

My cousin, author Karen Lynn Nolan: my heartfelt thanks for holding my hand throughout this process. For answering my many questions and for the sound advice, I'm forever grateful. I appreciate that you kept my head *Above the Fog*.

My sister Bobbie Foshee: thank you for reading my first drafts, for listening as I pondered plot when creating Charlotte and her friends. Your words of encouragement and your prayers sustained me. I love you, Sissy.

Our boys and girls: Ken and his family, Cecili, Piper, and Emerson; our other three boys Christopher, Adam, and Daniel, you have no idea how much it warms my heart to hear you say how proud you are of your mama or your DD. Let my writing journey be a lesson to you: it's never too late to pursue your dreams. If you want it badly enough, you can make it happen. I love all of you.

My husband, Jim: the first word would never have been written without your support. All the trips between Tampa and Asheville for all those conferences were worth it now, huh? Nothing like having my own personal road warrior. Thank you for so willingly driving Miss Debbie. Thank you for being there every step of this journey. You're my rock. I love you.

Finally, the Master Storyteller: You knew, long before I, that one day I would *need* a second voice. Thank you for this unexpected gift. My thanks are immeasurable. There are no words.

Chapter One

I only had one thing to say: if looks could kill, Boopsie Sweets would have been well on her way to the Promised Land. But I reckon it's a good thing looks can't kill, because my looks aimed at Boopsie would've had her bags packed and the Pearly Gates flung wide open.

I stood before the group assembled in the library's research area, the last five minutes seeming like an eternity. Since this was my first gig as the newly appointed director of the local historical and genealogical society, I wasn't all that comfortable to begin with. Dread filled my heart like a thousand horses pounding the Sahara. My dry mouth longed for any sign of an oasis. I picked up the glass at my right and took a sip of water, swallowing with a gulp so big, it echoed. I sat the glass down with shaking hands, then looked up.

Familiar people sat, hands hovering above every kind of writing pad imaginable, from the old Indian-head grammar school pads to three-ring notebooks filled with loose-leaf paper. Relief flooded as I sensed that they *seemed* eager to hear what I had to say.

Grayheads, redheads, precision-cut heads, bald heads, and even one person with her hair pulled back by a hippie head scarf, gathered around the table. English Leather mingled with Ambush, which blended with Chanel No. 5 and Old Spice. But what was that odd one . . .was that *peanut butter*?

Perspiration tickled my hairline and upper lip and my right hand shook as I lifted the wooden gavel. "I hereby call to order the first meeting of the Woodville Historical and Genealogical Society." I brought the gavel down with a bang, then grimaced. I've always hated those things . . . so archaic.

I took a deep breath, relieved to see Mama and Cousin Fiona in attendance, primed to witness this momentous event. And, of course, Aunt Becky. No way would she miss a chance to lend her support. She knew what Mama and Fee knew—this is what I was born to do. Genealogy pulsed in my blood; no pun intended.

My gaze settled on Fiona—Fee, to family and friends. She's—well, she's everything I wish I could be. She's tall and gorgeous and has fashion sense like no one I know. And let's not forget her amazing red curls, all thanks to her Scottish father. I, on the other hand, *barely reach the floor* as my recently departed Papa liked to say. Insert heavy sigh here. And, I'm a bit on the pleasingly plump side—also one of Papa's sayings. Or at least, I was until I began running around cemeteries. But that's a story for another day.

This old library was one of my favorite places in all of Loblolly. The unmistakable smell of old books, its worn-oak floors which creaked each time I shifted my weight, the old-fashioned oak catalog file cabinets, and even the old clock on the back wall, spoke to me. Together they seemed to say that I had finally returned home.

It seemed odd to think of Loblolly as home. I left eight years ago, right after graduation, at the tender age of eighteen. Glad as I was to leave, since that ill-fated day I'd felt a tug at my heart to come back. I'd had a lot of work to do on me before I could even think about that. Old hurts and abrasive words hadn't been easy to let go. Yet, there I stood, ready to face demons from my past and prove to everyone that I wasn't the ditzy, head-in-the-clouds girl they all remembered. The one who leaped and worried about looking later. Much later.

Like … eight years later.

I subconsciously grasped the blue-and-white-enameled Huguenot cross which dangled from a silver chain around my neck, seeking the solace it always rendered. With my left hand, I smoothed the nonexistent wrinkles from my summer dress. Confession—I hate wearing dresses. Always have. I'm a jeans-and-tees kind of girl. Comfort all the way. Plus, in my capacity as the genealogist for Woodville County, I was in and out of the dusty stacks and file rooms of old courthouses and libraries on a regular basis. And that's just a part of what I did. Those cemeteries were where I really get down and dirty. Dresses just didn't work.

But tonight, I needed to impress my boss, so I grabbed the first decent-looking thing I found hanging in my closet.

I shifted my weight from one foot to the other and the floor responded with its familiar creak. No sooner had I opened my mouth to begin the evening's agenda when Boopsie Sweets blurted out, "I believe we all know Charlotte isn't qualified to lead this group."

The collective gasp could be heard clear into the next county. And then, Boopsie's words were followed by those deadly looks . . . and every one of them aimed at Boopsie. The people of Loblolly had waited a long time for such a group. Now, *this*?

I froze.

"What's the matter, Char-*lotte*? Cat got your tongue?" Boopsie sat with her arms crossed about her ample bosom as she leaned back in her chair. Her right leg, crossed over her left, wiggled like a worm in the sun. "I know y'all heard me, but in case some of you forgot your hearing aids . . ." She stopped and rolled her heavily made-up eyes. "Let me repeat myself ... Let me repeat myself. Charlotte Graves has no business being the director of the WHS or anything remotely related to genealogy when she doesn't even know her *own* ancestors." Boopsie looked around the room, staring at each person, one by one, like one of those bobblehead dolls, seeming to dare them to disagree.

No. No. Not here. Not now. I swayed slightly. How on earth could this be happening? *Just stop her, somebody.* Blood rushed from my head so fast, I grabbed the edge of the table to keep myself upright and dared myself to be sick.

Boopsie continued talking, but her voice sounded as if she were speaking through a broken speaker at the drive-in while the clock on the back wall ticked away the seconds.

Tick.

Tock.

Tick.

Tock.

Anger crawled up my body from the bottoms of my feet all the way up to my face which flushed with heat. My head was on the verge of exploding. But I refused to buckle. Not to Boopsie. Why would this woman choose tonight to bring up these accusations—an old taunt she'd baited me with since grade school. Surely after so many years we'd matured enough to put our past differences behind us. Did she still hate me that much? Had *she* wanted this job? And if so, why hadn't *she* applied for it?

I paused long enough to get ahold of my temper and my wayward mouth. A miracle, believe me.

Olivia Woodville Lawrence, town society maven and more-or-less my boss, pushed back her chair with a scrape against the wooden floor. She stood and leaned across the table, slapping her hands palms down and looking straight into the troublemaker's smug face. "Boopsie Sweets, that will be quite enough out of you for one evening, little missy. We all heard your outlandish statement and have chosen to ignore you . . . as usual." Olivia returned to her seat and smoothed her already perfectly coiffed platinum hair. "Now, Charlotte, I believe you were about to tell us about our fine little town's founding citizens."

"She shore was." George Wilkins banged his age-spot-laden, boney fist on his thigh. "And high time somebody put smart-mouthed Boopsie in her place. I'm surprised somebody ain't shut her up afore now." He turned to peruse the other members of the group who nodded in agreement.

I picked up a book from the nearby table, the piece of paper holding my place shaking audibly. My voice cracked as I tried to speak. I cleared my throat, swallowed hard, and began again. I could do this.

"A-as I was about to say, local historian of the nineteenth century, Hiram Moore, did a great deal of research on the people who first settled our area. Parker Woodville Lanier and his wife, Caroline Simmons, were two of the earliest people to move here, a few years before Alabama became a state. They, um . . ." I looked down at the book, then back up. "They were the ancestors of our own Olivia." I smiled at Olivia who nodded, bolstering my confidence. If I could keep my mind from wandering to that outlandish outburst and direct my attention to the subject at hand, I would be fine.

"That's right," Olivia said as I took another sip of water. "Parker and Caroline were my four-times-great-grandparents." Olivia commanded respect, and when she spoke, people listened. "The county was named for them."

I continued my lecture about the Woodville family without further interruptions from Boopsie, who sat through the rest of the meeting in silence. That smug look, however, remained plastered in place.

At the conclusion of the meeting Olivia approached me. "Don't worry about that foolish girl. Her meddlesome mouth will catch up with her one day, no doubt." She pulled her stole around her shoulders, adjusting it slightly, revealing the owl pin she was never without.

I glanced over my shoulder at Boopsie. "Seems like she's all talk. Been messing with me all my life. Old habits are hard to break, I guess."

"Forget about Boopsie. You did a great job tonight. I'm looking forward to hearing many more lectures from you regarding the ancestors of our good citizens. This society is one of the best things that's happened in our town in a while." She waved to her husband, Max, who stood at the back of the room and smiled.

I smiled, too. I couldn't help but think how handsome he looked. Tall and dark with just a hint of gray at his temples, and always impeccably dressed. He and Olivia made a great pair. At least, on the surface. I didn't really know them as a couple all that well.

"Have to run," Olivia said with a light sigh. So light I almost missed it. "Max is obviously ready to go. As usual, he'll probably want to go back to the bank and put in some late hours after he drops me at home." She nodded to the group and left, her heels clicking on the wooden floors.

As I gathered my things and prepared to leave, a few people, including Mama, grouped around me and walked me to my car.

"I should have said something, baby," Mama said. "I'm sorry I didn't, but if I had, it wouldn't have been ladylike in the slightest. Best I kept my mouth closed, for once." She placed her hand on my arm. "Gotta get home and let the dogs out. Be careful driving home. See you soon." A peck on my cheek sealed her apology. She opened the door of her '64 Galaxy sedan station wagon, climbed inside, and drove away with a little beep of her horn.

I waved to Mama. I couldn't help but smile at her use of nonexistent dogs as a means of escaping unwanted conversations. Maybe it was time for Mama to get a real dog.

"Yeah, do be careful driving home." Serena, a woman I'd known since high school, and the one who wore the hippie scarf, whispered in my ear, "Come by The Copper Pot sometime soon and I'll have a nice hot cup of coffee for you. Maybe even something to eat." She gave me a quick hug. Bracelets jangled on both wrists as she tucked her new shag-cut hair behind multi-pierced ears—a true flower child if I'd ever known one.

As I inserted the key into the door of my '61 Chevy Impala— once pristine and the most edible shade of red but now sad and faded and beaten up—Boopsie grabbed my arm. "Won't do you any good to hide behind those folks." She waved in the direction of the retreating crowd. "You need to know, someone in that room tonight is your *real* grandmother. You just ask your mama. I can't believe you haven't figured that out by now, since you're such a smarty-pants gen-e-al-o-gist and all." Before I could open my mouth to protest, Boopsie turned, nose in the air, and swished to her brand-new T-Bird. "Don't you just love how the color brings out the glimmer in my delightful blue eyes?" she called over her shoulder.

I tried. Believe me, I *tried* to hold my tongue, but the words just wouldn't stay inside. I actually *yelled* at Boopsie's retreating back. "If you know something about my family you think I need to know, then you'd best be telling me or shut your mouth before somebody shuts it for you."

Members of the group turned toward us, their heads shaking.

Yes. Ditzy Charlotte was back in town. Leaping first. Looking later.

Being back in Loblolly was already a problem and I'd only been here for six months. How would I ever learn to deal with the woman who'd tortured me since grade school?

I climbed into my car and drove out of the parking lot. As I drove, the scene from that awful day on the playground played over and over. Fourth grade seemed long ago, but some things carried a lifetime.

I tried to shake the buried memory, but Boopsie's voice echoed through my mind. "*I heard my mama say so. Go ask your mama. She'll tell you.*" Her words put me on the proverbial edge of the Grand Canyon, about to tumble over. Boopsie hadn't changed one little bit. She was still as mean as ever.

I glanced at the clock on the dash. Just a bit after nine. I couldn't shake the barb thrown at me during the meeting. I reached for the radio controls and tuned to the local station. Right now, I needed a distraction and music has always been a source of peace. Mainly, I enjoy singing along with the current artists and groups and I don't care who sees me belting one out while driving. But tonight, I couldn't concentrate hard enough to follow the lyrics. My mind kept revisiting the meeting. What if Boopsie had told the truth? But . . . how could she know things about my family that I didn't know? How could Mrs. Sweets have known? And not Mama? Wouldn't Mama have said something if she knew? And who on earth sitting in that room could Boopsie be talking about?

I thought back to when I attended Loblolly's one and only high school. Mama helped me as I worked on our family tree for a history class. By the end of the project, I felt confident that we had all the right people in the correct trees. Everything was documented to the best of my abilities. Our teacher had emphasized the importance of having proof. Could I have missed something? Sure, that can happen, but something as big as Nana not being my grandmother? That didn't seem likely. Especially with Mama having never heard this little rumor.

Still . . . when it came to genealogy, anything was possible.

That was one of the many times I've wished Papa were still here. He always gave such good advice. Even though six months had faded away, my heart was still raw from his passing. Mama and I would never be the same.

"I miss you so much," I whispered into the empty car as a tear rolled down my cheek. I brushed it away with my fingertips, rough from years of literally digging through cemetery dirt as I pieced together family trees for relatives, friends, or clients. "If you were here, you'd know exactly what to do, where to go for answers, and mostly . . . what to say."

I sniffled as I drove around Loblolly's town square. My hometown was a peaceful, welcoming place which boasted a central park lined with ancient oaks laden with Spanish moss—like those in many southern towns, but not quite as heavily adorned as some. In its center stood a gurgling fountain. Soft light from old-fashioned streetlamps illuminated downtown. Year round, couples, young and old, strolled along the winding brick paths, hands clasped, reminding me of Savannah, Georgia . . . and Linden, who had been my fiancé once upon a time. But I couldn't think about that tonight—shouldn't be thinking about him at all, now that the scoundrel was a married man. At that moment, I had too many other things on my mind.

I drove past my old high school where Roan Steele had been the first to break my heart—years before Linden had done the same. I wondered why all these hurts and memories, and at the same time. I couldn't help but question if coming back home had been a mistake.

Papa's music store, Allegro, loomed ahead and reminded me of the task that awaited me inside. It would get my mind off things. I'd get some work done, too. The sooner the inventory was completed, the sooner Mama could put the business on the market. No way could she run it alone. She was a homemaker, not a businesswoman. And even though I'd worked alongside Papa when I was in my teens, I simply had no desire to run the music store. It was time to move on and find a new owner.

I drove the familiar way to the downtown store, passing Dairy Queen, where the gang I'd once run with gathered on Friday nights. The lot was full, even on a weeknight. I parked out front then walked up to the window. A chili dog sounded delicious, but I settled on a Coke. That would hold me while I worked.

It occurred to me that I should let Mama in on my plans. It was now just a tick past ten o'clock and I figured that, in spite of the hour, I could work a while and get out of the store before midnight. Once I got to the store, I phoned Mama to let her know my whereabouts. Even though I was almost thirty, she still worried.

Sometime later, my body begged for relief. I stretched, arching my back and reaching my hands toward the ceiling. Shoving boxes around wasn't fun, especially in a dress. After a few deep-breathing exercises, I climbed down the rickety stairs. At the bottom, I glanced at my watch.

Almost midnight.

I was intent on getting home, but the anger I felt earlier returned and refused to let go. Or . . . at this point, maybe it was more my curiosity. Either way, minutes after I left the music store, I found myself pulling up in front of Boopsie's home. I parked my old Chevy behind the shiny T-bird, a metaphorical reminder of the differences between me and my old nemesis. A distant streetlamp offered the only light illuminating the front entry. No visible lights on inside. Then again, it *was* after midnight.

Knocking at this hour was not an option, so I decided to leave a note in the door. First thing tomorrow, Boopsie would see it.

I rummaged through my pocketbook, then pulled out a notepad and scribbled: *We need to talk. Call me tomorrow. 5-6295. C.*

I made my way up the walkway but stopped at the bottom of the brick steps long enough to take in Boopsie's décor. Large urns sat at the bottom of the steps. A plant I didn't recognize boasted blossoms that cascaded over the rim. A statue of an angel stood off to the right in an area of manicured bushes. Really? An angel? That hardly seemed like Boopsie. In fact, nothing about the quaint little bungalow seemed like Boopsie to me. I climbed the steps and made my way across the porch to the door. I opened the screened door with the intent of wedging the note there but stopped when I saw that the front door was cracked open.

"Oh," I said, because nothing about this looked right. Or felt right. Boopsie wouldn't leave her door open . . . not even in Loblolly.

"Boopsie?" I pushed the door with the toe of my sensible black flats and peeked in. "Boopsie, are you here?"

Not a single light burned in the house—at least not as far as could be seen—which made it difficult to get around. Not that I should even be in Boopsie's home in the first place. Especially uninvited. And particularly in the dark. I called again, "*Boopsie?*"

I'd never been in Boopsie's house before and certainly had no clue as to the layout. And apparently, she liked her privacy, because every curtain in the place was pulled shut. Not one speck of light cascaded from the outside. *Pickled bricks.* I stumbled once, then managed to make it through the small living area, feeling my way, step by timid step.

"Boopsie?" I called out again, this time my voice stronger.

I stopped. Sniffed. The smell of popcorn led me toward a room in the back, presumably the kitchen. Light from a neighbor's rear porch eased through an unadorned window. Silhouettes of appliances, countertops, and cabinets came into view. "Boopsie, it's Charlotte," I called into the eerie stillness. "I just want to talk."

I didn't like this—not one iota. Every hair on my head stood on end as I settled my pocketbook strap on my shoulder and squeezed the note . . . still in my hand.

My heart pounded in my ears. "Boopsie, are you home?"

I paused at the door, allowing my eyes to adjust to the darkness, took a deep breath, then felt along the wall to my left and then the one to my right until I found a light switch.

I flipped it up.

And screamed.

Chapter Two

There wasn't time to stop and think. I dropped the pocketbook and the scribbled note where I stood, then scrambled over to Boopsie's body sprawled on the kitchen floor. A pool of blood gathered around her. An iron skillet was overturned nearby. Hands shaking like crazy, I placed two fingers on Boopsie's throat, feeling for a pulse. Thank God, I'd taken lifesaving in college.

I looked up, hoping to see a kitchen phone, but at the same time, two deputies burst into the kitchen from a back door I hadn't noticed before.

"Put your hands where I can see them."

I'd recognize that voice anywhere. After all these months of avoiding Roan Steele, here he was. Could this night get any worse?

"Help me. She's bleeding," I called over my shoulder. It hardly registered with me that he was talking to *me*. That he had his gun pointed directly at *me*.

"Put your hands up and stand. Slowly."

"It's me, Roan. Charlotte. You have to help me. Call an ambulance."

"*You* need to do what I said. Put your hands where I can see them."

Reluctantly, I did as I was told and backed away from the body. Roan motioned for his partner to check on Boopsie. She bent, checked for a pulse then looked up at Roan and shook her head.

"Charlotte Graves, you're under arrest for suspicion of the murder of Boopsie Sweets," Roan said.

What? Roan thought I'd done *this*? There was some kind of mistake for sure. "Wait. I didn't do this. I found her like this." I took a step toward Roan, who pulled my arms behind me. *Oh, pickled bricks*. I was going to be sick.

"Take her out to the car and stay with her while I call the sheriff.

He'll want to be here for this one," Roan told his partner.

The deputy grabbed my arms, now cuffed behind me, and pulled me toward the front door. "Come on."

"You *know* I didn't do this," I called as I was being forced from the room, followed by, "My purse. . . the *note!*"

***

The sheriff's department wasn't any place I thought I'd ever be. The only time I'd been there was when I was about seven and Papa had taken me to deliver toys for the needy at Christmas. This was hardly Christmas.

The deputy—Travis, her nametag read—took me to an interior room. Even though they hadn't thrown me into a jail cell, I still wore the handcuffs. Travis told me to sit in a metal chair beside a wooden table, worn smooth from years of use. As I slid into the chair, I glanced around. The room bore no windows to the outside. Hard concrete walls were painted in that awful shade of institutional green required for such places. Otherwise, why would any *sane* person choose such a disgusting color?

I sat and waited and thought. So, this was how I was to meet Roan after all those years? As if he hadn't already thought me a coward, now he thought I was a murderer? I'd been right to avoid him. No good could possibly come from seeing him or talking to him ever again. Some things and some relationships were best left in the past.

After what seemed an eternity, Roan and the sheriff walked in. Roan placed a cup of coffee in front of me. "Here, you may need this."

I looked at the cup then glared at Roan. "How am I supposed to drink this? Did you bring a straw?" I twisted and showed him my handcuffs. "Too bad the years haven't taught you common sense."

Roan set his jaw. The veins in his temples pulsed.

Good. He needed to feel guilty. "What am I doing here? You need to let me go. Mama's going to be worried out of her mind."

The sheriff spoke first. "My deputy tells me he read you your rights. Did you understand them?"

"What? What rights? What are you talking about?" I couldn't believe what I'd heard. Had I been . . . oh, what was the word? *Mirandaed.* Wasn't that it? That law was so new, how on earth had it made its way to Loblolly? But I, Charlotte Isabelle Graves— *Mirandized.* Yeah, that was right. Had I been? Maybe, though I barely recalled it. How was I supposed to remember anything when getting help for Boopsie was all that mattered?

"You can uncuff her now, Officer Steele. She won't be going anywhere." The sheriff sat in one of the chairs across from me as Roan unlocked the cuffs. To be honest, they didn't really hurt, but it seemed natural to rub where the foreign objects had touched my body. I stared at my wrists and hoped they cleaned those things between uses.

"I'll ask you again, Miss Graves. Do you understand your rights?" the sheriff said.

I had known Sheriff Theodore "Tank" Turner all my life. He'd never called me anything other than *Charlie.* Man. I figured I must really be in trouble if even Tank thought I was capable of murder.

"Maybe. Yes? I guess? I don't know, but any way you look at it, you *know* I didn't do this. Roan." I looked at him and held my hands out to him. "You know me better than . . . than anyone in this room and you know, you *know* I did *not* do this. I . . . I put spiders outside— even though I'm deathly afraid of them—rather than kill them, for Pete's sake." I waved my hands and slid to the edge of the metal chair. I leaned toward Roan, my eyes pleading my innocence. How many times had he gotten lost in my eyes? Now? Phooey. I'd been right to leave. Look at how he'd turned out.

Roan looked at the sheriff, who nodded. "Look, it isn't that simple. We have to follow procedure here, no matter who we bring in. It'll go easier if you cooperate and answer our questions. Do you think you can do that?" He leaned on the table, gripping its edge, his face too close to mine.

I so wanted to slap him. If I'd had the nerve, I would have. All those times in the past eight years I'd thought about him. Where he was, what he was doing. Did he ever think about me? Huh. Not likely.

What a waste ... "So, I'm under arrest then? For murder?" I furrowed my brow. "For *suspicion* of murder? Or as a witness? Which one? I have a right to know." I locked gazes with my old beau. And those looks that could kill? I imagined one or two of those about then.

"You were found over the body of an apparent murder victim," the sheriff answered in his thickly accented voice.

A body. So that was it. Well, I didn't have many rights, but I remembered one for sure. "I'd like to have Uncle Angus here, please. Once he's here, then I'll talk to you if he advises me to do so." I sat back, picked up the coffee, sighed, then placed the cup back on the table as I straightened. "Oh, and Mama, too. She has to be out of her mind with worry. I'm never out this late." And I'd told her I'd be home hours ago.

Roan Steele, indeed.

***

After going through the humiliation of being booked and fingerprinted, the deputy led me to a cell in the back of the department. As if having the tell-tale signs of that black ink on my fingers wasn't bad enough, the cell had two cots, both with stained, bare mattresses. A light, haphazardly folded blanket had been left at the foot of each. *Really?* The county couldn't afford a simple bedsheet? The place was even worse than I'd imagined. At least there was no toilet out in the open. That would be more than I could take.

The cell reeked, and I fought being sick. Every time I closed my eyes, I saw Boopsie lying there, surrounded by her own blood. As much as I never cared for the woman, I didn't want her dead.

Scrunched in the corner of one of the small cots, I pulled my dress over my knees, then reached for the blanket, unfolded and gathered it around me. *Please be clean. Please be clean. Please be clean.* I started to lean my head against the wall then thought better of it. I closed my eyes and let the tears fall as I thought of Boopsie and those who loved her.

***

"Hey." A voice startled me. "You awake?"

I stirred. Roan. When had I drifted off? "What time is it?" I ran a thick tongue over parched lips. I needed my lip gloss in the worst way. "Can I go home?"

"It's three in the morning. I just came to tell you your uncle is here."

I ran my fingers through my hair. My dress was a wrinkled mess. If Mama was with him, she'd be scared to death if I walked in looking as bad as I felt. As much as I hated having to talk to Roan, well . . . I had no choice.

"May I use the ladies' room before I see him? I need to wash my face." I got up and stood by the cell door. "And I don't suppose you have a clean toothbrush?"

"Sorry. We don't supply a lot of comforts." Roan called in Deputy Travis to accompany me, then unlocked the door. "My partner will take you. I'll be here when you get back."

True to his word, he still stood leaning against the bars when I returned. Why did he have to look so good? The uniform suited him. Fit him . . . nicely. The man definitely had Indian in his ancestry ...

"No, not in there. I'm taking you to Mr. Campbell." He took about twenty paces then turned to face me. "You're right, you know," he said, and I stopped. "I know you didn't do this. We just have to follow procedure."

A half-smile was the best I could do. "Sure." Just get to Uncle Angus, then I won't have to talk to Roan anymore. One foot in front of the other.

"You do know we have to talk, don't you?" Roan asked when we reached the door at the end of a narrow hallway. He reached for the doorknob, kept his grip around it, but didn't open the door.

"What's to say? The past is the past, and now Boopsie's dead. Let's just move on." I braved looking him in the eye.

"Later then." Roan opened the door and motioned for me to enter.

Uncle Angus rose from the same metal chair I'd occupied earlier. He came around the table and gathered me in one of his bear hugs.

Then the questions began.

This was going to be a long day.

Chapter Three

After what I'd seen at Boopsie's, I figured the iron skillet had been the weapon. Confident the evidence would fail to show my prints on anything except that light switch and the wall around it, I wasn't too worried. That and the note I'd dropped had to be enough to convince them that there was reasonable doubt.

Once Uncle Angus had his say, the sheriff released me. Mama, Fee, and Aunt Becky waited for us as Uncle Angus and I were ushered into the main room of the jailhouse by the sheriff.

Mama put her arms around me, pulling me close. "Baby, let's go home." I wasn't used to this after so many years on my own, but I had to admit, it felt good. We took a step toward the exit.

"Don't forget," the sheriff said, "you can't leave town. This is still an open investigation, and you're not out of the woods."

Mama moved quickly. "Right now, she isn't going anywhere but home, Tank Turner, and you should be ashamed of yourself, arresting my baby girl." She shook her finger in Tank's face. "And keeping her here practically overnight? You need to be out there figuring out who really killed that poor girl and keeping the rest of us safe." Polly Graves wasn't often riled, and she may have been petite, but when you messed with her only child, Mama wasn't about to let you off easily. She'd fight like a mother bear. I had to say, I was rather proud of Mama just then. My insides were dancing to their own little tune.

"It's okay, Mama. I survived. I just wanna go home, get a shower and some clean clothes. Can we just please go?"

***

By late morning that day, I paced in the back room of cousin Fee's boutique which she'd named *Soilse*—her middle name—from a Gaelic word meaning *light,* while The Box Tops' "The Letter" pulsed from a small radio perched on her French-provincial desk. A shower, clean clothes, and some of Mama's home cooking for breakfast had done wonders.

"I'm telling you. I don't think I've ever been as angry. And you know I have a terrible temper." I couldn't help it. I paced from one end of her office area, located in one corner of the room, to the other.

"Guns ... handcuffs ... that nasty, nasty squad car." I shivered. "Oh, don't even get me started on the jail cell. Filthy. No sheets. Pure raw filth. Horrible blanket that smelled to high heaven ... And they expected me to sleep on that." I pursed my lips. "They didn't even give me so much as a toothbrush." My rant went on for at least another solid minute of time. God bless Fee. She just let me go on and on.

"You through now?" Fee stared at me, unfazed.

"No." I said, ready to ask a question I'd been wondering all night. "How come Roan is still here in Loblolly? Why isn't he—I don't know—in Vietnam or—"

"Childhood asthma," Fee shot back. "He tried to enlist before they called his number but . . ." She shrugged as her hands came up then dropped to her sides.

I pointed at her. "Well, I betcha one thing. If he *had* of gone over there, the war would be started and finished before the Viet Cong and Ho Chi Minh knew what hit 'em."

Fee shook her head. "And people think redheads have bad tempers. They just haven't met my dear cousin." She fluffed her long red curls, took a sunflower-print minidress from a box and placed it on a hanger. "But, I'd be feeling the same if I were you. I mean, not about Vietnam. But, you know . . . you? Accused of murder? Outrageous. I don't know what the sheriff could've been thinking. Now, maybe I could forgive him for doing his job, but Roan? No way. Uh-uh. He doesn't get off that easily."

"Tell me about it. I've done such a good job of avoiding him since I've been home, and this is how we finally meet? Add to that, he thinks we need to talk. *Talk.*" I continued pacing, the anger coming to the surface. "You should have been there."

"Um, excuse me?" Fee hung the garment on a nearby rack before turning back to the box. "I, for one, am most relieved that I wasn't attached to your side, for once." Fee pulled another garment from the box. A lovely pink cashmere sweater.

"You know what I mean. It was like I'd walked into a nightmare. Boopsie lying there, bleeding . . ."

Fee held up a free hand. "Please. Spare me the details. It's enough to know the poor thing was hit over the head with her own frying pan. I won't ever look at cornbread the same way again." She shuddered as she hung the sweater beside the mini.

"Yeah. It was awful, but then Roan came in and pointed his gun at me. *He pointed a gun at me.* Me." I stopped, hands on my hips. "You know as well as I do, he knew the minute he saw it was me that I hadn't done . . . that. He knew and yet he let that woman read me my rights." I turned and looked pointedly at Fee as a song on the radio changed to Bobby Vee's "Come Back When You Grow Up." The irony wasn't lost on me. "You ever heard of that? Rights?" I asked, pushing all thoughts of the lyrics from my mind. "Ask your daddy about being Mirandized in case you ever need to know that. Anyway, he let her put handcuffs on me, and cart me off to jail. *Jail.* No wonder I moved away for college. That rat. Not only do I catch him kissing all over Boopsie at grad night, but he had to go and arrest me for her murder, too?" I flopped onto the flowery chintz-covered sofa in front of Fee's desk. "I should have stayed in Savannah. Dealing with Linden eloping with Sissy Jo Hart would be a whole lot easier than this."

"No. It wouldn't. You know you're innocent of this horrible crime. Linden is definitely guilty of jilting you and running off with that . . . that Sissy Jo what-ever-her-name-is." Fee waved her hand in the air. She pulled a stack of straight-legged slacks in a variety of colors from another box and plopped them on her desk.

I pursed my lips. "Awww. Thanks, Cuz. That's why you have always, always been my very best friend."

"And I always will be," she said as she flipped through the stack and began to sort them by size. "But that doesn't fix this situation. Somebody murdered Boopsie. She may not have been the easiest person to get along with, and Lord knows she had the biggest mouth of anyone in this county, but she was still a worthy human being and she didn't deserve this."

"You're right. I thought about that the whole time I was sitting in that smelly jail cell." I shuddered and rubbed my hands up and down my arms. "I've decided it's up to me to find Boopsie's murderer."

Fiona looked up from her work. "What?" The pants slipped from her fingers and fell to the floor. "That does not sound like a good idea to me. You're not in law enforcement." Fee came and sat beside me, perching on the edge of the little sofa.

"I know that, but I have skills. Look at all the genealogical mysteries I've solved." I jumped up to retrieve the pants and wondered if I'd like wearing them. Lucille Ball had worn them in *The Lucy Show* and I liked the way they looked on her. Then again, she was built for them.

I turned back to Fee. "Don't you think solving a murder might be somewhat like that? I mean, I can find dead people 'til the cows come home. Why can't I use those same tools and techniques to ferret out one that's alive?" I placed the pants at the top of the pile on the desktop.

"I don't know." Fee shook her head. "It could be dangerous. And you said it. The people you look for are *dead*. They can't hurt you. Besides, Tank and Roan aren't going to want you to interfere in their investigation." She raised one brow. "And then there's Aunt Polly. No. No. I don't like it." Fee shook her head again, the red curls shimmering beneath the overhead lighting. "You'd better think twice."

"I already did." I sat beside Fee. "I know the sheriff and Roan are capable of solving this, but what if I just use some of the stuff I know how to do to help them along a bit? I won't get in anyone's way and, if I'm careful and discreet, they won't even know."

"No. Let me repeat. I do *not* like it. Not one little bit." Fee chewed on her bottom lip and looked deep in thought. Finally, she answered. "Okay, wait . . . if you're *going* to do this, you definitely aren't doing it alone. I'll keep quiet, but you're going to have to put up with me being right by your side. Understood?" She looked me squarely in the eye.

I breathed a sigh of relief. Fee had responded exactly as I'd hoped. "Understood."

"So, where do we go from here?"

I pulled a notebook from a psychedelic-print tote bag Mama had made me for all my paraphernalia. It wasn't overly fashionable, but it suited my needs. "I thought you'd never ask."

Chapter Four

"Well, that's a good start." Fee and I had moved from the store to a cozy booth for two at The Copper Pot, our favorite place to go when we wanted to mull things over. I looked at the list of people we'd compiled. "This is a lot of folks. Did we leave out anyone who attended the meeting?"

"I don't think so. Let me look at it again." Fee reached over our burgers and fries to take the notebook from me and glanced at the list we'd begun at her shop and then completed in the diner. "Looks pretty thorough to me." She handed it back. "So, what's the plan?"

"Thought I'd start by asking questions of the people on this list. Maybe begin with Olivia. If anyone has the goods on the people of this town, *she* does."

"Makes sense. Just be careful not to say too much. You know how you are. You don't want to offend anyone." Fee leaned her elbows on the tabletop.

Fee was right, as usual. It seems I had a bad habit of opening my mouth and out poured stupid. One of the many things I needed to work on—getting my words under control. "Got it. Short and sweet."

"Want me to come with you?"

"To talk to Olivia? I don't think so. She's pretty harmless." I tucked the spiral notebook into my bag and slid across the red vinyl booth. "I'll let you know if I learn anything."

"What about all the people who aren't in the historical society? That's a considerable number. We can't forget that Boopsie had a way of offending just about everybody in Loblolly, bless her heart." Fee took a sip of her Coke. "Don't look now, but here comes Max Lawrence with Lanie Kellogg."

I looked over my shoulder toward the entry of the diner. What were they doing together? He was married. And to my boss, no less.

Fee kicked me beneath the table. "I said *not* to look."

"Sorry. Instinct." I rubbed my throbbing shin. "Wonder what they're doing."

"Likely business. Max is a banker, you know." Fee bit into a ketchup-covered french fry.

"I don't know Lanie. When did she move here?" I wiped at a crumb on the tabletop.

"A little after you left. She and her dad moved down from Massachusetts. I heard his wife had family here from her mother's side. I don't really know. He opened a pharmacy—or so I've heard—to give Lanie something to do when he retired. She's been running it for at least five years now. Rumor has it she wants to expand. That's why I'm thinking she and Max are talking business."

"Mmmm. Here in Loblolly or into other areas? The expansion ..." Because it didn't make sense to want to expand in Loblolly.

We had a couple of pharmacies and they managed to take care of the needs of the people who lived here.

"I have no idea. I'm not *that* in the know. That was Boopsie's domain. All I know is, she talks like a . . . a northerner." Fee made a face at me, then shook her head. She ate another fry before grabbing my hand. "Ewww. Don't look and I mean *don't look.*"

"What? What?" I started to turn but Fee kicked me again. "Will you *stop* that? I'm going to be black and blue." I leaned down and rubbed again at what was surely becoming a bruise. "So, tell me. Who or what am I *not* looking at?"

"Whom. It's whom. And it's Max and Lanie." She pasted a fake smile on her face.

"What is with you and that goofy face? Stop it and just *tell* me."

"She has her shoe off and she's rubbing her foot up and down his calf."

Before Fee could protest, I was out of the booth. "I'm going to the ladies' room."

Five minutes later I slid back into the booth. "She had her shoes on and was being a perfect lady when I passed by. Are you sure you saw that?"

"I'm sure." She pointed to her green eyes. "Twenty-twenty. And for your information, when you hopped up, she slid her last year's Size 7s back into those kitten heels." Fee wiped her mouth with the napkin. "Wonder what that was all about."

"Some business meeting from what I could hear. Maybe she's trying to broker a better deal." I waggled my eyebrows and wondered what kind of eye Fee must have had to know that Lanie's shoes were from last year's fashion selection. But on second thought, I nixed that idea. Fee always knew when it came to style.

"Could be worth looking into."

Serena Newton, owner of The Copper Pot, came to our booth. Her apron matched the tie-dyed band in her hair. "Hey, y'all need anything else? Refills on those co-colas?"

"Thanks, Serena." I looked at Fee. "Drinks to go?"

"Good idea. I'll be glad to have it while I'm getting the new inventory out." Fee crooked her finger at Serena, who bent down, bringing her closer to Fee. "So, what's up with those two?"

She dipped her head toward Max and Lanie.

"Those two?" Serena rolled her eyes and made a face. "If I knew, I'd tell you, but I haven't figured it out yet. They come in here about once a week for a *business* meeting."

"Fee says she wants to expand her pharmacy."

"No idea. They always clam up when I refill their cups." She straightened. "I'll get those drinks. Meet you at the register in a couple of minutes?" She wrote on her pad, tore out a page and placed it discreetly between Fee and me.

"Thanks, Serena. We'll be right there." I put away my notebook and leaned on the tabletop, bringing the paper straw to my lips. "Um, where were we before they came in?" I finished my Coke and wiped my hands.

"All the people Boopsie offended."

"Mmm. You're right. I wasn't thinking past the end of my nose." I stopped and thought for a moment. "Why don't you compile a list of anybody you think should be on that list. You'll know things I don't know since I was away for so long. We'll have two lists. The WHS group, and then everybody else."

"That's all good, but I could be working on it into next month."

"Oooo. That bad, huh?" I tapped the toes of my shoes on the floor, deep in thought. "Well, it'll just have to be long. If you make the list, I can go over it with you when I get back from talking to Olivia. Deal?"

"Yep. I'll get started right away. Be careful at Olivia's. You never know who may be listening."

"That's the plan." I pushed a five across the table to Fee as she slid from the booth. "This one's on me." I stopped at the register to pick up my Coke and waved good-bye.

***

Olivia lived in a stately mansion situated on about twenty acres just beyond the country-club subdivision. I was still surprised, even on this second visit, that it was a log home. But it far surpassed just a cabin. This was a massive Craftsman-style with typical wooden features, wide overhanging eaves, exposed rafters beneath the enormous front porch, cedar shake shingles, gable and roof brackets, and stacked stone features, to name the few I knew. The woman owned the lumber mill—I shouldn't have been surprised—but I always felt like I was driving up to The Ponderosa when I arrived.

After a quick look at myself in the rearview mirror, I got out of my car and climbed the wide stone steps leading to the front porch. A thought ran through my mind as I rang the doorbell: If there was something between Max and Lanie besides business, did Olivia know?

The front door swung open and I was greeted by the housekeeper, who led me to Olivia's office.

"Thank you, Della." Olivia raised her hand and waved me in. "Charlotte, do come in, dear." Olivia sat behind an ornately carved desk but stood and came around it to envelop me in a quick hug. I understood that this was the South, but all this hugging simply wasn't normal in my life. Well, for the past eight years, anyway.

Olivia moved to a sofa across the room and indicated for me to sit beside her. "How awful of Tank to arrest you last night. What could the man have been thinking? It seems that all common sense has left this world."

How had Olivia heard about my arrest so quickly? Loblolly was small, true, but this was record speed. I leaned into the pillows on the overly stiff sofa and decided then and there that luxury didn't necessarily mean comfort. "It wasn't a pleasant experience, to say the very least. But, as I told Mama, I survived."

"Well, before all that awfulness, you did *such* a good job telling us the history of our little town. I'm quite pleased." She smoothed her hair. "So, what can I do for you today? I assume you know that you still have your job."

"Well, to be honest, I wondered. After all, I no sooner began this job than I was accused of murder."

She fanned the air with one hand. "Anyone with good sense knows you wouldn't do such a thing." Olivia sat back in the corner of the sofa and tugged on the hem of her off-white jacket. The ever-present owl pin winked at me from the left lapel.

"Olivia," I began slowly, hoping not to draw too much attention to the direction of my question. "Would you happen to know of anyone who'd have a reason to kill Boopsie? Apparently, the whole town knows her reputation for being a meddlesome busybody. But has she had issues with anyone in particular?"

"I'm afraid I wouldn't know that, dear. I'm so busy running Woodville Lumber that I don't have a lot of time for gossip and such." She straightened. "Of course, I hear things like everybody else. That's why I had no problem last night telling her to sit down and hush." Olivia stood, then walked to the window overlooking an ornate garden. I waited while she seemed to study it for a moment and wondered what had her so fascinated. A gardener? A bee flitting around her roses? But then she turned to face me, leaned on the window ledge, and cocked her head to one side. "What's going on? Why these questions? Don't tell me you're thinking of trying to find Boopsie's murderer."

I shifted. "Is it that obvious?"

"Well, it certainly is now." Olivia crossed the room to a hidden fridge. She removed two small bottles of Coke from it and popped off the cap of one before bringing it to me. "What can I do to help?" she asked as she popped the second cap then came to sit beside me.

"Thank you." I took the familiar green bottle from her and took a sip. "I'm not sure. When I first thought about this, I thought I might be able to figure things out. . . you know, because I have experience with genealogical puzzles. I mean, how different could this be? A puzzle is a puzzle."

"Well, I'll give you that, but you don't have the experience that Tank and Roan have." Her brow rose a fraction of an inch. "Nor do you have the law on your side. But that *could* prove to be an advantage." She nodded, and the brow returned. "Perhaps people would be more forthcoming with you. They wouldn't feel . . . threatened." Olivia took a tiny sip of her Coke without losing so much as a smidge of her lipstick. "In that light, let me inform you that I came straight home after the meeting, had a cup of hot tea, took my sleeping pill, and went straight to bed. I didn't even see Max after he dropped me here." A change of expression crossed her face. "As far as Max is concerned, I can only assume he went back to work. Heaven knows what time he came in. He's always at that bank. Works all the time."

I made a mental note to check into that. But after what Fee had seen today, was Max *truly* always at the bank? If he was having an affair, working late could be a good cover. But in such a small town, how could he possibly cover all his tracks? Someone was bound to know something. Could that someone have been Boopsie?

I brought my hand to my chest. "I appreciate that information, but I didn't consider you a suspect for one second." I wanted to jot a few thoughts into my notebook, but I'd need to place the Coke bottle somewhere first. One look at the coffee table in front of me told me *that* was a no-go. Mama would have a fit if I were to put a wet bottle on *her* good furniture, so I decided to just hold it and make mental notes.

"I suppose that's good to hear." Olivia gave a little laugh. "But, seriously … let me know if I can help in any way." She went to a cabinet near the little fridge, opened it and retrieved napkins. She handed one to me. "Now, if you'll excuse me, I really do have to get back to work." She pressed two fingers to her temple. "Quarterly taxes are due, and I have papers to review."

I placed the wet bottle on the napkin and, with more questions than answers, exited the Lawrence home and climbed into my Chevy. "You and I are both out of our element in this neighborhood, old girl." I patted the dash and pulled my trusty notebook from my bag. I made a few notes about Max and work, Olivia and sleeping pills, then went back to look over my list of names until I came upon … *Mrs. Sweets.* I chewed on my bottom lip. Should I skip this one? Now wasn't an appropriate time to question her. But if she knew of someone who would want to harm her daughter, she may be willing to talk. The notion that I should get Fee to come with me crossed my mind.

I pulled through the circular drive and headed toward Soilse.

***

"Now remember, sympathy first. We don't want to be too obvious. Maybe something will just slip out." I was glad we'd thought to stop in at the local bakery before arriving at Boopsie's mother's home. The sweet aroma of the red velvet cake we'd purchased slipped through the edges and folds of its white box and filled the car. Such baked goods were always welcomed in a southern home. Especially at a time such as this. One thing Southerners did best was to take care of the grieving.

We made our way through the throngs of people gathered on the front porch. A few looked surprised to see me. As we entered the small home, the familiar smell of home-cooked food made my mouth water.

I wasn't prepared for the outburst of Boopsie's brother Bubba, whose given name was Robert James. Boopsie, on the other hand, had been named Barbara Sue, but Bubba—unable to pronounce it properly as a toddler—had changed it to Boopsie. I felt a little sorry for Mr. and Mrs. Sweets; neither of their children ended up being called by their given names.

I hadn't seen him but a time or two since returning home. He looked about the same as he had when we were children, just older and heavier. "What are you doing here? Outta jail?" Bubba grabbed my arm, his beefy hand pulling me toward the door. "They let murderers just walk around mingling with the good folks of Loblolly?"

Fee stepped in and blocked his way. "You take your hands off her, Bubba Sweets, or you'll be finding yourself sitting in that nasty jail. You know full well Charlotte wouldn't be here if the sheriff thought she'd killed your sister."

"You ain't wanted here. Neither one of you. You're gonna upset Mama. You just need to git." He waved his free hand in the air.

I pulled my arm from his grasp, thankful that Fee carried the cake. "We just came to offer our sympathy to you and your mama. We didn't mean to upset anyone. We'll go, but you may have answers no one else can give."

Mrs. Sweets made her way through the group gathered around the three of us. "What's going on here?" She looked at me, hate burning behind cold eyes. "What's she doing here?" She stood there, arms perched on her hips, looking none too pleased to find me standing in her living room.

"That's what I was asking. That dumb sheriff done turned her loose."

"He released me because I didn't do anything. I only found ... Boopsie. That's all."

I'd almost said, "the body." Thank goodness I hadn't.

Bubba took the cake box from Fee and sniffed at its contents. "You can leave this, but then you need to go on now. Like I done said, you ain't wanted here."

"You need to leave well enough alone, Charlotte Graves," Mrs. Sweets said. "Always making trouble for my girl. Look what you've gone and done now. Just leave things be. Stirring up a pot of trouble, that's all you're doing." Mrs. Sweets was built like Boopsie, medium height, skinny. But Mrs. Sweets' hair had turned gray long ago while

Boopsie's had been dark. Very dark. And Mrs. Sweets looked tired. Very tired. I chalked that up to a hard life . . . and grief. "Just go."

But seriously? Mrs. Sweets thought *I* was the troublemaker? How had things gotten so mixed up over the years? Something was out of whack ... and I was determined to find out just what that was.

"I really am sorry about Boopsie. She didn't deserve this." I meant it whether they believed me or not. My heart and my conscience were clear. And whether they liked it or not, I intended to find Boopsie's killer.

Chapter Five

Thrilled to be the passenger as Fee drove her sweet 1968 Ford Mustang Shelby GT 500—silver with black racing stripes slicing down the middle—to Mama's house, I relished the scenes unfolding along the way. Summer would soon give way to fall, my favorite season. I could almost smell the crisp autumn air filled with smoke from chimneys awakened from a lazy summer of rest. A long time had gone by since I'd experienced fall in Loblolly. Long-ago memories of Halloween carnivals with candy apples threatening to break my teeth and the scent of cotton candy wafting through the crisp air brought a smile followed by a heavy sigh. *Hurry, fall. And bring the fair.*

"Thanks for offering to drive, Fee." I turned my thoughts from the thrill of Tilt-a-Whirls and footlong hotdogs to peruse the notes inside the notebook resting in my lap. "I haven't thought of anything significant yet, but I know it's there." I glanced over at my cousin. "You remembered to call Aunt Becky?"

"Sure did. I don't know about you, but I'm scared to death of the conversation we're about to have. Mama and Aunt Polly are going to pitch a hissy fit." Fee took a quick sideways glance at me.

"Fee, if we don't ask, we won't know. And if they get offended . . . we'll just have to ask for forgiveness later on, as the saying goes."

Fee pulled her car into the drive beside her mother's truck. "I don't get that generation wanting trucks when you could have a nice little sports car." She gestured to her mother's Ford. "I get that Aunt Polly likes to sit higher, but Mama is as tall as I am. She could see over the dashboard in a Corvette if she had to."

Silently, I agreed with my cousin, but I'd never say it out loud. My own mama sometimes drove a big old truck. Said she had to have it to haul plants, and dirt, and other gardening stuff, not to mention the old furniture she liked to drag home and make new again. Mama was quite the gifted decorator, if I did say so.

I used my key and entered the home I shared with Mama, then held the door open until Fee followed me into its coziness.

The interior had changed dramatically since Papa's death. Mama refused to leave the home they'd shared for over thirty years, but that didn't mean she couldn't make it look different. The memories were in her heart, and changing the décor made it easier to remain in the familiar dwelling place. I recognized Fee's helping hand in the modern touches that were so unlike Mama. Knowing Fee had helped made me smile, but it also reminded me that I should have been here for both Mama and Papa. A wave of guilt ran up my body and I shuddered.

"Hey, Mama. I'm home. Fee's with me," I called.

"We're in the den. Come on back," Mama said.

Both of us stopped to give our mothers a quick kiss and hug. I dropped my tote bag at the end of one of the sofas which sat vertical to the fireplace. Fee did likewise.

"So, what's up with you two that you needed us together twice in one day?" Aunt Becky said.

"Oh, just some thoughts we've had. You know. About Boopsie's outburst last night," I said.

"Uh-oh." Mama looked at Aunt Becky, who sat beside her on an off-white-and-gold damask sofa. "This sounds ominous."

"No, wait, Aunt Polly." Fee looked across the brass and glass coffee table at her aunt and mother. "Just a few questions."

"Questions about what?" Aunt Becky asked, her defensive tone apparent.

"Well . . ." I drew out the word then inhaled deeply, blowing it out slowly. "When Boopsie said that Nana isn't our *real* grandmother, what was she talking about?" I bit my bottom lip as I looked from Mama to Aunt Becky. "Because if Nana *is* our real grandmother, why would Boopsie *say* such a thing?"

Mama and Aunt Becky looked at me as if I'd just claimed to be from Jupiter. And at this moment, that fit my description precisely.

"Charlotte Isabelle Graves. What on earth has gotten into you? Of course, Mama was my mother—and Becky's too, which, in case you've forgotten, makes her—your and Fiona's—grandmother." Mama picked up a *Good Housekeeping* magazine from the coffee table and began to fan with it. "Give me strength, Lord, just give me strength."

Aunt Becky looked at her sister. "Don't get too excited just yet, Polly." She patted Mama's hand. "Let's hear her out." Aunt Becky crossed her arms over her flat stomach and sent me and Fee a look that said, *this had better be good.* "Then we'll pitch ourselves a good fit."

I looked from one sister to the other. They looked about as much alike as their daughters—which meant, they looked nothing alike. While Mama was short and dark, like me, Aunt Becky was tall and lanky, like Fee, only Aunt Becky sported blond hair, not red. For the first time ever, I took note of the differences. Could it be that Boopsie's statement held a modicum of truth? Had the sisters been adopted? I felt deep within that there existed at least a grain of truth there, but what? And was it more than skin deep? Furthermore, did I really want to know?

Mama continued to fan, not quite as furiously as before, but I knew my mother was still mad as a wet setting hen and Aunt Becky looked just about as pleased as Mama. She tapped her foot in rhythm with Mama's fanning.

"I'm only asking," I said, "because this is where the investigation has brought me."

With her eyes narrowed, Mama scooted to the edge of the sofa. "Investigation? What investigation?"

"The one where I find out who really murdered Boopsie." I sounded braver than I felt.

"Unh-unh," Fee added. "That would be *we*. Where *we* find out."

"*Are you out of your minds?*" our mothers yelled in unison. It wasn't so much a question as a statement of "yes-you-have" fact.

I looked pointedly at my mother. "You can't get mad at me for trying to find out the truth, Mama. You always told me that knowing the truth sets us free."

"You know full well that's *not* what that means, young lady." Mama fanned harder.

I looked at Fee. Where was her gumption when I needed it most?

"Don't look at me, Cousin, I'm just the sidekick. My only job is to keep you out of trouble. This is your show." Fee sat back and pulled a pillow from behind her to hug against the flat of her stomach.

Okay, so I was on my own. No help was going to come riding in from anywhere. How had I gotten into such a mess? Yep, I should've stayed in Savannah. Deep inside me lived a brave soul—one whose appearance was long-past due. I took a deep breath, grabbed my tote bag, and pulled out my faithful notebook.

"Okay, then. Well, I only know that something weird is going on." I opened the book, flipped through the pages, and scrolled through my notes. "Mrs. Sweets told me I was just stirring up a pot of trouble . . . like always. Now, since when have I been a troublemaker? You tell me that." If I sounded defensive, so be it. "I may have had my head in the clouds, and I may have made some bad choices, but I've always been the good girl who stayed out of trouble." I poked the spot on the page with my index finger, emphasizing each word. "Yet, Boopsie's mother thinks that *I* was the one who always started things with her daughter. And we all know that's not true."

Mama fanned a bit more slowly. "You're right about that. I remember Nina calling me once when you and Boopsie were just girls and telling me you were picking on her daughter. Funny thing, you told me Boopsie was picking on you. So, which one of you was lying?"

My mouth fell open. "Mama! How could you ask that? I've never lied to you. Not once." I squared my shoulders, ready to defend myself.

"Yeah, you have." Fee played with the fringe on the pillow. "Remember the time we told them we were going to Marcia Rogers's house and we drove to the lake instead?"

"For Pete's sake, Fee. You aren't helping here. And that's beside the point. We were both young and foolish." I ran a hand through my hair, felt the curls twist around my fingers. "Tell them. It was always Boopsie. Always." I dared her to say anything that disagreed with me.

"She's right. I was there and it *was* Boopsie. She started it *every* single time. Just like she did Tuesday night."

"Thank you," I said. "Now maybe we can get somewhere." I settled into the corner of the sofa, pulling my feet beneath me. "As I said, things are just weird. Why would Boopsie tell me that someone in that room is my real grandmother and then her mother tells me I'm stirring up trouble? Something is just off-off-off." I drummed my fingers on top of the notebook to the tune of the repeated word. "What kind of trouble? For whom? More importantly, why would she say such a thing?"

Mama stood and walked to the fireplace. She rearranged the things on the mantel, adjusting the old perpetual motion clock, positioning it squarely in the center—an old nervous habit.

"Okay, Mama. What gives?" Mama always rearranged something when she was thinking or upset. Always.

"I just remembered something." She turned and faced the other women. "It may not be anything, but it is rather odd. I thought nothing of it at the time, but now that I'm … older … it seems . . . peculiar."

"Polly, what on earth are you talking about?" Aunt Becky glared at her sister.

"When I was a girl, I used to visit Rose Haven. You know that big house, estate actually, out in the country, about ten miles out of town? It belongs to Miss Marge Mayhew now. Back then, her daddy was still living. Mama would get me all dressed up and I'd go out there and spend, well, I guess holidays, now that I think about it." She returned to the sofa. "There was an enormous tree during Christmas with loads of ornaments and silky icicles and colorful lights. And at Easter there was this funny sort of naked-limbed tree that sat on the dining room table. It had eggs hanging from colorful silk ties on every tree branch." She reached for her sister's hand. "Do you remember that, Becky?"

Aunt Becky pulled her hand out of Mama's grasp. "No, Polly. I don't. I never went to Rose Haven. I've *never* been to Rose Haven, as a matter of fact. But I do remember Mama driving *you* out there. You stayed and I came back home."

Mama's shoulders drooped. "That's right." Her hands flew to her mouth. "I'd forgotten that. I was always so lonely when I was there. I wondered why Mama made me go and not you. You were *never* there, Becky?"

I wrote as fast as the sisters talked. "That has to be significant in some kind of way, don't you think?"

"Oh, I just remembered something else."

I looked at Mama as my hand hovered above the page. "What, Mama? Don't keep us in suspense."

"Boopsie's grandmother, Norah, was the housekeeper and cook."

"What? Are you sure?" I asked.

"Of course, I'm sure." She turned toward her sister. "And she had a child with her. A boy." She appeared deep in thought. "Think, Polly," she said to herself as she banged her fist on her forehead.

Aunt Becky spoke up, "Why have I never heard these stories? What on earth did you do in that home, and who was that boy?"

"I don't remember. It was so long ago I'd nearly forgotten the whole thing. Maybe it'll come to me later. I do know that that boy didn't call Norah 'Mama.' I always thought that was strange because she certainly acted like his mama." Mama rubbed the back of her neck.

Aunt Becky grimaced at her sister. "I can't imagine our mother leaving you in a house full of strangers. How old was this boy?"

"He had to have been about my age. Maybe five or six. Couldn't have been much older, if any. I just wish I could remember more about that time. Why was I there? And why did Mama just leave me?"

Chapter Six

While Mama read in her bedroom, I attempted to forget about things for a while by watching an hour of *Hawaii Five-O* on CBS, followed by a switch to ABC at 9:00. I giggled through an episode of *That Girl,* even though—truth be told—Donald Hollinger looked an awful lot like a certain someone I'd left behind in Savannah.

I decided not to watch the local news, fearing what I might see. Instead, I got ready for bed and hoped for a good night's sleep. Instead, thinking about the meeting with Mama and Aunt Becky created a sleepless night. If I could only make sense of all this. And what did it have to do with Boopsie? The pieces weren't connecting like most of my genealogical puzzles. Talk about brick walls . . . this one screamed *insurmountable.* Sometime after dawn, I threw back the covers and slipped my feet into fuzzy house shoes and my arms into a quilted cotton housecoat and tied the wide satiny sash.

The smell of cinnamon buns and coffee lured me into the kitchen. Mama stood at the counter, filling a cup with the steaming brew. I laid my head on her shoulder. "Good morning. It smells good in here."

"It does, doesn't it? Your daddy loved my homemade cinnamon buns. Said they were better than the ones you can get at the bakery."

"He was right." I removed a cup from the white wooden cabinet and poured myself a cup from the percolator.

"I wonder if I'll ever get used to him not being here," Mama said as she blew across the surface of the brown liquid before taking a tentative sip. She then took her cup and a plate full of buns, dripping with thick icing, to the table where I now sat.

"I don't know how you could. I still miss him. More every day." The rolls were *huge.* I cut one in half, put it on my plate, and took a bite. "Mmmm. So good, Mama. You need to teach me to make these one day."

"I just need to make sure I get all my recipes written down for you. I'll worry about continuing the cooking lessons later."

"I'm sorry I'm such a disaster in the kitchen. I try, but my food just doesn't taste like yours, even when I do every single thing you've taught me." I added cream to my coffee then took a sip and shuddered. I'd forgotten to add sugar. Two tablespoons later and it was just right. "My cooking is just missing something."

"Love. Plain old-fashioned love. Makes all the difference. Once you start cooking for somebody you love, your food will be delicious. You'll see." Mama took a bite of her roll.

"Must be why Linden always complained about my cooking. I just didn't love him."

"Hmm. Seems he may have done you a favor by eloping with that girl."

"You may be right." I pointed at Mama to emphasize my agreement. "Things with him just didn't feel right. You know. Comfy, like you and Papa."

"Or like you and Roan used to be?" Mama raised her eyebrows.

I gathered my dishes and took them to the sink. "*Used to be* being the operative phrase. As in the past. Roan and I moved on a long time ago. No use in dwelling on what might have been." I walked to the fridge to put away the cream.

"He still loves you, you know." Mama kept her eyes on the cup of coffee in front of her.

I felt a stab of pain. "No, Mama. He doesn't. That was too long ago to even go there." Then why was my heart dancing and smiling over Mama's statement? I wouldn't, couldn't consider that. Had to listen to my own advice. I returned to the table. "So, are we just going to avoid the obvious?"

Mama's head came up. "What?" She looked puzzled.

"Last night's conversation. Are we going to talk about it or just let it stand there stinking up the place?"

"Oh. That." She played with her fork. "I don't know what to think. I do know it's odd that I spent so much time at Rose Haven. Even more odd that Becky never went."

"Well, I thought about all of this last night." I gave Mama a knowing look. "I didn't sleep much." Mama nodded in understanding. "You want to know what I think?"

"Of course, I do. Even if it makes me uncomfortable. As you pointed out, it's best to know the truth, no matter what that may be."

"I think Boopsie must have known something. Something so big that someone—I don't know who yet—but someone was willing to kill her to keep her quiet." I looked at her expectantly.

"I hadn't thought of that. But, you could be right. Especially with her mother telling you to butt out."

I jumped up. "*Pickled bricks.* If Boopsie knew, then her mother probably does, too. Which means she could be in danger." I ran to the green-lacquered wall phone next to the fridge. "I need to call the sheriff."

"Don't call him. Just go." Mama waved her hand at me as my index finger jerked the first of four digits to the right. I'd tried to convince Mama to get one of the newer models with push buttons, but she'd said the rotary was just fine for now. "He'll see the fear if you're right in front of him."

"I agree," I said, then quickly showered and changed into a pair of straight-legged yellow slacks with a matching floral top. I slipped my feet into a pair of flats, then climbed into my Chevy and prayed it would start. Man, did I need a new car. Well, not new, but different. One that was reliable, not this cantankerous old thing.

I let out a sigh of relief when it cranked on the second try.

***

The last place I wanted to be was back at the jail. But what choice did I have? People's lives could be in danger. One more death would be my undoing, for sure. I dreaded talking to the sheriff. Running into Roan would be even worse. I steeled myself then walked up to the front desk.

"I'd like to see the sheriff, please. It's urgent." I leaned from one foot to the other.

"It always is." The desk attendant finally looked up. "You? I thought we let you go yesterday. You like us so much you just had to come back, huh?" His laugh had the other two officers in the room looking.

"Very funny." I leaned toward the officer. "Seriously. I need to speak to the sheriff."

"Well, he's out. Best I can do is see if Deputy Steele will see you."

My worst fear. Oh, well. I had to deal with this. "Fine. Deputy Steele will do." Roan's shifts must have changed to days. Just my luck, his shifts coinciding with my life lately.

The sheriff's department still smelled of burned coffee, old cigars, and—somewhere in the recesses—dirty cells . Digging up good, clean dirt in graveyards was one thing, but having to work or be in conditions like this place was quite another. Freshly turned earth smelled good . . . well, earthy. This place did not.

Five minutes later, I paced in Roan's office, biting at my fingernails while he sat behind his desk watching me as I shared my concerns for Mrs. Sweets . . . and Bubba. His expression declared that he and I were not on the same page. "Why can't you see what I see? It's as clear as, well … it's clear."

"First, we have to have more to go on than gut feelings and the mother of our victim telling our first suspect to back off." He leaned back in his swivel chair and twirled a nubby No. 2 pencil between his fingers.

"But it makes sense. Boopsie knew something. Something that got her killed. If her mother and her brother know it, too, they could be next."

"Tell you what. I'll go see them, ask a few questions. But if I don't get any vibes that tell me they're afraid or hiding something, that's the end of it." His eyes widened. "Got it?"

"Got it. That's all I'm asking." I opened the door to leave, then turned back to find Roan staring at me. "You probably won't tell me, but did you find anything at Boopsie's that would support what I just told you?"

"I guess there's no harm in telling you that we didn't. Not a thing. Made a thorough search and left the place neat as could be. That's how we operate."

"Thanks."

I started out again when Roan cleared his throat and I looked over my shoulder at him. "You look nice in those slacks," he said with a wink.

I frowned. "Thanks," I said. And with that, I beat a hasty path to my car. I sat inside, windows down, thinking. Within minutes, it finally came to me. What I planned required assistance, but I wasn't sure Fee would be on board for this one.

***

I found myself in *Soilse*. Again.

I had to stop this before it became a habit. Fancy clothes were Fee's domain. A simple pair of slacks was my style. And in the winter it wasn't unusual for me to don a man's tee, add a flannel long-sleeved shirt, and if needed, a jacket, and I was good to go.

"Are you crazy? Seriously. Have you completely lost your mind?" Fee towered over me.

"It'll be dark. We'll dress in black. In and out." I pointed with my index fingers toward the door, then away from it. "Dash in, dash out. Quick."

"It's just too dangerous. You *just* got out of jail. You want to go back so soon?"

"Fine. I'll do it. A-lone. What's one more night in that nasty place? I was kind of getting used to it, anyway." I picked up my tote and headed toward the door, pretending to leave her store.

Fee grabbed my arm. "Wait." She sighed. "All right. I'll do it. But only as a lookout. Don't ask me to do anything other than to stand outside and give a whistle if Roan suddenly drives by."

"He won't," I said with a grin. "He's working day shift right now."

"How do you know?"

"Because that's the way it works down there. They serve a week or two of night shift, then a week or two of day shift."

"Well, aren't you just Sherlock Holmes."

"More like Dr. Watson … you know …Basil Rathbone." Was that right? Or was he Sherlock? "Whichever actor played Dr. Watson."

Fee leaned against her desk, then looked me squarely in the eye. "Heaven help me. What have I just agreed to do?"

Chapter Seven

Fee and I agreed to meet at Fee's garage apartment. We couldn't do what we needed to do at Mama's. She'd be far too curious.

Fee answered the door, clad head to toe in black. "Hey, you need to hurry and change."

"Thanks for getting a couple of things for me. I couldn't have left home dressed like that." I nodded at Fee's attire then dropped my tote on a nearby chair. "Mama would have known something was up for sure. I never wear all black."

"Well, hurry up and change. Your clothes are on my bed. I'm nervous as a cat in a …" Fee hesitated. "Nervous as a cat."

"Yeah, a cat *burglar*." I laughed as I pulled on the black stirrup pants Fee had brought from her store. I topped that with a black sweater, about three sizes too large for me. It hung to my knees and looked more like a dress. "Yours, I presume?" I curtsied to Fee.

"Hey, it's the best I could do on short notice." She smiled at the reference to my diminutive size.

"Very funny." I pulled on worn-out Keds. "It's a good thing these are old and not so white." I tied the laces, then stood and grabbed my tote. "Got everything?"

"Yep. Just as instructed. Flashlight. Soft cloths." She zipped her bag closed. "Did you get the face paint?" She pulled her bag onto her back. "And, by the way, that stuff *better* come off."

"It should." I took one last look inside my own bag then zipped it.

"You'd best be making that an 'It will,'" Fee said.

"No worries. The theatre uses this stuff. I went by the high school and picked some up. Told them I have a project. They wouldn't use it if they couldn't remove it." I hefted my tote onto my shoulder. "You ready?"

"To break into Boopsie's house? Hardly. But I can't leave you to the wolves."

***

After a debate about whose loud car to take—my beat-up Chevy or Fee's souped-up Mustang—we opted for my rattletrap. More people in Boopsie's area of town drove cars like mine than like Fee's, Boopsie's T-Bird having been the odd one out.

We parked a good two blocks away and made our way to and through back yards. The first of many-to-come fallen leaves crunched beneath our feet. Fall was on its way. An occasional dog barked, and outdoor lights came on at a couple of homes. But, for the most part, we arrived at Boopsie's without incidence.

We approached the back entry of Boopsie's home as quietly as possible. The sheriff had draped a rope across the doorway, as if that would keep anyone out. I lifted it and held it for Fee, then checked the door. Oddly, it wasn't locked. My eyes widened toward my cousin, who shrugged. How had the cops overlooked that? No way I could even ask.

We tiptoed over the threshold.

I whispered, "You stay here. I'll go check out her room. Let me know if you see or hear anything." I headed across the kitchen, careful not to look at the spot where I'd found Boopsie. Once in the hallway, I aimed my light in search of a door that indicated a possible bedroom. The beam from the small flashlight barely illuminated the way.

There was only one bedroom. If Boopsie were to hide something, where would she put it? The bed looked too neat. Had it not been searched? I opened the bedside drawer. Nothing special there. A pad. Pencils. Chapstick. The dresser drawers were a mess. Roan said they'd left it tidy. This was far from orderly.

That bed still bothered me. I knelt at the near side and ran my hand between the mattress and the box springs. Nothing. I adjusted the spread, smoothing out the wrinkles. On the far side, I repeated the motions, but this time I reached as far as I could, running my hand top to bottom. Bingo! I grabbed whatever it was, smoothed that side of the spread, then made for the kitchen. Dogs barked and, in the distance, sirens wailed in the dark night.

"Come on," I said when I reached Fee. "Let's get out of here." I tucked the find into my tote and hoisted it onto my back.

"What? What is it?" Fee said, her voice quaking.

"I'll tell you later. Let's get out of here."

We made our way through the same backyards as before, weaving in and out of trees and away from lights shining from homes. We arrived at my car out of breath. Sirens alerted us to approaching police vehicles. We squatted until the cops moved on.

First Fee, then I, tumbled into the Chevy. I turned the key and prayed the car would start. The noisy, ramshackle engine sounded like a sweet lullaby.

Fee pulled the cloths from a plastic freezer bag and handed one to me. "Here. This better work." She began wiping at the black paint on her face.

I took the cloth but placed it in the dash as a minty scent wafted through the car. "I'm getting us out of here before I clean me up." I drove to a remote area near Fee's home, pulled over and began to wipe my face, noticing that Fee had thought to dampen the cloth and slap some Noxzema between the folds. I glanced in the rearview mirror. "Smart girl," I said.

"I thought so."

I turned the mirror at an angle toward her. "Use the mirror, Fee. Quickly, though. We need to scoot."

"Ewww. What a mess. Hurry up and get us home so we can scrub." Fee continued to rub at the black smears. "The things I let you talk me into."

***

I made the drive to Fee's in record time—the garage apartment had never looked so good. We didn't dare speak another word until we were inside, the door locked behind us. I threw my tote onto a nearby chair.

"Did you see what I saw?" Fee said as she removed her own bag and entered her bedroom.

"You mean two figures dressed in black, sneaking through backyards?"

"Yes, and I don't mean us." She threw the bag onto her bed and grabbed clothing from a dresser drawer.

"Somebody besides us has been in that home tonight. Do you think they saw us?" I stripped off my black clothing, replacing them with my usual jeans and a tee. Fee did the same, but she pulled on printed pajama pants and a tee boasting the words, *Crimson Tide*.

"Let's hope not. Otherwise, we could be on a murderer's short list." She picked up her discarded clothing and motioned to me. "Give me your stuff and I'll hide it along with mine, then come into my bathroom. I've got good cold cream in there that'll get the rest of this black mess off."

"Cold creams? Really, Fee? When did you start using that stuff? We aren't even thirty yet."

"Just be glad I do."

After using Fee's high-end cream and wondering what was wrong with the Pond's our mothers used, we gathered in the living area. Fee grabbed sandwiches stored in the fridge, placed them on plates and plunked them onto the old, glass-topped tool chest which served as a coffee table, then tuned her TV to the opening credits of *Judd for the Defense*. She went back to the kitchen, retrieved Cokes and chips, then handed one to me, now settled on the sofa.

"Good thinking, Cuz." If anyone came to question us, we'd been here watching TV. I settled on the sofa and propped my feet on the coffee table. We nibbled at the turkey and cheese sandwiches and potato chips.

Fee popped a chip into her mouth, crunching away as she talked. "So, you gonna sit there all night or you going to share what you found?"

I picked up my tote and pulled out a small diary, the kind little girls keep. "I found this tucked between the mattress and box springs. Wonder how Sheriff and Roan missed this. Doesn't seem like them."

"You're right. I can't see them missing this."

I checked the lock. Broken. Good. No key would be needed. I ran my hand along the worn front cover and thumbed through the pages.

"Planted?"

"Possible. When I first entered her room, I thought her bed was just too neat. It was freshly made actually. Her dresser drawers, on the other hand, were a mess. Stuff pulled out, strewn everywhere. But her bed was made. Don't you find that odd?"

"Sounds like someone figured another someone would go snooping and was trying to throw them off the trail." Fee took a sip of her Coke and placed the bottle on the coffee table.

"Or else, they wanted this to be found. Either scenario makes about as much sense as anything else at this point." I uncrossed my ankles and crossed them the other way.

Fee leaned over my shoulder. "Hurry up and open it. Let's see what it says." She took a glance at the page. "You read it aloud. You're better at deciphering handwriting."

"*This is the diary of Barbara Sue Sweets*," I began. "*Do NOT read this. If you do, your eyeballs will fall out!*"

"Seriously?" Fee reached over to turn the pages. "How old is this? Did she date it?"

"Stop that." I held the book out of Fee's reach. "Give me a minute and I'll look." I turned to the first entry, dated *June 3, 1950*, which I pointed to so Fee would have her answer. "Hopefully she did that throughout." I flipped through quickly, seeking more dates, and nodded. "Okay. Apparently, she did a pretty good job of that."

"Read some more. Go back to the beginning."

I flipped back to the first page as Fee wiggled around for comfort. "We were what? Seven or eight?" I had to think a moment. "Yeah." I settled against the loose pillows on Fee's sofa. "Are you ready?"

Fee nodded and I turned to the first page.

"Okay. Here we go ..."

June 3, 1950

I don't much like going to Rose Haven. No kids there. Just old folks. Even Mama is old. MeeMaw's even older. She's the cook. I like her cooking. I just wish I didn't have to go to that big old house to get it. Mama says if we don't, we'll go hungry cause Daddy left us. I don't know why he left, but I'm glad he did. He was loud. He yelled at me and Mama and Bubba all the time. And he smelled bad. Mama said it was the drink. I don't know what that is, but it stinks. He tried to kiss me when he got home, but I always ran away and hid. I didn't like it. I didn't like him.

I stopped and looked at Fee. "I knew her dad had left, but I didn't realize things were that bad. Do you think he . . ."

"Don't, Charlotte. Don't even think that." Fee shook her head as if to clear the thought. "Just read."

I nodded. "You're right." Swallowing a sip of my drink first, I continued.

June 5, 1950

We went to Rose Haven again today. It's a big old house with fancy, curvy stairs and a big, big light that Mama calls a shandyleer. It's pretty and sparkly. When I grow up, I'm going to live in Rose Haven and be a fancy lady like Miss Marge. Mama says I'll have to be the cook or housekeeper, but that's not true. I'm going to be a lady, and it's going to be my house. And I'm going to live there with Roan Steele cause he's going to marry me. And he won't stink like my daddy.

I put my finger in the book and looked at Fee. "*Roan?*"

Fee's mouth fell open. "Crumbs! She was dreaming about Roan way back then."

With a shake of my head, I opened the book again, skimming the entries. Most of them were ramblings on about going to school and hating math and how the kids picked on her. Some had even called her vile names. As much as I'd always disliked Boopsie, I could say without question that I had never mistreated her. Mama and Papa had taught me better than that. Argue with her about things? Yes, I did that. But I never called Boopsie names. Ever. At least not out loud. I wasn't perfect, but I wasn't mean, either.

"Look at this . . ." I pointed to a left page in the diary. "Aunt Sarah

..." My words faded as my lips continued in a silent read.

"Aloud, please," Fee said.

"Sorry."

August 23, 1953

I don't understand what Mama said today. About Aunt Sarah. She said she had a baby. But Aunt Sarah isn't married. You can't have a baby unless you're married. Mama said so. Then I heard her say Aunt Sarah isn't the only one. Besides, Aunt Sarah is old. Old people don't have babies. If folks knew, they'd sure be surprised. Aunt Sarah isn't the only what? I'm too young to understand this stuff. Mama and Grandma said Aunt Sarah should be Miss Marge. I don't understand that either. How can she be somebody else? If I could be somebody else, I'd want to be Charlotte Graves. Her daddy loves her. I can tell when I see him with her in town. And Roan likes her, too, so I'd like to be Charlotte.

"Whoa," Fee said. She'd leaned forward during the reading, but now fell back against the pillows behind her.

My eyes met Fee's. "Could that have been part of her issue? She wanted to *be* me?" All this time I'd thought Boopsie hated me because I was ... *Charlotte.* But in reality, Boopsie had hated me because Boopsie was not me. "I don't even know what to say to that."

"She was just a kid." Fee waved her hand in the air as though a pesky mosquito had invaded her space. "All little kids are jealous of somebody." Fee leaned forward again. "But what's that about Miss Sarah having a baby? You ever heard that?"

"No. But give me a second here. I'm still trying to get my head around the wanting to be me thing." I grimaced. "What were you thinking, Boopsie?"

Chapter Eight

I thumbed through the next few pages, my eyes scanning for the right words. Finding them, I said, "Okay, okay. Here we go. The next time she talks about Rose Haven is in October."

"I'm listening," Fee prompted.

October 16, 1953

At Rose Haven again. They never pay any attention to me. Not MeeMaw or Mama, not Miss Marge, and not Aunt Sarah. I can hide in places only I know about. There are secret rooms they don't know I've found. Well, maybe not secret, but rooms that are locked. But I can open them. I found a key. They don't know I've been in there. I like to go in and pretend it's my house. One is a baby's room. The other one is a fancy lady's room. There's a picture there of Miss Marge holding a baby. I wonder who the baby is. I hear things when I hide. They don't know I hear. It's just my secret and no one else's. They talk about some people called the Laniers. At least, Aunt Sarah and MeeMaw do. I don't know them. The Laniers, I mean. They must be bad people. Aunt Sarah and MeeMaw say they hid someone's grave and if they ever find it, it's going to be big trouble for a lot of people in Loblolly. I can't ask about it. They don't know that I know. I hope I never run into the Laniers. Maybe they'd want to hide me."

"Wait, wait, wait," Fee said. "Read that first part again. Did she say a picture of Miss Marge ... locked? In a room?"

"The picture of her holding the baby was in a locked room." I stopped and gazed around, not really allowing my focus to zero in on any one thing. I had to think. Something about this added up ... as though I knew the sum of the equation but not the addends. Which left me more or less knowing the answer but not the question. I held up a finger. "The first part of the equation is: who could that baby be? That's addend number one." I held up another finger. "And the second addend is: where is that room?"

Fee's brow rose a half inch. "Addends?"

I grinned playfully. "Bet you never thought I paid attention in math class."

"Nope," she sighed.

"Hah. Had you fooled. I didn't like math, but I did pay attention. Had to. It didn't come easily to me like it does to you." I shifted around a bit. "Back to the questions." I wiggled my fingers.

"I have no idea, but I'm sure you have plans ticking away inside that mathematical head of yours and I'm positive I'm not going to like them." Fee cocked her head and looked me. "You may as well keep going."

"Wait ... let's go back to the Laniers. Do you know anyone with that last name?"

Fee shook her head.

"Me either. But the name sounds familiar. Maybe one of the WHS has it in a family tree." I made a mental note-to-self. "I'll have to check on that."

"You do that. Check on it later but keep reading now."

"Patience never was your best trait." I looked back to the book.

December 24, 1954

I overheard Aunt Sarah say it's been over a hundred years since that woman died. I thought they said Boopsie and that they were talking about me. But I'm not dead. And I'm not 100 years old. Aunt Sarah says this house will belong to Uncle Max one day.

Fee and I exchanged a look.

But they have to keep the grave hidden. I think they said Josie. I don't know Josie, but I feel sorry for her. Her grave has been hidden for a long time. I wonder who she is. I'll have to be quiet and listen some more. If Uncle Max wins Rose Haven, I hope I can live with him. I used to hate it here, but I like knowing secrets. Rose Haven has lots of secrets.

Fee grimaced. "This is getting weirder by the minute. There were some crazy things going on in that house. Either that or Boopsie had one vivid imagination." Her brow shot up again. "Especially for a kid. Wait a minute ... how old would Boopsie be at this time?"

"Let me think … 1954? We were twelve, right? Right. But what about this Max … Do you think that's Olivia's Max? And how old would he have been? Do I dare ask Olivia?"

"Just finish reading. We can worry about all the particulars later."

"All right already …" I thumbed through the passages until I found another entry that looked interesting. "Ready?" I asked in redundancy.

"Always."

January 30, 1955

Today I turned thirteen. I guess I'm a woman now. Except I've read things that say that I'm really not. I'm not sure how to go about it, but I've gotta make sure I become a woman soon. I think thirteen is old enough. Mama talks about some singer she listens to who got married at thirteen. I wish I could marry Roan.

Fee gave a faux shudder. "Who thinks about getting married at thirteen? I hadn't even been *kissed* at that age."

"Seriously? You told me that . . ."

Fee's hand shot up. "Stop. Right there. I was a kid and kids fabricate stories to make themselves appear to be worldly. Now that's the end of that." She crossed her arms.

"Mmm-hmm." I thumbed through the pages, my eyes scanning the words. "She isn't saying much here. Just about movies and birthday parties … buying makeup. That sort of thing. "Oh, look. The next big event is another birthday."

January 30, 1958

I turned sweet sixteen today. Roan Steele told me happy birthday. I'm so happy. He really razzes my berries! If I could just get that awful Charlotte Graves out of our lives, I could have Roan all to myself. I vow on this, my sixteenth birthday, I will have Roan Steele if it's the last thing I do. He's so handsome. That Charlotte thinks she's going to have him. But he's mine. All mine. I'll die before I let Charlotte have him.

"Pickled bricks," I said. "She hated me. She wanted to be me, but she's always hated me. And all because of Roan." The book fell out of my hands, onto my lap.

"Well, she doesn't hate you now. She's dead. Which is why we're reading this. To try to figure out who killed her." Fee grabbed the book, flipped back pages in search for an entry and once found, pointed to the line about Uncle Max. "I'm ready to talk about this some more."

"Yeah. Uncle Max. I've lived here all my life . . . well, other than the eight years in Savannah ... and I've never heard anything about Mr. Lawrence being Boopsie's uncle. Have you?"

"Could be another Max. Who's to say this guy is Mr. Lawrence?" Fee tossed the book to the sofa, then went to the fridge. "Want another drink?" I didn't answer, but Fee grabbed two bottles anyway and brought them back to the sofa. She handed one to me then took a long swig from hers.

"I guess you're right, but I don't know any other Maxes. Do you?" I set my bottle on the coffee table next to my propped-up feet.

"No. Not that I recall. No Laniers either. Although, I agree the name sounds familiar. And from the sounds of them, I'm glad of it." She shivered dramatically. "Who hides a grave? We need to keep reading."

I thumbed through the diary again, skimming over what looked like uneventful days. But May 20, 1960 nearly jumped off the page when I spotted my name. "Look. She made note of Grad Night."

May 20, 1960

Finally! Roan is going to be mine and Charlotte won't be able to do anything about it. After all these years of planning and plotting, I finally got him right where I want him. And all of it witnessed by little Miss Goodie-Goodie, Charlotte. He didn't see it coming, but I did. There we were, in the boys' locker room. Just Roan and me. I finally managed to lure him into my trap. I made sure Charlotte was looking before I pulled Roan to me, right on one of the benches. I'd practiced long and hard to make it look as if Roan was the one kissing me. Ha! Charlotte thought Roan kissed me. She's so dense. Such a fool. Such a little girl. What Roan sees in her is beyond me. He needs me—a woman—not that simple, silly, little Charlotte.

I stopped reading long enough to digest the words. Weights bore down on my chest, making it difficult to breathe.

"I never thought I'd see that. I mean. I've been blaming Roan all these years and it really *was* Boopsie." The pressure grew in my chest.

"What have I done?" I looked at my cousin, whose mouth fell open only enough to let a bug in, had there been a bug. "Fiona, what do I do about this?" Blood rushed from my head and my heart pounded. I inhaled slowly, the breath coming in jagged spurts, then pursed my lips and allowed what little intake I'd managed, to ease out. "How do I fix an eight-year mistake?"

"With Roan?"

I nodded.

"Just don't think about that now. You have plenty of time to figure it out. Roan isn't going anywhere, and neither are you. If you act in haste …" Her eyes widened. "Like before … you could make an even bigger mistake. And this one you won't be able to fix."

Fee, ever the voice of reason.

"You're right." The best thing for me to do now was to read on. Half an hour later we came to the final page, but this time we read each entry to ourselves.

"Wow." Fee stood. "So, Boopsie was definitely privy to some heavy conversations."

I lingered on the last page, then looked up. "Wow is right. I wasn't expecting any of that. I'll look into this … check it against courthouse and cemetery records."

"Do you know any of these names? Aunt Polly ever mention any of them?"

"Not that I recall. But remember, between us, we have three sides. Our mothers', your dad's, and my dad's. We don't know if any of these people are in any of our trees."

Fee's hands went immediately to her hips. "What about that history project we had to do with our family trees way back in the day? Remember? Did any of their names come up in yours?"

"I don't remember. But I didn't go back very far. Just to three-times-great grands." I flipped through the diary again, searching for surnames. "I bet Mama still has that report. She keeps everything."

"I'll ask mine too. Sisters. It's in the genes." Fee picked up our empty plates and started for the kitchen area of her studio. "But what about that historian you talked about at the WHS meeting?"

"Hiram Moore."

"Yeah. If he's a historian, wouldn't there be a book or something in the library written by him? Maybe these names will show up there?" Fee shrugged as she placed the plates in the sink.

"I checked it out. Not the book. Well, yes, the book … but I didn't check it out."

Fee turned and rested her hips against the countertop. "But you just said you did. Did you or didn't you?"

"Pickled bricks, Fee. You're confusing me now." From the look on Fee's face, I wasn't the only one with a scrambled brain. "I mean I went to the library to see if there was a book by Mr. Moore. A different one from the one I used at the meeting. There was, but it wasn't there. When I asked Kilene when it was expected back in, she said it wasn't checked out."

"How could that be? She's the most meticulous librarian Loblolly's ever had."

"Probably stolen." I retrieved then crunched on a chip dropped on the coffee tabletop. "Only thing it could be. Because it wasn't checked out by anyone on record."

"Who on earth would want an old, dusty history book?" Fee scrunched her face in disgust.

I wiped my fingers on the used napkin. "Someone who didn't want some part of Loblolly's history to be known—that's who." Or a host of folks working on their family genealogies. But who could that be?

Fee returned to the sofa and plopped onto it, which gave me a toss. "Now what do we do? This is mindboggling, and if it's connected to us in any way, it could also be lifechanging." She twirled one long red curl around her fingers. Old habits came out when nerves kicked in.

"Right now, I have no clue." I leaned my head in my hand. "It's just too much. But my gut is telling me, we need to go to Rose Haven."

Fee reached for the diary and then held it up. "And we need to hide this lovely piece of evidence."

Chapter Nine

Mama and Aunt Becky plus Fee and I gathered in Mama's living room. Meeting like this was going to become a habit if we didn't watch it. Seemed that every time I opened my mouth lately, something awful happened. And here I stood, about to make another request. After reading Boopsie's diary, it was obvious that some answers lurked behind the old walls of Rose Haven.

Mama may have been acquainted with Miss Marge, but as far as I recalled, the historical society meeting remained the only place I remembered seeing the older woman. She'd carried the title of "town matriarch" since Moses was a boy. But apparently, Miss Marge and Mama shared some kind of connection. At least as it concerned Rose Haven.

So now I smiled at my mother and aunt. "We thought you'd like to go with us. Both of you."

"To Rose Haven?" Mama narrowed her eyes, appearing totally confused. "What on earth for? I had enough of that place when I was a child. I see no reas—"

Aunt Becky held up her hand, palm out. "For once, just don't argue the point, Polly," Aunt Becky commanded her big sister. "Of course, *you* can't see any reason to go. You've been there a thousand times. I want to see this place Mama shipped you off to. It's about time I got to go, too." She looked and sounded like a sulking child.

"Mama?" I looked expectantly at my mother who stood near the fireplace glaring at Aunt Becky.

"Oh, all right. I'll go. But it's under protest. I want that understood." She fiddled with the whatnots on the mantel, but only slightly this time. Did that mean she *wasn't* as upset about going to Rose Haven as I'd dreaded she'd be?

I waggled my eyebrows at Fee, who grinned and gave the okay sign. Rose Haven, here we come.

***

Rose Haven appeared before us, perched on a slight hill like the proud old lady she'd become. I'd expected a large home, but this was grander than it was large, and like something straight out of *Gone with the Wind.* Ancient oaks lined a crushed-shell lane which wound its way to the front walkway, lined with red Alabama clay bricks. The thirty-foot walkway led to the expansive verandah. Stately columns supported the lower roofline and the upper balcony and roofline. Rocking chairs lined the porch from one side to the other . . . at least a dozen.

A little white clapboard church stood off in the distance. The paint peeled away from the boards in curls, and the cross on the steeple listed to one side. Behind it loomed what I suspected was the family burial grounds, its perimeter surrounded by a rusted old iron fence. A meadow filled with wildflowers stood on the opposite side of the big house, and behind that rose a big, red barn, its paint faded and peeling. A large pond nestled smack in the middle of the colorful meadow and glistened in the sunlight, its smooth surface broken by the wake of a family of ducks. One could easily imagine children from years past jumping into that pond and running through the meadow. Had Mama enjoyed a summer's day along the banks or within the coolness of the water?

"Oh, my." Mama's hand came to her mouth as she exited the car from the rear. "It's just as I remember. Not one thing has changed."

Aunt Becky exited from the opposite side of her sister and took charge. "Come on, y'all. I've waited all my life to see inside this big old house. Time's a-wastin'." She slammed the car door and made for the massive oak doors of the home, then lifted the knocker and banged it three times.

The door swung open on squeaking hinges to reveal none other than Miss Marge Mayhew herself. She was a short little woman, a bit on the heavy side. But just a bit. Her short, practical hairstyle curled about her round face, much like my own hair, but it was gray, not chestnut like mine. She wiped her hands on the flower print apron tied about her waist.

"My goodness, what a lovely surprise." Her hand flew to her chest and her eyes sparkled at the prospect of having visitors. The place was a good ten to fifteen miles out of town. Not too many people would venture out this way without a good reason. She backed into the entry hall and beckoned us inside. "Come in, come in."

Mama spoke first. "We're so sorry to just intrude on you, Miss Marge. I think you know everyone. I'm sure you remember me. I'm Polly Graves. Ummm. Mary Jones Graves."

Miss Marge reached for Mama's hand, took it, and then gave a light squeeze. "Of course, I remember you, Mary."

Mary? I knew Mama's given name was Mary, but this was the first time I'd ever heard her referred to that way.

Mama turned to me, but Miss Marge didn't release Mama's hand. "This is my daughter. You might remember that she presided over the WHS meeting Tuesday night. And this is my sister, Becky Campbell, and her daughter, Fiona."

"Our mother was Sophia Jones," Aunt Becky inserted. "You may remember her as well."

The elderly woman flinched and swallowed hard. A light blush made its way across her face, then quickly faded. "Why, yes. Yes. Of course. What a lovely surprise." Only then did she release Mama's hand.

"Come in, please," Miss Marge continued. "Just follow me."

Following the lady of the house, we stepped farther into the entry hall. An ornate curved staircase hugged the left-hand wall and the ceilings soared to the top of the second floor. An enormous crystal chandelier hung from the center, its prisms dancing in the light shining through the front floor-to-ceiling windows. The one Boopsie mentioned in her diary. The largest medallion ever in the history of medallions crowned the chandelier, its carved surface adding to the opulence of the room. Austere, somber faces stared at us from what I assumed to be family portraits which graced the stairwell, step by step.

Hearts-of-pine floors stretched from room to room. This home would vie such estates, anywhere.

Miss Marge led us through a parlor, to the left and back of the home, and into a hallway which opened into the conservatory. The room boasted floor to ceiling windows, curved along the back. Potted plants were everywhere, from the smallest ones timidly pushing through the soil, to huge palms residing in enormous pots. The furniture was mostly old—an eclectic mix of days gone by, but surprisingly, a couple of mid-century-modern pieces laid claim to one area of the grand room. Throw rugs scattered here and there covered Mexican terra-cotta floors.

"Sit, please. And do excuse me while I go and gather refreshments. It isn't every day I have such a lovely bevy of visitors."

Mama and Aunt Becky chose to sit on a green-and-white checkered sofa. Fee and I moved to the matching loveseat, positioned at an odd angle to the sofa. We left the club chairs empty for Miss Marge. I bent to sit when I heard Mama's telltale throat clearing. A nod of Mama's head told me what was expected.

I quickly caught up with the little lady. "Let me help you, Miss Mayhew."

"Oh, thank you, dear." She kept walking and I followed. "And it's Marge. *Miss* Marge if you prefer."

"Okay. Miss Marge it is." Some things in the South went deep—far deeper than we may have imagined, and manners was one of those. We never called our elders by their given names. We always preceded it with Miss or Mister, depending.

Miss Marge smiled. Funny. There was something endearing and familiar about the woman's smile. Something that, perhaps, I'd seen in one of the old portraits of the town's founders. Maybe ... I couldn't quite put my finger on what exactly, but I knew it would come. It always did.

After teacakes, a pot of tea, and freshly squeezed lemonade, we all settled down to talk. Head-on was always the best approach.

"Miss Marge," I began, "I've been looking into the murder of Boopsie Sweets. I understand that her grandmother worked here when

Boopsie was a girl."

"Oh. Wasn't it terrible about that dear child? And her poor, poor mother. Bless her heart. And that's right, dear. But it wasn't just her grandmother, Norah. Her mother and her great-grandmother worked here as well. I remember them fondly. They served as our cook and housekeeper." Miss Marge smiled weakly. "At one time, we had quite a large staff. Then Mama and Papa passed away and the parties stopped." Her shoulders drooped. "Oh, I just remembered. These teacakes were from Mama's great-grandmother's recipe files. She made them for me when I was a child."

Mama took another cookie and bit into it. She closed her eyes. "I remember these. I knew there was something familiar about them. I couldn't quite get there. It must have been Boopsie's grandmother who made them." She glanced at Becky who munched on her own cookie.

"Oh, no, dear Mary. Norah didn't make them. Each time you came to visit, it was *I* who made the teacakes for you." Miss Marge sat up straight to offer a genuine smile.

Why would she have done that? Especially when they employed a cook. I took a quick glance at my cousin and raised one shoulder. *Are you thinking what I'm thinking, Fee?*

"I had no idea you'd made those, Miss Marge. What a lovely gesture. But I do have to ask." She sat her teacup on the glass-top table in front of the sofa, clasped her hands together, then leaned forward, resting her elbows on her thighs. "Why did my mother bring me here? And why never Becky? I have so many questions about that time in my life and I do hope you can answer some of them."

"That was all so long ago." The older woman looked away, then down to pull at the hem of her house dress. "I dare say that I just do not remember the precise reasons you were here and never Rebekah. I do recall making the teacakes and that Papa doted on you so."

"But the visits stopped. Suddenly. Can you tell me why?"

Miss Marge stiffened her upper lip and squared her shoulders. "I can only tell you that Sophia decided, out of the blue one day, that the visits should end. And that was the end of that. No explanations and no further visits." She smiled, and her countenance lifted. "Until today."

"I don't understand." Mama looked at Aunt Becky, who shrugged her shoulders, then back at Miss Marge.

What were we getting into here? Nana had brought Mama ... and yet she was the one who had stopped the visits? Things were getting more complicated by the minute. I didn't want to push my luck, but I had to know ... "I have a couple more questions, if you don't mind." I took a sideward glance at Fee. Why hadn't she chimed in? She was never this quiet. Hopefully she was thinking about all of this and trying to connect the dots.

"What would you like to know?" Miss Marge chewed on her bottom lip.

"First, who was the young boy Mama remembers being here when she visited? And have you ever heard any mention of a hidden grave?" There. I'd dared to mention the secret grave.

Miss Marge let out a little chuckle. "Oh, that young boy would be Norah's son. He often hung around his mother in the kitchen. But a grave? Let me think." She seemed deep in thought. "Now that you mention it, I do recall my grandfather, Evan Lanier, saying he wished he could find someone's grave. I don't recall who that may have been. My father never spoke of it." She stood, gathered the dishes, and placed them on the tray with the almost empty pitcher. "I am afraid I have not been of much help."

Aunt Becky stood and took the tray. "Here, let me get this. Just lead the way."

I exchanged a glance with Fee, who raised one brow. Who did Aunt Becky think she was fooling? She just wanted to get a look at more of this house. Fee stood and scurried to catch up with her mother.

"Here, Mama. I'll carry that heavy pitcher. It'll lighten your load."

I shook my head as I retrieved my notebook from my ever-near tote. After making a single notation—*Evan Lanier, grandfather of Marge Mayhew*—I looked at my mother who stared at me thoughtfully, then I closed my pad and tucked it into my bag. "Care to join them?"

Mama led the way with me on her heels. So, Miss Marge was related to the Laniers. That must be why the name was a bit familiar when we came upon it in Boopsie's diary last night. And hadn't Olivia mentioned that name at the WHS meeting? My mind hadn't worked properly since I'd been arrested. I'd need to look over my notes. All these connections had to mean something. Didn't they? But what?

Boopsie may have unearthed a family secret. But had that knowledge gotten her killed? This investigation was far from over and it commanded many more questions. *I'm getting closer, Boopsie.*

Chapter Ten

We dropped the sisters off at Mama's. After watching them offer a quick wave from the front porch, I looked up an address in the phonebook I kept in the old clunker. I backed out of the drive and headed toward the next stop in our investigation.

Fee turned in her seat. "All right. Out with it. Where are we going now?"

"To Miss Sarah's."

"Why? What are you expecting her to know?"

"Who knows? I don't even know if she'll talk to me. But it doesn't hurt to ask. Did you pick up on Miss Marge saying the boy was Norah's son?" She took her eyes off the road to glance at Fee. "But Mama said he never called her *Mama*."

"That's strange. Especially back in those days. I know it wasn't that long ago, just a generation or so, but back then you wouldn't call your mother by her name, or something besides *Mama* or *Mother*." Fee shrugged her shoulders.

"Why would Miss Marge say that? It doesn't make sense." I cast a sideward glance. "And I'll never get used to calling her *Miss Marge*."

"Sure, you will. Just repeat it to yourself a dozen times. I think it's actually twenty-one times. Or is it twenty-one days?" Fee cocked her head to one side. "Oh, well. You get it. It'll become a habit."

"Thanks, but I doubt our relationship, if you can even call it a relationship, will last that long." I pulled my Chevy in front of a cottage-style home directly across from Boopsie's. How had I forgotten where Miss Sarah lived? No wonder her address had sounded so familiar. But eight years away messed with some memories.

"Cute house." Fee leaned over me and looked through my window.

"Yeah, it is." The little yellow cottage boasted white porch railings and shutters. A white picket fence surrounded the front yard. Colorful zinnias, snapdragons, and orange-and-yellow daylilies danced in the slight breeze in the bed hugging the picket fence. "Right out of my dreams."

"This?" Fee indicated the little cottage. "You?" Fee looked at me, puzzlement on her face. "No way."

"I didn't say they were recent dreams."

"Oh, I get it. When you and Ro—"

"Stop. Just stop. We're not going there." What was it with my family? They all seemed to think Roan and I were going to have some kind of future together. That wasn't going to happen. *They* hadn't been the ones burned by Roan's actions with Boopsie. But—and I couldn't forget this but—Boopsie's diary indicated that I'd been wrong about that. All these years. Still . . . for now I had things to do besides think about what might have been.

"Sorry. I'll try not to mention it again." Fee settled into the passenger seat.

"Let's go see if Miss Sarah's home. And pray she knows something." I stepped onto the sidewalk and glanced across the street at Boopsie's home. The ropes which screamed *keep out* were gone, leaving the place looking sad, deserted.

Fee joined me on the sidewalk. "I see that look on your face. Don't think about it, Charlotte. You're innocent and we're going to find out who killed Boopsie."

"I know." We headed toward the walkway leading to Miss Sarah's front door, but I stole one last glance at Boopsie's home.

***

Sarah Harkins seemed surprised to see us. Sarah, the twin of Boopsie's grandmother Norah, was built much like Boopsie and her mother. Tall and slender, but she had an air of … what? Sophistication? Snobbery? Which, I didn't know, but I made a mental note. It could be significant.

Miss Sarah looked from me to Fee, then let her gaze settle on me. "What on earth are you doing here?" Forget about everyone in the South having southern charm. Miss Sarah sounded anything *but* charming. Who could blame her, really? She thought I'd killed her niece. Didn't she? "I know I'm the last person you want to see. But let me assure you that we're only trying to help find Boopsie's real killer."

Miss Sarah stood in the doorway looking from me to Fee . . . again. She shrugged and pushed open the screened door. "May as well see what you have to say." She held the door wide for us to enter, then latched the hook.

Fee and I stood in the middle of the tiny but charming living room that screamed an older woman lived there. The furnishings were like those at Rose Haven, old and out of style, with doilies on every surface, but with no effort toward anything modern. It also carried that musty roses grandma-lives-here smell, too. The only thing that seemed out of place was a rather expensive looking exercise bike stationed in the far corner, with two what I assumed were hand weights perched on the seat. "Nice bike." Miss Sarah didn't fit my idea of someone who would enjoy exercise. At all.

Miss Sarah glanced at it dismissively. "When you get to be my age, you like to stay in shape as best you can," she said as she sat in a Queen Anne chair and indicated the small sofa to me and Fee. "Sit, please."

We sat, our knees practically digging into the cherry coffee table in front of us. I pondered how to begin. "Miss Sarah, would you mind answering some questions about the night Boopsie was killed?" I peered out the front window in the direction of Boopsie's home. "I didn't remember that you lived so nearby."

Miss Sarah followed my gaze. "It was awful. A terrible tragedy. The poor thing was too young to die." She shook her head, her lips drawn into a thin line.

"It *is* a tragedy, Miss Sarah. That's why we're trying to figure out this mystery." I leaned forward and rested open hands on my tender knees. I couldn't imagine the agony Fee must be in. "Did you see or hear anything out of the ordinary that night?"

"No, I didn't. As I told Theodore—that's the sheriff, you know—I'm a sound sleeper. I take out my hearing aids and don't hear a thing."

She smoothed the skirt of her modest dress.

"Did you ever see anyone lurking around, looking suspicious?" Fee said.

"I really don't spend much time up here in the front of my home. I have a lovely little back porch where I sometimes sit. It's screened, you know. Oh, and my bedroom and den are in the back as well. So, I don't pay much attention to the comings and goings out front." She looked pointedly at me. "My neighbors' lives are none of my business."

"I understand that you're Boopsie's aunt. Is that right?" I wasn't sure I should let my knowledge of their relationship be known, but how else was I to learn the truth?

"Why, yes." Miss Sarah's hands went to her chest. "She was my great-niece. Her mother is my niece. Norah was my twin sister."

Maybe things weren't such a secret if Miss Sarah was willing to share this information, especially with me. "So, you were probably a visitor at Rose Haven when they worked there?"

"I wasn't just a visitor." She sat up straight, squared her shoulders, and lifted her chin, looking almost regal. "When Margie's mother passed, I moved into Rose Haven and lived there for many years to help assuage Margie's grief. Her father was such a prominent businessman, you know, and he needed someone to take over as hostess when Constance passed away." Miss Sarah gave a faint shake of her head. "Margie simply wasn't up to the task, so I volunteered to step into those duties." Her eyes widened. "Goodness, I lived there until the thirties."

"I didn't know that, Miss Sarah." I couldn't imagine being in such a position. "Was it hard on your sister, having to work in the kitchen and head up housekeeping while you were acting as mistress of the manor?"

"Norah didn't seem to mind. I think she was just happy to have a job. Rose Haven was a good place for Maxwell to grow up."

Maxwell. I looked at Fee who shrugged.

"Oh, dear. I feel I've said too much."

"Please don't worry about what you say to us, Miss Sarah. We're only trying to discover who might've killed poor Boopsie. That someone is still out there, and they could be dangerous."

Miss Sarah clasped her hands, wringing them, putting a stop to my words. "Oh, dear. Oh, dear. I do think you ladies had best leave now. I'm afraid I've said far too much, and this is all very upsetting to me." The older woman stood and walked to the door, unlatched it, pushed it open, and stood with her back against it.

Fee and I took her cue and walked out to the front porch.

"Thank you for your time, Miss Sarah. Be sure to keep your doors and windows locked. And please call me if you think of anything else." I pulled my notebook from my tote, pulled out a page and wrote my name and Mama's phone number on it. I handed it to Miss Sarah then motioned for Fee to go before me.

At the bottom of the stairs, I turned back to Miss Sarah who stared at us, a strange look on her face. One of almost . . . hatred? But why? Did she honestly think *I'd* killed Boopsie? Had to be it. What other reason could she have for such a look? I hesitated for a moment, then decided I would ask one last question.

"Miss Sarah, when you were living at Rose Haven, did you ever hear anyone mention a hidden grave or perhaps a lost diary?"

"I've told you all I know. You girls need to leave well enough alone and let Theodore figure out this mess. No good can come from digging into the dirt of the past. Some things are best forgotten. Now, if you'll excuse me. I have a headache." With that, she turned and entered her home.

Miss Sarah hooked the screen door then slammed the solid door hard enough for half of Loblolly to hear it. If she truly had a headache, it was going to be a lot worse after that loud bang.

***

"So, where do we go from here?" Fee pulled down the visor to block the afternoon sun.

"How 'bout to your house or mine to regroup?"

"Better make it mine. Aunt Polly will be at yours. At least Mama will be in the main house and busy with Daddy this time of day. Privacy." She waggled her eyebrows at me then turned up her radio as Diana

Ross and the Supremes' song "The Happening" started up. "Gosh, I love this song," Fee all but shouted, then wiggled her shoulders to the beat.

Ten minutes later we sat on the sofa in Fee's garage apartment. I pulled my notebook from my oversized bag. "Here's the list we made of all the people at the WHS meeting." I shoved the notebook toward Fee.

"That's a lot of people, but still . . . I thought there'd be a lot more who had a beef with Boopsie. You were gone so long, you don't know, but she rubbed just about everybody in Loblolly the wrong way. Always sticking her nose in, making a fuss, mostly about nothing." Fee rubbed the back of her neck and let out a sigh.

"You're right about me not knowing. I've caught bits and pieces here and there since I've been home, but I've been so busy with the music store and trying to organize the historical society, I haven't spent a great deal of my time thinking about Boopsie and her obsessions." I took the notebook when Fee handed it back to me. "So, since you know things I don't know, you talk, I'll write."

"Okaaay. Tell me what you want to know. I'm not much for gossip. Never have been."

"I know that, but this is different. It isn't gossip if we're trying to piece together facts that could lead us to Boopsie's killer."

"That makes sense, but I still don't like it." She got up and went to her small kitchen. "I'm gonna get us a Coke first." She opened her fridge and peered inside. "I'm down to one for each of us. Need to add that to my grocery list for next time I go to the A&P."

I began writing. "You got any snacks? I'm getting hungry. Thinking does that to me."

Fee brought the bottled drinks and the bag of Golden Flake from earlier and placed them on the coffee table. "I know she had words with Jeff Briton at choir practice on more than one occasion. I know because I was there. You can ask anybody in the choir. And Rachel Peters will back that up."

"The organist?" I entered the two names.

"Yes. You've met her, haven't you? Cute as a button. Sweet, too. Hard to believe she's old enough to play for church now."

"I used to babysit her. She *is* cute. What was going on between Boopsie and Jeff?"

"You know Boopsie. She didn't like the way he conducted, or where he sat her, or that she didn't get the solo, or her robe was too big, or too little, or so long that you couldn't see her pink kitten heel pumps." Fee shook her head.

"Really?" I looked sideward at my cousin. "She was that picky? At church? And since when could she carry a tune? Last I heard, she was fresh out of buckets."

Fee punched my arm. "Be kind, Charlotte, the woman is dead."

"I think I *know* that, but let's move on. Who else should go on this list?" I rubbed my arm. It didn't hurt, but I could pretend it had, just as I'd done when we were children.

"Stop that. I didn't hit you that hard. And Max. Rumor is, they had a fling. I don't know if that's true, so it really *is* gossip. Unless you hear it from somewhere else, don't put him on the list." She munched a chip and took a swig of her Coke.

"You mean Olivia's husband? That Max?" My eyes opened wide.

"We've already established that he's the only one we know. Yes, that Max."

"Pickled bricks. You'd think she'd be too smart to mess around with the likes of him."

"I said it's just a rumor. I can't verify or prove it." Fee looked at me. "And where and when and why did you start saying *pickled bricks*?"

I took a sip from my bottle. "Mmm. When I began doing genealogies. When you can't find someone, you hit a brick wall. Saying *oh, bricks*, just evolved into *pickled bricks*." I threw Fee a slanted smile.

"Oh, I . . . guess that makes sense . . . I . . . suppose."

"Getting back to our investigation, I can't see Olivia allowing Max to have an affair with Boopsie for one second." I added Max and Olivia to the list. "I'm putting both of them on here, but it makes me very uncomfortable. They're some powerful people." I shook my head. "Wait a sec … this is unbelievable," I whispered. "If Max is Norah's son, that would make him Boopsie's cousin. An affair with your cousin? Ewww. I say we for sure consider this to be rumor and gossip and nothing else. Let it be. I'm not adding his name." I erased what I'd written. "At least, not now." I shuddered. What a horrible thought.

An hour later, the Cokes had been drained, the bag of Golden Flake lay crumpled and nearly empty, and new additions were on a list I looked over one last time. "Well, you were right. Boopsie had issues with most of the movers and shakers in Loblolly, and a few on the fringes." My notebook went into my bag. "Makes you wonder how she managed to have a halfway decent life if so many people had issues with her."

"Yeah. Know what you mean." Fee gathered the empty bottles and the nearly empty bag of chips and headed to the kitchen. "So, what's our next move?"

"I'll take this home and do some research at the library tomorrow or the next day, see what I can find."

"I'd have no idea of where to begin. Did you learn all that stuff over in Savannah?"

"Yeah. Lots of it. Genealogy is a lot of poring over dusty old records. Wills, land grants, deeds, census records, stuff like that. But they can tell you a lot about folks if you know how to look at them with a critical eye." I stood, ready to go. "And you have to remember to look at who the neighbors were. Odds were, they were related in some way."

"I still can't imagine. Glad it's you and not me having to do that. Give me a rack with some clothes on it—or a fashion magazine—any day. That's my kind of research."

"Well, I need to get on this," holding up my bag. "I'll let you know if I turn up anything."

Once in my car, I let my mind wander to the names on the list. Way too many. Narrowing it was the only way to go. But who to eliminate? And who to keep?

Chapter Eleven

I plumped up the pillows and settled against the iron headboard. One thing Mama had done when Papa passed was to buy all new furniture. It wasn't *new* new, but it was different to Mama. Like this old iron bed she found in a rundown farmhouse where the owner had died, brought it home, cleaned it up and painted it white.

The new look of my old room made my heart happy. No more little-girl décor for me. Gone were the pink bows and glittery-shimmery curtains. In their place were reds and blacks and white, and an old quilt folded at the foot of my bed. Even my bathroom had been remodeled. Now, instead of pink, the tiles and fixtures were black and white. The curtains were black-and-white checks, and red towels added a pop of color. A girl could get used to this.

"Careful, Charlotte," I said aloud as the thought crossed my mind. "Don't go getting too comfy. This isn't going to be your permanent home, no matter what Mama thinks." I'd been at Mama's for over six months now. Maybe it was time to think about finding my own place.

But where on earth would I go in Loblolly? Apartments were not that readily available. Mama, unlike Fee's parents, had no garage apartment.

Fee had lucked out in that respect. They turned the upper level of their garage into an apartment when Fee was in high school and Uncle Angus's mother had moved in with them. When she passed a little over two years ago, Fee accepted her parents' offer of the place. They even helped her remodel it to her own tastes. It was now a lovely contemporary home, perfect for Fee until she met the man of her dreams and moved on.

Man of her dreams. What about the man of *my* dreams? How and when had things gone so wrong with Roan and me? I'd thought I knew him. Then I found him in a not-so-innocent-looking embrace with Boopsie at grad night. Then and there I promised myself that I would move on and make something of myself. And not look back. I'd planned to never return to Loblolly, no matter what.

That old saying about making plans reared its ugly head. My plans changed in the broken beat of my heart once Linden eloped with Sissy Jo. And then, Papa dying became the catalyst that brought me back home. I couldn't stay away when Mama needed me so badly. Besides, there was nothing left for me in Savannah. With Linden and his new bride both working at the historical society, I couldn't even keep my job in the city I'd come to love.

But now, I'd have to adjust my thinking about Roan if Boopsie's diary entry were true. And why would it not be? Most girls I knew would never lie to their own diary.

"Oh, my goodness," I said aloud. I hadn't thought about the music store in days. I needed to get back down there and finish the inventory. Poor Mama couldn't do anything until that store sold.

I jumped up, pulled on a pair of jeans and a tee. I grabbed my tote and slipped my feet into flipflops. I stopped by Mama's room on my way out, only to discover she'd turned out her lights. I stole a glance at my Timex. Technically, it was still early, but ... I supposed Mama was tired. Seemed that was the way of it since Papa died.

Oh, well. I'd just leave a note in the kitchen.

***

Downtown twinkled in the darkness. The city had done a good job of putting up beautiful lampposts. Light flooded the storefronts. I parked in front of Allegro, grabbed my tote and pulled out my keys. I unlocked the store, and flipped on the lights as I entered, careful to lock the door behind me.

I'd finished with the downstairs and needed to start on the storage area in the attic. I climbed the creaky old stairs—not the easiest thing in the world in thin flipflops meant for beachcombing—and pulled the chain on the naked light bulb. I ran my fingers over the top of a nearby box. Mama had been here, no doubt. Instead of inches of dust covering the multitude of boxes, there was now only a mere sprinkling. Hmm. Most things were well-labeled. Mama's touch again. Old sheet music, broken instruments, spare parts, music books, and just about anything related to music. Where to start? The back, for sure. If anything of value was in here, it would likely be in a place to be stored away for a long while.

I walked to the back and pulled out an old box. It felt sturdy enough to hold me. I sat on top of it, removed my notebook from my tote, then began pulling out one box after another, going through each one, making a list of its contents. Thus far, most of the things were of little value. A sheet music collector seemed a likely source for selling the old pieces. *Contact auction houses*, I wrote. This was far too important to forget, thus, a note in my handy little book.

One box held some old hymnals. So old, I suspected they could have some value due to their condition, which was good.

After a while, my back ached. "Gracious," I said to my watch, which told me it was after three in the morning. I stood, stretched, and walked around the room again wondering how old the building was and what had been its use previous to Papa moving in.

Papa's store had only been here since the 1940s. He'd bought it from the previous owner, who'd retired. Papa and Mama made a good living from the store. It also provided me with a job I'd loved and the money to buy things I wanted when I was in my teen years. It taught me good work ethics, too.

I started back to work, but then decided I was too tired to continue. I pulled the box of old hymnals to the edge of the stairs, pulled the chain, and climbed down.

Just as I turned the key to lock up, movement caught my eye. I walked to the curb and looked in both directions. Nothing. I opened my car door and peered into the back seat. Nothing there. Blessed relief. With one last glance over my shoulder, I climbed in. Inside the safety of my vehicle, I blew out the breath I'd held. Maybe Fee or Mama should come with me next time.

***

Morning came far too early. Why on earth I had felt the need to go down to the store at such a late hour the night before was beyond me. No, it wasn't. I had a job to do and I needed to get it done in a timely manner. Mama counted on me. In fact, a lot of people counted on me these days.

The promising aroma of something good to eat wafted from the kitchen and drew me out of bed and to Mama's side.

"Smells so good. Whatcha making?" I kissed her cheek and headed for the coffee pot.

"Hey, you. Scrambled eggs with ham, peppers, and onions. Toast. Jelly. Coffee. Nothing special."

"Anything you make is special, Mama. And always yummy." I stirred cream into my cup and remembered the sugar.

Mama brought the food to the table and sat across from me. We ate in silence for a few moments.

"You look sleepy. Did I hear you leave rather late?" Mama spread mayhaw jelly on her toast.

"I didn't mean to disturb you. Yes, ma'am, I did leave fairly late. You didn't find my note? I've put off the work at the store. Between being arrested and trying to solve a couple of mysteries, I just plain ole forgot about it. I'm so sorry. I won't let that happen again."

"Mmm. I did find your note but wanted to hear it from you." Mama laid her hand on top of mine. "Don't you give that store a second thought. Your freedom and finding Boopsie's killer come first. Allegro isn't going anywhere." She took a sip of her black coffee. "Is there anything I can do to help you?"

"Well, now that you ask, yes, there is. I have a feeling the boxes in the back of the attic storage are full of really old music books, old sheet music. Things with some value. I just don't have the time it'll take to get all that inventoried. Not by myself, anyway. Would you be willing to help?"

"Why didn't you tell me this before? I didn't even think about helping. I guess I just dreaded going without your daddy being there." She took a deep breath. Straightened. "But he's in a better place, and I know that. I can certainly go and help. Tell me what you want or need."

"We're going to need to hire someone to carry heavy boxes down the stairs. I don't think either of us could do that. You know anyone offhand?" I ate the last of my eggs and carried the dishes to the sink.

"I think the Cecil boy might help. He was helping your daddy before . . . well, before."

"I'll call him today. Do you think we could get started on that tonight? It's tedious, let me warn you."

Mama took her own dishes to the sink and rinsed them before filling the sink with hot water and suds. "I don't mind tedious. It'll keep my mind off John and give me something to do at the same time."

I paused a minute, glad Mama was distracted with filling the sink. It was odd to hear her call Papa *John*. When I was in high school, I'd never heard them call one another anything besides Mama and Papa when they were in my presence. I let out a heavy sigh. "Good. I'll be home by five. Dinner's on me. We can grab a quick bite at Serena's. Sound good?" I gave Mama a quick peck on the cheek before heading back to my room to get ready for the day.

***

Fee's shop was beginning to feel a bit too comfy. I'd spent way too much time there lately. I lounged on the flowery sofa, pad in hand, while I waited for her to finish with a customer. By the time Fee was able to join me, I had a couple of pages filled with what we knew thus far.

1. Boopsie had died between 9 p.m. and midnight.
2. She'd been hit with her iron skillet.
3. She'd made strange accusations at WHS meeting.
4. She obviously knew something, but what?
5. Mrs. Sweets warned me not to meddle.
6. Miss Sarah warned me not to meddle.
7. Boopsie's grandmother and mother had worked at Rose Haven.

8. Miss Sarah had been hostess at Rose Haven. Was hostess all she'd been? Hmm.

9. Norah had a son, Maxwell.

10. There is a hidden grave.

11. There is a missing diary.

12. The ridiculous notations in Boopsie's diary, written when she was nine years old.

For sure, people in Loblolly knew things they didn't want known. Secrets. Like Mama says, the truth sets you free. And I was determined to learn the truth.

I sat up when Fee walked in.

"Sorry to be so long. Mrs. Adams can never decide what she wants to buy, but she always buys some of the most expensive things in the boutique, so I give her my undivided attention." Fee sat next to me. "Today she purchased the most awful lime green chiffon hat—"

"If it's so awful, why do you have it in the store?"

"Because women like Mrs. Adams like lime green chiffon hats."

"Oh."

"I tried to talk her into this adorable Audrey Hepburn type ..." She paused to gawk at me. "You know, you'd look swell in that hat."

"No. No way."

Fee waved her hand close to the side of her head. "It has a cute daisy petal, black and white ... oh, never mind. I'll just keep buying for customers like Mrs. Adams and hope you come around one day to see style and fashion for what it is."

"Ha, ha. But believe me, I understand. The music store was the same way. Unless someone bought a new instrument, we didn't really have big spenders. That's why we loved music teachers and their students." I held out my list to Fee.

"What's this?"

"What we know thus far." I waited for a response.

"You forgot the most important thing."

"What?" I craned my head around her.

"That they arrested an innocent person."

I nodded and shrugged. "True, but I don't want that on my list. I just want to forget about it and find the person who did this." I sat back on the sofa. "I think we need to speak to Boopsie's mother again. She *must* know something. After all, it was her family who worked at Rose Haven. I have a feeling our answers all lie there and to those connected with the old estate."

"Let me make sure Iris can handle things here, and I'll tag along. I don't want you walking into that den of vipers again."

***

Mrs. Sweets stood on the other side of her screened door, staring hard at us. "What would make you think I want to see you again? You need to leave, right now." She yelled over her shoulder at someone—likely Bubba—to call the sheriff.

"Mrs. Sweets, please. I have reason to believe that you and Bubba could be in danger. Please hear me out."

"The only person I know of who could put me or my family in danger is *you*, Charlotte Graves. Now you need to git."

"Will you please wait until the sheriff arrives?"

"And why would I do that?" She stood, arms akimbo, as she waited for Fee and me to leave.

Something in her tone must have startled Fee because she grabbed my arm and dragged me down the steps and back to the car. She opened the passenger door and threw me in and ran around to the driver's side. She hotfooted it out of there before the sheriff could arrive.

"Humph. That went well, now didn't it?" Fee said. Buffalo Springfield played on the radio—one of *my* favorite songs this time—but Fee flipped the switch to off.

"I don't know why that woman hates me so much, other than the fact that I was arrested for her daughter's murder. Which we both know I didn't do." I stared out the open window and twirled a curl in my hair around my fingers. I turned toward Fee. "It just makes me think even more so that they know something. I can feel the danger in my bones. She may not know or believe it, but I know it's there. Just waiting."

"Let's just let the sheriff and Roan figure out all that. How about if we just concentrate on what we do best and find that missing grave?" Fee pulled into a space at the back of her boutique. "Come on. We're going to walk over to The Copper Pot and grab some lunch. Then, we're going back to Rose Haven."

"Sounds like a plan."

Chapter Twelve

After a quick bypass to my house where I dressed in a decent skirt with matching sweater and even a pair of pantyhose and two-toned Oxford flats, Fee and I headed out to Rose Haven, this time taking my old car. I turned the ignition and switched on the radio. "Hey Jude" blasted out of the speakers of the old girl. "Have you heard this yet?" I asked, pointing toward the dash.

"Just the other day. Their latest."

"I like it," I commented, "except at the part when they kinda scream."

Fee nodded toward the radio. "You know, this car may be a bit on the old side, but the radio works just fine."

We rolled down the windows to let the breeze blow our hair as we belted out the top hit of the day, both of us *nah-nah*ing as loudly as we could, as if we were still in high school without a care in the world.

But I had grown quiet by the time we reached Rose Haven. Seemed funny to me that I hadn't been out this way in a long while and here I was coming for the second time within a few days. The drive had been pleasant. My little Chevy appreciated that I wanted to enjoy the drive. And I couldn't help but think that I'd been in Savannah so long or cooped up here in Papa's store or at Mama's, it was nice to get out into the wide-open spaces. We'd passed several old farms with animals, mostly cattle, out in grassy fields. An occasional field held horses, but they were workhorses with stringy manes and bowed backs. Definitely not the kind owned by the Cartwrights on *Bonanza*.

Familiar farmyard odors wafted through the lowered windows. Those nasty smells held memories, but I still didn't care for them. Right then I was just thankful the last vestiges of honeysuckle mingled with the yukky ones. Honeysuckle and good clean dirt. There was nothing quite like the smell of freshly turned earth as farmers prepared for the next season's crops. Yes indeed, autumn was just around the corner.

As we turned off the main road onto the one that led to Miss Marge's, I had to brake for an old dog that chased alongside us. At least the poor thing wasn't chained to a tree as were so many out in the country. No animal should be forced to live that way. Like the message of a movie I'd seen back in Savannah with Linden —"Born Free"—I believed we were created to roam without shackles. Not a Charlotte Graves axiom, but a good one.

A few more miles and an abundance of homes with old rusted-out cars or trucks in the yards spoke volumes about where we were—out in the country, not within the city limits. Some things didn't change. Around here, you kept things until they didn't work any longer. And even then, you kept them around for parts. Frugality was a way of life. It was a matter of necessity. Not too many folks lived in big houses like the one Miss Marge owned.

This time, as I drove around the shell drive, the estate didn't seem as daunting. Still expansive, but somehow just knowing Miss Marge a bit better and having spent an afternoon there made it feel homier than it had on that first visit.

"I still can't believe she lives way out here alone," I said as I stopped my out-of-place Chevy at the front of the mansion.

Fee pulled on the handle and opened her door by bopping it with her shoulder. "I'm not sure I could do that. As if the house itself isn't big enough, throw in all the outbuildings, the church, and the graveyard and it's kind of ... well . . . creepy."

Once out of the car, we walked to the end of the long walkway before I replied, "You think so? I was just thinking how lovely a home it is." I tilted my head to gaze up at the house. "Big, true, but still quite a pleasant and peaceful place."

"I'll have to work on that. I just don't see what you see."

We stood at the massive oak doors where I lifted the heavy knocker and banged it three times. "Maybe we should have called. She could be in town or busy or ... whatever one does in a big old place like this."

The doors swung open to reveal George Wilkins, a member of the WHS. "Why, Charlotte," he drawled. "Fiona … what brings you ladies out this way?"

"Mr. Wilkins," Fee said over my shoulder. "How nice to see you." She stepped around me and craned her neck to peer into the vast foyer. "Is Miss Marge home?"

"Shore is. And I know she'll be glad to see you." George held up a white container of baby powder and a small paint brush. "I was just fixing some of the squeaky floorboards for her. Nothin' works near as good as the old-fashioned stuff." He motioned us in, then closed the big doors behind. "I'll go back to the kitchen and let her know you're here." He took a step. "Aw, shucks, just come on with me. She won't mind you seeing her covered in flour." He chuckled beneath his breath. "Follow me." He headed toward the dining room to our right.

Fee stepped back to let me take the lead. "Covered in flour? She's baking?"

"Not really," he said, stopping to look at us. "She was cleaning out the pantry and dumped the whole bag on her head. I told her she should'a called me to fetch it for her. She's not quite as tall as you, Miss Charlotte, so things put up high always cause a problem." He gave us a knowing wink before turning to push the swinging kitchen door. "Lookie here who I found on the front stoop." He turned and winked at us.

"George, I can barely see." Miss Marge was, indeed, covered head to toe with the white powdery flour and doing her best to clean it from her face and hair with a dishcloth, but without a lot of success. "Who is it? I do look a sight, I'm sure."

I threw my tote into a kitchen chair and rushed to her side. "Here, Miss May—Marge. Let me help you with that." I took the cloth from the older woman and began to swipe at the flour.

Fee placed her hand on George's arm. "I'll grab the broom if you tell me where it is."

"I'll get it for you." A second later, he removed the broom and dustpan from a closet at the rear of the kitchen and handed them to

Fee while I led Miss Marge to the sink.

"Can you lean forward a bit and let me try to get most of it out of your hair?" I ran my fingers through the older woman's gray hair, flour kicking up a cloud of dust. "I'm afraid that's about the best I can do. You're going to have to shower for sure." I shook my head as I bit my lip to keep from losing it, but I couldn't help myself. I burst into laughter and was quickly joined by George and Fee. Within a moment, even Miss Marge joined in.

"Lands sake. I must look like the Ghost of Christmas Past." She took the cloth from me, dampened it and wiped at her face, making raccoon eyes in an otherwise, pasty white mask. "Let me scoot into my room and take care of this. George, do serve the young ladies some lemonade." She waved a hand toward a far corner. "And there are still a few teacakes in the pantry. I'll be quick as a wink."

"This floor is going to need a vacuum and a good scrubbing, I'm afraid." Fee emptied the dustpan into a trashcan at the end of the sink area, then laid the dustpan on the floor. She leaned the broom against the counter. The white powder had settled into every crack of the old pine planks.

"I'll take care of that after I get your drinks." George opened the refrigerator and took out a pitcher half filled with lemonade.

I took the pitcher from him. "Here, Mr. Wilkins, let us get this. I think I'll take it out to the front porch. Do you think that'll be okay?" I wasn't sure what George's job at Rose Haven was, but he obviously knew his way around the place.

"If that's where you want to be, Margie won't care a'tall." He took a tray from the butler's hall and placed the pitcher of lemonade on it. He then put the plate of cookies from the pantry and added three glasses to the tray before handing it to me. "It's heavy. You sure you got this?" He looked at me, brows raised.

"I'm sure," I said, my voice strained. "If Fee will take the pitcher, I can get the rest."

Fee got the hint as George motioned to the front of the house. "Go on out there and I'll tell her that's where you are. Just shoo Oreo out of your way if she's taking up one of the rockers."

Minutes later we'd settled in a couple of the rockers, a white wicker table between us hosting the goodies. We took our time sipping the tangy drink and nibbling on teacakes. The aroma of honeysuckle mixed with climbing roses, and I breathed in, feeling as languid as I had in days, despite the way I had dressed for the occasion.

Well, since Boopsie's murder, to be exact.

Ducks down on the pond quacked away in faint unison as mockingbirds called to one another from a nearby tree, drawing my attention from one slice of nature to the next. I smiled, almost startled, when the black-and-white cat jumped from one of the rockers at the opposite end of the porch. Neither Fee nor I said a word as the cat sashayed its way toward us, then twirled around my feet. Oreo, no doubt. The old cat stretched out to her full length and settled on a rag rug in the sun.

I gave a full-on grin to my cousin. "See what I mean?"

"I see what you mean. This is a lovely place. Not creepy at all. In fact, it's downright relaxing."

"True. I was just thinking that I hadn't—well, a girl could get used to this place." I sat back and closed my eyes, taking in the sounds and the summery smells surrounding us, nearly ready to take a short nap. But the door squeaked open and we were joined by the lady of the manor, now cleaned of the flour.

"You've found my favorite place in all of Rose Haven," Miss Marge said. She took the rocker next to me.

I lifted the pitcher from the table, one of many strategically arranged around the porch. After pouring a third glass of lemonade, I handed it to the elderly woman, noting briefly that the front door had been left open. Fee passed the teacakes. "Miss Marge?" she offered.

Miss Marge shook her head as she brought her glass near her lips.

"So, what has brought you two beautiful girls out to see this old lady? Two visits in one week?" One brow shot up. "I know something is up." She took a sip of lemonade. "Tell me how I can help."

I placed both Oxfords on the porch and brought the rocker to a stop. "Miss Marge, we were wondering if you've remembered anything else about the hidden grave."

Miss Marge nodded as if she'd expected this to be my first question. "I thought about that a great deal after you left yesterday." She wrapped her gnarled fingers around the glass and brought it to rest on the table at hand. "I recall that Grandfather Evan related every now and then that he wished he could find his mother's grave. But it wasn't anything the family ever spoke of." She leaned her elbow on the chair's arm and shifted closer to me. "A taboo subject, you understand. And I only heard it mentioned a time or two. Now my father ... my father *never* mentioned it."

"But your grandfather told you this?" I shifted toward the older woman, mindful of Fee behind me.

Miss Marge's eyes widened. "Oh, no. I just happened to overhear. In those days children were seen and not heard." She chuckled lightly.

I only offered a brief smile. There sure were a lot of overheard conversations at Rose Haven. "Do you think your father may have left information for you about the grave?"

"Well now ... if he did, he hid it well. I've been through all his papers. At least those in his office. There was nothing like that there."

I took a bite of cookie and chewed slowly while I thought. "Well, if you do find anything like that, would you mind sharing it with me? It might help to solve the mystery of the hidden grave. Maybe even tell us why Boopsie was killed."

Miss Marge cocked her head and turned to look directly at me. "What does a lost grave from so many years ago have to do with Boopsie's death?" Miss Marge put her hand on her cheek and turned abruptly, nearly spilling her drink. "Oh. I have an excellent idea." She placed her glass on the nearby table, then she clasped her hands and looked expectantly at Fee and me.

"Yes?"

Even Fee stopped rocking.

"What if I pay you to come and do an inventory of my estate? I've been meaning to do this for years but I'm just too old to do that now.

If you find something … well, that would be wonderful. And as for me, I'll know what all is in this big old place." She looked from me to Fee and back again.

Still clutching my near-empty glass of lemonade, I leapt from the rocker, went to the rail, and propped against it. "It sounds like a good idea, but I'm not sure I'll have time for that. I'm still helping Mama with the inventory of Papa's store. She can't sell it until I get that done."

"For goodness sake, Charlotte." Fee crossed to where I stood and placed her hand on my shoulder. "You need to do this for Miss Marge. I can help with the music store and I'm sure our mothers can pitch in. It'll keep them out of our hair while we work on other things." Fee nodded toward the graveyard.

Miss Marge's suggestion made sense in practical terms. But could I pull it off? Add in my WHS work, the music store, and now this? "I don't know, Fee. Mama's been kind of squirrely about going into the store without Papa there." I bit my bottom lip and thought for a moment. "But she did offer to help browse through the boxes."

"How about if I get Mama to help Aunt Polly?"

"I suppose that would work." I curled my fingers through one flip of my hair. "We'll need to make sure they're truly up for it, though."

"Oh, that sounds wonderful," Miss Marge said. "I just know Mary and Rebecca will do this." Her smile expressed her eagerness. "But why don't you bring the things from the music store here and let them work from my home? I have plenty of room to spread things out. That way, if any of you needs something from the others, you would all be right here."

I looked at Fee, brows raised in question.

Fee held her hands palms up. "I know Mama would love doing this. She hasn't said so, but I know she was jealous of the time Aunt Polly got to spend here when they were children. Maybe this would ease of bit of that old hurt."

Miss Marge brought her attention back to me and I said, "I like it. It'll make my job easier. I just need to arrange for those boxes in the attic at the music store to be brought out here. Lots of old stuff up there."

Miss Marge smiled as she raised a finger. "Did you know that your father's music store was once the offices for Grandpapa's lumber company?" She reached for a teacake and took a little nibble.

What? I looked at Fee, who had returned to her rocker. How could I not have known that? Had Papa known? Even if he had, why would he have brought it up? He'd had no clue about this convoluted mess. At least, to my knowledge he hadn't.

I sat between Fee and Miss Marge, ready to talk out the facts.

"Grandpapa kept his offices there just as his father had done," Miss Marge said. "You know how things have a way of changing with modern inventions. Those buildings were empty for quite a while. Then young people began moving back and opening businesses, like your father, and like you, Fiona." She smiled and rocked as she gazed out at her surroundings and munched on the tiny teacake. "Well, the town is becoming a vibrant place again."

"Let me get this straight." I stilled my feet, stopping the to-and-fro action of the rocker. Could we possibly find something helpful in the attic? I lightly touched Miss Marge's hand, which gripped the arm of the rocker. I let my hand rest on Miss Marge's, emphasizing my words with a light tap. "The building in which Papa had his music store, where it still is, was Woodville Lumber Company's offices at one time?" I wasn't confused. Certain of what I'd heard, I wanted validation in case I had misunderstood. I focused on the older woman's face.

Miss Marge brought her own rocking chair to a standstill. She placed her other hand on top of mine. "That's right. The old WLC was housed there. For years. No telling what you'll find there when you begin to clear it out. I'm sure my father wasn't so meticulous that he took *every* little thing with him when he moved."

I slid my hand from Miss Marge's. "So, some of your father's and maybe even your grandfather's papers could be stored away or—lost— in Allegro?" I scooched to the edge of the rocker and looked intently at Miss Marge.

"I suppose that, yes, they could."

My mind whirred with this new information. Could those papers reveal the hidden grave? Could they contain some secret Boopsie had overheard? And if they *were* in Allegro, I needed to get them ... and fast. But minding one's manners was always expected in the Graves household. Mama would never forgive me if I were to be rude, especially to my elders. Still, curiosity was getting the better of me. "Miss Marge, this has been a wonderful visit, but Fee and I need to run and let you get back to your pantry." I stood and lifted the tray with the treats.

"Now you just leave that." Miss Marge motioned for me to put the tray down. "George will come clear away these things."

"I don't mind—"

"No, no." The older woman waved her hand again to indicate she meant business.

Not one to argue with my elders, I smiled as I set the tray back on the little wicker table. Fee laid a half-eaten teacake on the tray then joined me at the top of the steps. "Thank you so much for the lemonade and teacakes, Miss Marge. And the good company."

"I look forward to seeing both of you and your mothers very soon." The little woman rose and walked to where we stood. A second later, George walked out the front door to join Miss Marge on the porch. I looked from where he now stood to the opened door. Had he been listening to our conversation? I chewed on the inside of my mouth. There surely was an awful lot of that going on at Rose Haven.

Past and present.

"Charlotte?" Fee said, jolting me back to the here and now.

"Oh ... yes ..." I smiled, gave Miss Marge a quick hug, then wondered why. Hugging was unlike me. At least hugging people whom I didn't know or who weren't related to me.

After a final good-bye wave, we climbed into the Chevy and pulled out of the driveway, the crushed shells crunching beneath the wheels. "That was interesting," Fee said as she pulled the visor down to look at herself in the mirror.

"Mmm," I agreed, then stole a quick glance in the rearview mirror. My eyes widened. There stood Miss Marge and George on the porch, their hands clasped.

That wasn't what I'd expected from this visit, but if it would bring us closer to solving a mystery and a murder, then the drive out had been well-worth it.

But a new question had now risen. Could those diaries be in Allegro?

Chapter Thirteen

After a quick run to the Tastee-Burger, I parked behind Soilse. Fee got out with her bag of TB and a mention that she had a mountain of paperwork to take care of. A glance at my watch after she walked into the store told me the time was just after five. Good. The sun would be up a while longer. Though anxious to get to those boxes in the music store, I wasn't about to go alone. I'd wait on Fee to finish her work. Besides, I'd needed to clear my head a bit and get a take on the revelations of the past couple of days. A walk through the park in the square summoned my weary, overloaded mind.

I exited my car, darted into the store to let Fee know where I was going.

"Wait for me before you go into the music store," she said. "Promise me."

"Promise," I said, then left and headed up the street, TB bag in hand. Approaching Allegro, I stopped for a second. Curiosity pulled at me. But a promise was a promise, and I'd told Fee I'd wait. Besides, the park was a great place for a quick dinner and some deep thinking.

Another five-minute walk brought me to the town square. I loved this park. As beautiful as the ones in Savannah are, they never held the special place in my heart this lovely little park occupied. I'd made memories here, splashed in the fountain as a child, chased Fee and Roan through the winding trails. As a teen, I'd spent summer days lolling on a quilt, a good book in my hands. Roan and I had shared our first kiss on the bench I now occupied.

Sneaky, subconscious mind.

Roan.

Ignoring Boopsie's diary entry wasn't a possibility when it came to him. I'd been my typical old self back then and had run away from the issue. If I'd been stronger, more confident, I'd likely be married to him with a couple of kids by now.

I pushed the thought aside with a shake of my head. Nothing ever came from any what-might-have-been.

Fee was right. I had to think through how to handle Boopsie's revelation. One thing was certain, no longer would I run from my problems. There were other, better ways to deal with them. Running solved nothing and only created other issues. My life had played out as a perfect example of that.

With a heavy sigh, I placed my tote bag on the ground. The aroma of french fries called to me as I opened the bag of food and removed the burger and those rumbling-stomach-inducing fries. I popped one into my mouth and savored the familiar yumminess.

When I'd finished my meal, I tossed the crumpled-up bag into a nearby trash can. I returned to the bench and settled in as comfortably as possible, then removed the notebook from my tote bag, pulled my legs up and crossed them, and rested the pad on my left knee. I searched through until I found my notes from Boopsie's diary, then added what I'd learned today at Rose Haven. Could Allegro contain further secrets? It was almost too coincidental that these mysteries would come full circle. And one thing for certain—I didn't believe in coincidence.

A quick five-minute walk took me back to Soilse. I entered the boutique and called out to Fee.

"Hey, I'm back here," she called from the rear. "I'm finished up. You ready to go?"

"Yeah. Dinner in the park was good—a choice place to think . . . and eat."

"I barely know I ate mine. Check this number, take a bite." Fee came out, dressed in what she considered play clothes. They looked way too nice to me. "I'm ready if you are."

"Let's go then. Allegro awaits."

***

For once, I didn't give a second thought to the soaring temperature in

Allegro's attic. Eager to get into the uncomfortable space, I climbed the stairs as quickly as possible, wondering the whole way if the boxes held secrets from Rose Haven. Were we moving closer to finding clues that would lead us to who'd killed Boopsie?

I pulled the chain on the single bulb and let my eyes adjust to the dim light.

Fee climbed the stairs and joined me in the musty space. "This place is creepy."

"You think everything is creepy." Once my eyes could make out the different areas, I made a beeline for the back of the room and those curiosity-killed-the-cat boxes. "These I've labeled are the ones I thought I'd take to Rose Haven. But . . . I didn't find anything related to the lumber company in any of these when I was here before. Maybe I need to look more closely for something that Mr. Mayhew may have left behind." I turned to Fee and stood with my hands on my hips. "What do you think? See anything that looks like old WLC stuff?"

Fee turned in a circle, taking in every corner of the attic. "Will they be labeled? You know . . . have you found any that were?" She bent to read the labels on a stack of nearby boxes, their sides caving in. "Nothing here that indicates the lumber company. Want me to look inside?"

"Maybe. Let's keep looking first. I have no clue if Papa ever found stuff up here that had belonged to the previous owners. If he did, I certainly never heard him mention it. Of course, . . ." I opened a nearby box. ". . . he wouldn't have known any of the things we've discovered lately. And he'd have no reason to share that info with anyone." I tried unsuccessfully to lift a box. "This one is way too heavy. If they're all like this, we'll need help getting them out of here."

"Here, move over and let me try to lift it." Fee bent and strained to pick up the box. "I see what you mean." She sat it down with a *thud* and read the label. "This looks like your handwriting. *Old hymnals.*" She punched me on the arm. "Must have carved them on stone tablets."

"Cute." I rubbed my arm as I counted the boxes. "Looks like dozens upon dozens."

We rummaged through boxes for what seemed like forever, opened a few and found nothing that looked related to the lumber company. We separated the boxes as we went, shoving aside those we thought were Allegro-related. I rubbed my back, sore from all the bending, and looked at the rows of boxes. Way too many. "We're definitely going to need some help."

"Agreed. So, let's go then. Do more of this later." Fee walked across the room and to the top of the stairs.

I turned and stared at the boxes one last time. What if they held nothing but old hymnals or music-related stuff? *Please, please, please* have a clue. Anything that will show me where to go from here. I joined Fee at the top of the stairs and pulled the chain, which cloaked the attic in darkness.

"Why'd you do that? I can't see a thing," Fee said.

"Sorry. Give me a minute." I fumbled for the tiny flashlight I'd tucked inside the back pocket of my jeans. I turned it on and aimed the beam at the stairs. "Go ahead. I'll hold the light."

Fee took one step then took a quick glance over her shoulder. "If it's not too late, let's go over to The Copper Pot for some coffee and pie. That little burger didn't do much for my hunger pains and climbing up and down these stairs feels like ascending to Mount Sinai. I need nourishment." Fee carefully made her way down the remainder of the stairs. "What time is it anyway?"

"You always need nourishment. But I agree. Coffee and pie sound great. And I'll tell you the time when we get down these stairs." Halfway down I stopped and shook my head. "Oh, I get it. Stone tablets … Mt. Sinai. Very funny, Fiona." I pretended to laugh, but deep down, I hoped Fee would never change. She was forever a bright spot in a sometimes-dark world.

***

A quick glance at my watch reminded me why, other than a song piping from the jukebox, The Copper Pot was so quiet. We slid into our favorite booth in the back. I breathed deeply, taking in the pleasing aromas of coffee, fried food, and bacon. Always bacon. Serena sauntered over, looking as if it had been an excruciatingly long day.

"Hey, y'all. You're not normally here this late. What gives?" She looked first to her watch and then back at us.

I slid to the edge of the booth's seat. "We're hoping your decaf coffee is still fresh."

"Now you weren't gone so long from Loblolly, you forgot we always have fresh coffee. Regular *and* decaf. And plenty of pies and cakes. And for you girls, it's on the house."

"Serena, you can't keep doing that. You're giving away your profits."

Serena waved the hand that wore the familiar jingle-bracelets in the air. "Don't worry about my profits. Besides, if you come in late enough, the desserts are free anyway. Bake 'em fresh every morning. That's our way."

Fee's eyes brightened. "And what time would *late enough* be exactly?" she asked with a smile.

"Right around ten, 'bout now." Serena nudged Charlotte with her elbow. "And Roan is usually right on time, too, for free pie."

I frowned. "What's that got to do with me?"

"Oh, yeah," Fee interjected. "Pretend all you want."

Serena laughed, the sound reminding me of her bracelets. "So just stay right where you are and let me bring you some pie and coffee." She walked away, tucking her pencil behind her right ear, then turned and said, "You said decaf, right?"

We both gave a nod.

"You're right, you know," Fee said. "She is giving away her profits. I need to have a talk with that girl about how to run a profitable business." Fee removed the silverware from the napkin wrapped around it, then carefully placed the napkin on the tabletop, the silverware beside it.

"You about finished with your accounting degree?"

"Mm-hm. Two more classes. It's just a BS degree. No biggie." Fee pulled a napkin from the dispenser on the end of the table and laid it across her lap.

"Yes, it is. You've wanted to do that since we were kids." I followed

Fee's example with the silverware, but I laid my silverware on the napkin. Germs. Everywhere, germs. Things like this and that nasty jail cell always gave me the heebie-jeebies. "Okay. Back to those boxes in the attic. Mama said we could get the Cecil boy to help with them. I think I'll give him a call in the morning."

"And I'll talk to Mama about helping Aunt Polly. Like I said before, I'm sure she'll jump at the chance to spend more time at Rose Haven."

Serena arrived at our booth with ice water, coffee, and two slices of pie, one chocolate and one apple. "If you don't like these, there's more in the kitchen. Pecan and cherry along with slices of coconut cake and some good 'ole lemon cheese layer cake." She removed the items from the tray, then flipped it beneath her arm.

"Oooo. I love lemon cheese layer cake. Can I swap one of the pies for that?" My mouth watered at the thought. My great Aunt Coty had made the world's best lemon cheese layer cake. I missed my aunt…and the cake. I wondered if Mama had her recipe. I made a mental note to ask.

"Sure thing, but keep the pies. You never know who might come in and want to join you." Serena waggled her eyebrows at me, then went to retrieve the additional dessert.

"So, shall we just meet you at Rose Haven tomorrow or all go out together?" Fee stirred half the little silver-toned pitcher of cream into her coffee before attacking the chocolate pie.

"Let's all go together. That way we can talk about things in the car on the way there and back." I had second thoughts about the coffee and pushed my cup toward Fee. I picked up the glass and took a sip of ice water.

"What? No coffee?"

"No. I haven't slept well as it is. This'd just make it worse, even if it is decaf." But I dove into the cake as soon as Serena sat it in front of me. "Mmmm. This is so good." I let the tangy-sweet taste of the lemon icing roll around in my mouth and savored the smooth texture of the cake. "I wish I could bake like this."

"You could if you really wanted to."

"I don't like to cook. But if I could make this, it just might be worth the effort." I took another big bite and closed my eyes. "Mmmmm. So good."

We spent the next few minutes in silence as the desserts in front of us disappeared to nothing but crumbs. We were about to leave when the sheriff and Roan walked in and took the booth across from us.

"Ladies." Sheriff Turner removed his hat and sat it on the bench next to him. "You ladies staying out of trouble?" Tank pushed his hair back.

Roan looked at me then back at the sheriff.

"Nothing or nobody to be in trouble with, Sheriff." I slid from the booth, turning to grab my tote from the far side of the booth.

"That's not exactly how Mrs. Sweets put it. Says you been asking her a lot of questions." The sheriff turned in his seat, resting his left arm along the back and pulling his knee up onto the bench.

Hmmm ... "It's against the law to ask questions now?" I sounded like a shrew, but pickled bricks, the man had arrested me. Well, Roan had, which was the same thing.

"Depends on who's asking and why." The sheriff drummed his fingers on the tabletop.

"Whether she wants to believe it or not, and you, too, for that matter, I only went by to warn her that she could be in danger. It's not my fault there's a killer on the loose." Fee's hand gripped my elbow, hard. Okay. Maybe that sounded too accusatory. Without question the sheriff was doing his best, but could I help it if my woman's intuition was on high alert?

Roan leaned on the tabletop, his hands clasped. He took a deep breath, blew it out, then spoke. "Just let us do our jobs, Charlie." He looked up and locked gazes with me. "There are some rough people out there and we all know a killer is on the loose. You don't need to do anything to draw attention to yourself. Butt out, okay? Just let us handle this."

I didn't flinch, not even a little as fire blazed behind my eyes. "My name is *Charlotte*. I don't know anyone named *Charlie*." With that, I walked out of the diner.

***

My temper still raged when I crawled beneath the bedcovers. The nerve of Roan calling me *Charlie*. Once upon a time, that special name made my heart skip and breath catch in my throat. Now, it was just a painful reminder of what might've been. And it was Roan who had gone and ruined it all.

Or, had it been?

That thought had plagued me for so many years. It wasn't easy to accept that it might not be the truth. But Boopsie's diary said she'd planned it all along. Should I believe her? Probably, since I reckon no one lied to their own diary.

I dabbed at the tears that came unexpectedly. Oh, Roan. I had loved him. Probably still did if I was honest with myself. And why did he have to look so good after all these years? He was just a boy then. I knew that now. Just an innocent boy being manipulated by the likes of Boopsie Sweets.

I turned over, adjusting the pillow beneath my head.

A boy then ... yes. A grown man now. Was it too late for the two of us? "Don't be stupid, Charlotte . . . let it go."

A sliver of a smile crept up from my lips. Sounded like a good title for a country song.

Chapter Fourteen

The next morning, we four women piled into my car and created quite a ruckus. I thought of a gaggle of geese as Fee, Mama, Aunt Becky, and I talked, often over one another, on the way to Rose Haven. I was getting accustomed to the sights along the way. As we sped down the dirt roads, dust flew up, creating a reddish-orange cloud behind us.

I loved seeing the farmers in their fields. Most people around here only farmed what their family could eat. A few still had endless fields of cotton or peanut crops. The bolls or peanuts wouldn't be harvested until well into the fall. Since the invention of the mechanized harvester back in the 1940s, farmers who could afford one, had one. They did the work of eighty to one-hundred people. Expensive? Yes, but not when compared to labor costs, I suppose.

It wasn't long before we turned off the main throughway onto the little dirt road that led to Rose Haven. Aunt Becky leaned toward the front of the car as we approached the stately mansion. Her hands gripped the seat behind Fiona, who sat in the passenger's seat. "I cannot believe that I'm finally getting to browse through this big old house."

"It's just a house, Becky." Mama looked up at the rearview mirror and caught me looking at her reflection.

"You're right, Mama. It is just a house. A *big* house, but only a house, nonetheless. Let's simply all go in and do our jobs and not think about anything else." Poor Mama. I felt her discomfort, saw it in her eyes. Mama had nothing to do with being invited to Rose Haven as a child while her sister was forced to stay home, a fact that still bothered me. Somewhere in all of this existed a reason and I wouldn't stop searching until I discovered exactly what that was.

For the third time in as many days, I pulled my Chevy to the end of the walkway leading to the house. We all piled out. Mama and Aunt Becky stood at the end of the long brick walkway, each one looking at the structure looming before them. I almost read their thoughts. Mama reliving childhood memories, straining to recall specific bits and pieces. Aunt Becky eager to see all the things her sister got to enjoy while their mother denied her the same.

Mama laid her hand on my shoulder as we reached the door. "You knock since you're the one more or less in charge of this little venture."

I shrugged, lifted the heavy iron knocker, then banged it three times.

"This is becoming a habit," Fee said, rather matter-of-factly.

"Shhh," Aunt Becky whispered. "Mind your manners."

The massive oak doors swung open to reveal Miss Marge, this time without her apron.

"I've been expecting you," she said. "Come in, come in." She pushed the doors back and stepped out of the way for our little group to enter.

Fee and I stood aside to allow our mothers to enter first. Another of those southern good-manners things. Mama looked up at the enormous chandelier. Her eyes roamed over the hundreds of individual crystals, rainbows dancing as they swayed with the breeze from the open door, while Aunt Becky seemed to take in every aspect of the grand entry hall.

I moved to help Miss Marge close the heavy oak doors. "Here, let me do that." I pushed the doors until the now-familiar *clunk* signaled the latch had caught its mark.

"Thank you, dear. These old doors are getting heavier with each passing year. I guess I need to think about getting rid of this old place. It's just more than I—even with George's help—can take care of." The older woman stood in the middle of our group, wringing her hands as she gazed around at the big space. "But where are my manners? Come, come." She motioned for us to follow her as she headed for the parlor.

Dozens of boxes sat in neat stacks along the far wall, in front of bookcases filled with old volumes. Surely, they weren't the boxes from Allegro … were they?

Slowly, and as unobtrusively as possible, I made my way over to one of the stacks. I sneaked a peek at the labels. They *were* from Allegro. But when and how had this happened? I looked at Fee, eyebrows raised in question.

Fee shook her head slightly and simply shrugged. Obviously, she had no idea, either.

For the first time, I noticed bookcases brimming with old volumes. Why hadn't I noticed all those books before? Could an old history book be resting on one of those shelves? I needed to get a closer look … later.

Mama turned and faced the older woman. "I see that the boxes arrived, Miss Marge. Thank you for arranging the pick-up."

I jerked around at Mama's words. She'd arranged this? That was so out of character. Things had really gotten peculiar lately.

Miss Marge looked up at the mention of her name. She smiled warmly. "It was nothing, dear. I've known the Cecil family for years. And thank you for meeting him at the store this morning. He told me how much he loved your John. He was delighted to help out."

So, that was where Mama went early this morning. I'd heard Mama leave, but I thought she'd gone for a walk or an early-morning breakfast with a friend or Aunt Becky. That wouldn't be unusual. But to Allegro? Without *me*?

"Now, you all make yourselves at home." Miss Marge stood in the wide doorway. "You move things around in here however you deem necessary." She waved around the room at the furnishings. "There's always coffee in the kitchen, and food in the icebox and pantry. Dishes are in the cabinets in the kitchen. Just open them until you find what you need. I'll stay out of your way." She took two steps then turned back. "Oh, and my handyman George is out and about. If you should need him, just ring the old dinner bell on the back porch. He'll hear it from wherever he is and come running."

Handyman, huh? I'd never held hands with my handyman, and I doubted Mama had either. A story grew at the same rate as Jack's beanstalk, but this wasn't the time for *that* either. There was much work to be done.

Fee sat on the Oriental rug covering the parlor floor and played with Oreo, who'd made an appearance, while I showed Mama and Aunt Becky how to look over each book or item and document their findings in the notebook I'd purchased for the task. Afterward, Fee and I went searching for Miss Marge. We left Mama and Aunt Becky, eagerly working on the task at hand.

We walked from the parlor through the entry hall where those prismatic rainbows danced on the walls. The chandelier was beautiful, but hardly my taste. I preferred more simplistic décor, like what I'd seen once in a magazine display of Frank Sinatra's living room. Clean lines. Simple comforts, in spite of his wealth and good fortune.

After making our way through the formal dining room, we pushed open the same swinging door George had gone through yesterday. We found Miss Marge bending down, peeking into the oven.

The aroma wafting through the room caused my mouth to water.

Fee closed her eyes and breathed deeply. "Mmm. What is that delicious smell?"

"Oh, you startled me!" Miss Marge stood straight and closed the oven's door. "It's nothing, really. Just some zucchini bread. I'm doing my best to use what's left of the summer garden before fall gets here." She pulled off the oven mitts. "Seemed like a good thing to make. And you know how I do love to bake." She giggled at her unexpected rhyme. "Oh. I guess I'm a poet but didn't know it."

We politely joined in the laughter.

I ventured farther into the kitchen. "It smells so good, Miss Marge. If it's half as good as your teacakes, then you've got another winner."

"Oh, thank you, dear. I hope it will be tasty. My old recipes haven't failed me yet. I'll take some to your mothers as soon as it's done."

I leaned against the counter. "Mama and Aunt Becky are going to have fun working together. It's been a long time since they got to do stuff like this." I crossed my ankles. "Miss Marge, would you mind if Fee and I wander the grounds before we get started on the inventory? I'd like to get some idea of what all we may encounter along the way."

"Of course, I don't mind. Land sakes, child. That's why I offered you the job in the first place." She filled a tea infuser with Earl Grey. "I need to know what all is stored on the estate. I haven't walked the property in ages. You just go anywhere you want or need to. I own all you can see for miles, so have at it." She waved her hand in the air then took a cup from one of the cupboards. She took the kettle, which now whistled away on the back burner, and poured boiling water over her infuser. "My only admonition is that you be careful. I have given permission to a few select gentlemen and even some ladies to hunt on my land. It's too early for deer season, but they could be out and about looking for squirrel or rabbit." She pointed out the windows above the kitchen sink. She looked thoughtful. "I have a good idea. You wait here and I'll be right back."

I picked up the tin of tea and read the label until Miss Marge returned.

"Here you go." She held out her hand to me and pressed something into mine when I extended it. "This should help you find your way. It was my great-great-grandfather's. It's laid on Papa's desk for so many years, I mostly don't see it anymore. But it seems like a good idea for you two young ladies." She smiled broadly.

My hand held a compass. I didn't think it was necessary . . . but if it made her feel better, then I'd certainly slip it into my pocket. "Thank you, Miss Marge. We promise to be careful." I turned to Fee who was leaning over the old farm sink, peering out the windows. "Won't we, Fee?"

She turned at the sound of her name. "What? Oh, sure. Yes. We'll be careful."

***

The scent of pine surrounded us as we entered the line of trees behind Miss Marge's home. The woods were thicker than they appeared from the kitchen windows. We listened for any noise which might indicate hunters in the area. Thus far, we'd only heard an occasional whippoorwill or some other bird whose call I didn't recognize. And, every now and then, small animals scurrying to-and-fro caught our attention. Would we have any luck finding that missing grave? Or were we headed in the wrong direction?

"I don't like being out here, Charlotte," Fee whispered.

"Why are you whispering?"

Fee grabbed my arm. "Shhh. Don't be so loud. I thought I saw smoke when we were in the kitchen. We don't want any hunters to shoot at us."

I looked heavenward. "They're a lot more likely to shoot at us if we *aren't* talking. If we're talking loudly, they'll know we're human and not a ... a squirrel or a ... rabbit," I fairly yelled.

"Oh. That makes sense. I guess." For half an hour, Fee followed me through the deep woods. "You should have told me you had a hike in the woods in mind. I have on sandals, in case you haven't noticed." Fee leaned one hand against the rough, sticky bark of a pine tree and reached down to pull straw from her open shoes.

"Look." I pointed at what seemed to be a clearing. "What's that?" I took a few tentative steps forward.

"It's so dark in here, it's hard to tell."

"Come on. Let's go a bit farther." I didn't like the darkness of the forest any better than Fee, but if I showed any sign of fear, my cousin would flee for sure. And I did not want to be in these woods alone. Or maybe not so alone, if hunters—or even worse, a killer—lurked behind the next tree.

Light spilled into the dark forest not a hundred feet—give or take an inch—from where we now stood. Indeed, there was a clearing with a small cabin smack in the middle. The cabin didn't look like much. It was obviously either extremely old or neglected ... or maybe a bit of both. The clearing around it covered about twenty feet on all sides of the structure. Pine straw covered most of the ground, with patches of Alabama red clay peeking through in several spots.

Why didn't George, or someone, keep the old cabin in better shape? Or did Miss Marge know it was even there? Did she remember it? She said it'd been years since she walked the grounds. Did that include the woods? Questions and more questions.

We stood at the edge, trying to conceal ourselves behind the largest trees we could find. Fee had been right. A small ribbon of smoke rose from the rickety stone chimney.

"Look," I whispered as I pointed to a couple of vehicles parked near the rear of the cabin.

"So, what do we do?" Fee clung to her chosen tree. "I mean, other than turn around right now and go back to Rose Haven?"

"No ... something's up and my instinct tells me we need to know more."

Fee shot me a look. "*Weeee* do *not* need to know more."

"Okay, then ... I do."

Fee's eyes widened. "Charlotte, *what* are you going to do?"

"Knock on the door?" I had no clue. I'd wound up in some strange situations in looking for the dead, but this was one for the books. Maybe I should have listened to Roan. *And* the sheriff. "There's a face at the window. We've been spotted."

"Well, isn't that just the cat's meow," Fee hissed toward me. "No turning back now." She looked from me to the cabin and back again. "Maybe if we make a lot of noise as we approach, they'll come out," Fee said.

"Good idea. Let's pretend we just saw it."

"Didn't we? *Just* see it, I mean."

"Yes, Fee. You know what I mean. Act natural." I looked at my cousin. She was shaking from head to toe. "Stop that shaking. We don't want to appear to be afraid."

"But I *am*. And you said to act natural."

"Come on. Just follow my lead." I took a step into the clearing and began to laugh. "Oh, Fee. You are so funny. Hey, this must be a hunting cabin." I tried my best to sound cheerful and unafraid. Maybe I was trying too hard.

"Ha, ha, ha. I have no idea what it's doing here. It must be a hunting cabin." Fee's acting abilities bordered on horrendous.

I hadn't taken one step when the door opened, and three men

walked onto the covered porch. "Oh, hello," I called from the edge of the woods. "We were just out for a . . . *Cam?*" I squinted against the sunlight and held up my hand to shield my eyes. "Is that you?" The one in the middle looked exactly like Cam Lawrence, Olivia's son. The old town bully. The other two held rifles. Oh, good. Pointed straight at *us*.

"Charlotte Graves. As I live and breathe." He sounded like something straight out of one of the westerns my father and I used to watch together on Sunday afternoons. John Wayne. Alan Ladd. And, my favorite, Gary Cooper, because he reminded me of Papa.

But the man standing in front of me, gunless, was the same old Cam I remembered. James Dean good looks. He even wore his hair like the late actor and walked with the same swagger. "What on God's green earth are you doing in the middle of the woods?" Cam stepped down to the next step. The other two men stayed on the porch. They still held those rifles.

I didn't know much about hunting, but I knew enough to know that one didn't point a gun at a human. Nope, those guns should be open, the barrels pointing down. I didn't like this. "Hey, Cam." I raised my arm and waved, hoping my internal quivers weren't apparent. "It's been a while. What're you doing out here?" I pointed to my cousin. "Fee and I were at Miss Marge's and we decided to take a walk. But ... I think we got off the trail." I sent a smile his way. "I mean, if you can call what we were on a trail."

"Now, these woods aren't any place for two pretty young things like y'all." He walked down the remaining two steps and sauntered over to me. "You hear me?" He reached me and then, James Dean easy, touched my hair.

I tried my best not to flinch. To not show fear. Roan had warned me to stay away from Cam and his buddies when we were in high school. Said he was no-good and a bunch of other stuff he wouldn't say back then. Even though Cam tried more than once to corner me in the hallways, Roan was right there to stop him. Maybe my luck was about to run out. Or maybe Cam had changed?

For pity's sake, where was Roan when I really needed him?

"You sure you're just out walking? Not looking for something?"

The smirk on his face was enough to make me want to run. Not that I'd leave Fee out here alone. I decided on a new approach. "Well … actually, Cam … we *are* looking for a missing grave. You know I do genealogies, right? You know, looking for people's long-ago relatives." I smiled again. "I've gone to work for your mama."

But Cam didn't flinch a muscle.

"Well, anyway," I said, breathing out, "Miss Marge is trying to find one of hers. She thought there might be a grave somewhere on the property. Seemed natural to follow what looked like a trail." I tried one more smile even as an inner voice told me to hush. To stop prattling and let Cam get a word in. If he would.

Cam looked over his shoulder at the two men on the porch. Unlike Cam, they didn't have movie-star appeal. They looked downright menacing, not to mention filthy. "You guys seen any graves out here?"

They shook their heads. I was surprised a flock of vultures didn't fly out of their nasty hair and beards with the movement. I stifled a shudder and took a quick glance at Fee to see how she was doing.

"Other than Miss Charlotte *Graves*," Cam continued, "I haven't seen any *graves* out in these old woods. But now that you're here, may be that I need to take up a new hobby." He walked a circle around me, wrapping one of my curls around his finger as he came to a stop in front of me. The men with him laughed. Not a funny, ha-ha laugh, but more like a threatening, lecherous laugh.

I couldn't help it—I shuddered.

Fee suddenly appeared beside us. "Now that's about enough of that, Cam Lawrence." Times like this, Fee's Scottish temper took over her reasoning. "We'll just be going on our way and let you guys get back to your hunting. If you *do* find a grave, by all means let us know. I'm sure Miss Marge and the sheriff will want to hear about it." She grabbed my arm and dragged me toward the path we'd followed to the cabin.

Behind us, Cam and the two men roared with laughter.

Chapter Fifteen

The laughter of the three men bounced off the trees and echoed within the forest. As soon as we were out of sight of Cam and his friends, Fee and I took off at a run for Rose Haven, with Fee's long legs carrying her faster than my nubby ones.

"Wait up, Fee. I can't breathe." I stopped and leaned over, hands on my knees.

Fee came back. "Sorry ... sorry ... to run off ... run off ... and leave you behind," she said, panting. "That was thoughtless. And careless. And sinful. Downright sinful. Please ... please ... forgive me."

"What?" I scrunched up my face. My heart pounded so I could barely hear her, but what I could hear was beyond strange. "No. I mean ... yes," I said through my own pants. "Sure. I forgive you." I blew out air and filled my lungs again. "Whooh!" I straightened fully. "There's nothing to forgive. You just have longer legs." I walked in a slow circle, breathing in and out, hands resting on my hips.

"You good to go on now?" Fee glanced in the direction of the cabin.

I took one last breath, nodded at Fee, then motioned for her to continue. I glanced over my shoulder. Surely those guys wouldn't try to follow us to Rose Haven. Chances were, they were still back at the cabin laughing.

I stole a glance at my wristwatch between jogs then did some mental calculations. It had taken us over an hour to get to the cabin. How long would the trip back take? Of course, we walked *to* the cabin; now we were running. Stopping to catch our breath and rest a minute lengthened the return for sure. Now, dark shadows cast by the towering pines enveloped us and I wasn't even sure we were still on the trail.

My need for answers had overruled common sense.

Fee stopped about three feet in front of me. "Can you see the trail?

She turned in a circle, searching for signs.

I followed Fee's lead and did the same. "I think we may be lost. I don't see anything that looks like a trail."

"We couldn't be *that* far off. I mean, we kind of went straight to the cabin and then straight back." Fee turned in another circle. "You know those novels we read where some character always makes a stupid mistake and winds up in a bad situation or, worse . . . dead?"

I nodded.

"I think we're living one."

The height of the trees combined with the thick, overgrown bushes and brambles meant we had managed to get ourselves into the thick of mid-morning dark. Why hadn't I brought my tote with me? We'd have a flashlight at the very least if I'd remembered it. Yep. Just like the novels . . . except . . . "Fiona Campbell, don't you dare say that. We are not going to die, and we are not stupid." At least I hoped we weren't. What did I have? I patted my pockets and remembered the compass. "Hey," I said, pulling it out. "I forgot I had this. You know how it works?"

"I have no clue. Never needed one before and I dropped out of Girl Scouts same time as you. I know my way around Loblolly." We stood shoulder to shoulder as she peered down at the gift in my hands. "How can it be so close to noontime and yet so dark in these woods? I can barely see it."

"Yeah, me too. I don't even know what all this means."

"Degrees. You know, like degrees of latitude or longitude."

"Is that true or did you just make it up?" I turned the unfamiliar object around in front of me. The red pointer moved every time I moved. "Okay, I know we can figure this out." I stared at the thing in my hand.

"I didn't make that up, Charlotte. Latitude and longitude have degrees. Thermometers have degrees. And apparently . . . so do compasses."

"Okay. Let's just stop and think about this." I propped my left hand on my hip. Even in the cool shade of the woods, sweat beaded up and down my back and my tee clung to skin. "So, the little red arrow thingy always points north." I turned in a circle again. "I should have paid better attention to Linden when he tried to show me how to read one of these."

"Well, you sound as if you know what you're doing. You heard at least some of what he said, so let's trust the red arrow." At least she was encouraging me rather than doubting me.

"Okay. So, that day when we sat on the front porch of Rose Haven, the sun was setting in front of us. Today when we left the sun was rising in front of us. So that means the house faces west and we walked toward the east." I held up the compass. "If we want to go west, and north is that way . . ." I pointed to the right . . . "that would put the back side of Rose Haven there." I pointed straight in front of us. "So, we've got to go straight ahead to go west." I looked up at Fee with brows raised.

Fee grinned at me and nodded. "Sounds good. Let's do that."

"As long as we keep north to our right, and we go straight, we are heading toward Rose Haven." A blackbird cawed close by, startling us both. "Let's go."

We started off once again, all too aware of the *what if* that loomed before us. Every now and then, we stopped to make sure we still traveled west.

"Fee?"

"Yeah?"

"I just had a thought." I turned to my cousin, who brought up my left. "We *cannot* let our mamas know about all of this. They'd have two hissy fits and they'd never let us out of their sight again."

"You're right about that."

We continued walking, dodging branches and all manner of flora. An occasional small animal scurried near us. "I hate being out here like this. I don't mind being in cemeteries, but *this* is spooky."

"I need water. Why didn't we bring a jug of water?" Fee stopped. "We've been walking forever. You sure we're going in the right direction?"

I stopped and leaned on a nearby tree, mindless of the sticky sap that likely oozed its way onto my clothing. "I'm about as sure as I can be. I don't *really* know how to read a compass." I waved it at Fee. "It's still saying north is to our right, which makes straight ahead where Rose Haven should be." Maybe Fee was right to be concerned. We'd been walking such a long time. *Please let us find our way back.*

"Listen," Fee said. "Did you hear that?"

In the distance, a bell clanged. "It must be Rose Haven." I glanced at my wristwatch for the time. Just after noon. We hadn't been gone for as long as I'd thought. "They're either looking for us or calling us to lunch." I blew out a deep breath of relief.

Ten minutes later we entered the meadow near the pond. How on earth we'd gotten so far off to that side of the house I'd never know. But thank goodness Rose Haven loomed in front of us like an old friend, welcoming us home.

***

After lunch, Miss Marge went to her room for an afternoon nap while Mama, Aunt Becky, Fee and I settled in the parlor. I looked over the work Mama and Aunt Becky had done. "This looks good, y'all. Pickled bricks, you even separated the books into categories for the sale." I looked around and noted boxes labeled the same.

"We tried to make it as easy for you as we could," Mama said. "Some of the sheet music is so old, it will likely be snatched up by a collector."

Aunt Becky indicated a pile near her. "Check out the colorful artwork on the covers."

Mama pointed to two old books laying on the coffee table, now shoved against the wall. "Oh, I put aside a hymnal or two I thought you'd like to see. They appear to be different from most of them here and could be a bit more valuable. You may want to check them out."

I went to the table and picked up the books. Opening each, I noted publication dates. Early 1800s. I closed them and ran my hand over the designs on both. Mama was right. The covers appeared to be leather with ornate tooling. Though well used, they were in remarkably good shape for their age. "I'll put those in here and look through them tonight." I placed them in my tote bag with a mental note to remember.

Fee flipped through the sheet music her mother had mentioned. "You're right, Mama. These are beautiful. You know, I don't remember the last time I bought a piece of sheet music. Do they still make that kind of stuff?"

"Of course, they do," I said, shock raising my voice. "When's the last time you were in Allegro? You didn't notice it there in the racks? Visible to all who entered?"

"You don't have to be so sarcastic, Cuz. I'm not the musical one in the family. You got those genes. Remember?" Fee continued browsing through the stacks of music.

Fee was right. Mama and I had musical genes that neither Fee nor Aunt Becky possessed. Another mental note to add to the family genealogy records. Would I find the musical ancestor? Maybe. With a bit of luck and a lot of hard work—just maybe.

We were winding down for the afternoon when Miss Marge joined us. "I do hope that you have found my home a good place to work."

"Yes, ma'am, we have," Mama answered for all of us. "Did you have a nice nap?"

"Oh, I always have a nice nap. I've been blessed with the ability to rest peacefully in all manner of circumstances." She sat in a Queen Anne side chair. "Now, tell me about your findings." She clasped her hands in her lap and looked expectantly from one face to another, finally settling on me.

"Fee and I did find something unexpected." I scooted across the floor and sat at the feet of Miss Marge. "Did you know that there's a cabin in the woods behind your home?"

"Land sakes." She slapped her hands against her cheeks. "I'd forgotten about that. It's been years since I've wandered these woods. I bet that's Grandpa Evan's old hunting cabin. It's still standing?"

"It's not in great shape, but it's standing. Could use some TLC, a good cleaning. It smelled funny." I scrunched up my nose. "Like . . .dead plants, or wild animals or something. But the men there didn't seem to mind it, so it must not be too bad."

"There were men there? What men, dear? Did you know them?"

"Three. Two I didn't know though they seemed familiar. Could be I knew them from high school. But, of course, I recognized Cam Lawrence, Olivia's son." I shifted positions on the floor and rubbed at the tingle in my leg. "Must've been a hunting trip. The two guys I didn't know had rifles."

Mama and Aunt Becky exchanged looks and they didn't look pleased.

"Oh." That was all Miss Marge said, but the look on her face and her clenched fists spoke volumes. She was concerned, to put it mildly. But why? She'd told us about expected hunters. But obviously not Cam and his friends. Mental note to check on that. I was making way too many mental notes. Something would be forgotten, for sure.

I looked at the organized mess around us. "Miss Marge, I forgot to thank you for arranging the pickup of all these boxes." Change of subject. A good thing. "Mama and Aunt Becky are doing an amazing job." I turned to my mother. "Mama, you're going to be able to sell Allegro soon. Once this is done, I can arrange for the sale of things and then just clean it up for the new owners."

Mama nodded, then brushed a tear from her eye. "Look at me, getting all sentimental."

I crossed from the table to the sofa and sat beside Mama, slipped my arms around her shoulders. "It's okay, Mama. I'll miss the store, too. Almost as much as I miss Papa."

"Life is just never going to be the same, is it?"

***

A few hours later, I unlocked Allegro for the umpteenth time that week. I'd be relieved when this task was behind me. Being in the store without Papa was bad enough, but to have to resort to late-night forays into its bowels was too heavy a burden.

Mama had done a good job of getting all the boxes delivered to Rose Haven, but she had no knowledge of the lumber company having offices in this building. Could I have overlooked something this morning? I wouldn't know unless I looked one more time.

I climbed the stairs and pulled the chain on the lightbulb, then got to work looking for boxes—or anything—from the lumber company. With all the music-related boxes moved to Rose Haven, there were fewer to peruse, making this task much easier this time around.

After an hour in the attic, I was spent. My search had produced old ledgers from WLC. I stuffed them into a box, pushed it to the top of the stairs, then pulled the chain, throwing the attic into darkness. Somehow, I navigated the stairs with the box and my tote. I sat it down at the door so I could manage the lock, then shoved the box over the threshold with my foot and locked the door behind me. I lifted the box, took two steps toward my car parked not ten feet away and stopped abruptly. Light from streetlamps spilled over the car and onto the street. Broken glass glistened all around my old Chevy.

I dropped the box and looked up and down the street, thankful I still held the key to Allegro in my hand. "Come on, Charlotte. Hurry." I managed to unlock the door in spite of my shaking hands. I locked the door behind me, then ran to the phone behind the counter.

Less than five minutes later, none other than Roan pulled the cruiser behind my car. He climbed out, slammed the door behind him, then walked to where I hunched behind the doors of the store. "It's after midnight," Roan called through the closed door. "What are you doing out here alone at this hour? Or have you forgotten there's a killer on the loose?"

I opened the door and walked out onto the sidewalk. "How could I forget? I was arrested for the deed. Or did *you* forget?" I yelled. Not at all like me, but he just made me so mad. And I was frightened. None of this was my fault. None of it. Yet, Roan seemed to blame me for everything that happened in the past eight years. I wanted to scream at him. Pummel him. *It was you, Roan. All of this is your fault.* But that wouldn't solve any of this. It wouldn't bring Boopsie back. It wouldn't erase the past. It wouldn't make the future better. It wouldn't even make standing here, this close to Roan, any more bearable. How could he still possess the power to crush my heart?

He walked away and I followed him to the Chevy.

"You haven't finished with the store yet?" He took my elbow and pulled me away from the car back the sidewalk. "Here. Just stand over here out of the way while I do my job. I need to call in for help."

I shrugged off the electricity that coursed up my arm from his touch. *Stop it. Change the subject.* "By the way, Roan, I was at Rose Haven today. Took a walk in the woods and ran into Cam Lawrence and some rough-looking guys with him. Said they were hunting." I leaned against the front window of Allegro.

"What? Now why on earth would you even think about going into those woods? Do you have any idea how easily you could get lost in there?"

Boy, did I ever …

Roan pulled out a notepad and pen. "And what's this about Cam and guns?"

"I wasn't looking for trouble or trying to get lost. There was a trail. Not a very good trail, but still, a trail." I waited while he wrote. "I was looking for a missing grave. It's what I do, in case you didn't know it."

"How could I not know it? The whole town knows it." He tucked his pen into his breast pocket then walked around in a circle. He removed his cap and slapped it against his thigh before putting it back on his head, then took a deep breath. "Listen, Charl—Charlotte. You've got to be careful. You can't just run all over town asking a bunch of questions that—that could get you killed. And for sure, you have no business running off into the woods or being at this dadblamed store at this hour of the night." He waved toward the storefront as he clenched his jaw. He sounded angry and disturbed and a lot of other things I didn't want to think about at the moment.

I took two steps away from the window toward Roan then stopped at the look he gave me. "I can't do my job if I'm not out roaming through woods and cemeteries. And I can't help Mama without being here. Daylight hours are spent doing my job, the one Olivia hired me to do. And Miss Marge, too. I can't help it if it sometimes puts me in harm's way." I sounded defensive. But for Pete's sake, he needed to give me some slack.

He pointed at me, ducked his chin, and drew his brows together. "You have to promise me you won't go out in those woods again, Charlotte. We've had a lot of trouble out that way. Folks've been complaining about odd occurrences and strangers lurking about." Well, at least he wasn't yelling. He took a breath before leaning forward to look inside my car. "Can you tell if anything is missing?" he asked.

"I don't know. I didn't really look, but there wasn't anything of value there. It's all at Rose Haven or locked up inside." I pointed to the store.

Roan ducked his head back inside my car, careful not to touch anything.

"And by the way, with all that's going on out that way, why on earth would you not have a deputy standing guard at Miss Marge's home? She's a single, elderly lady."

"She has George. He lives in one of her cabins." Roan put away his notepad. "Yeah. I'm calling in help," he said. "Ordinarily, I wouldn't. I'd call it an act of vandalism and wish you luck with your insurance. But with all the other ..."

I waited patiently while Roan walked back to his squad car, radioed in the call, then walked back over to me. "In case you hadn't noticed," I said, "George is old, too." What was wrong with the people in this town? Things had changed so much in the eight years I'd been away, I barely recognized the place I'd once navigated, up one side street and down the other.

Well, one thing for sure, if Roan and Sheriff Turner weren't going to protect Miss Marge, then I would. Moving in was no longer an option. Plenty of rooms made up Rose Haven, and one of them was about to house Charlotte Graves.

Chapter Sixteen

"**A**re you sure it's okay for us to do this? Did you have the decency to ask?" Mama always worried about the little things. Always.

"No, Mama. I didn't ask. Miss Marge needs us and we're going to stay here until they catch this murderer." I pulled my heavy suitcase up the brick steps, its weight challenging my strength. I flashed a tentative smile at Mama, then picked up the iron knocker and banged it three times.

George opened the door before I could say much more to my mother. "Why Miss Charlotte, Miss Mary, wha—?"

"Hey, George." I pushed past the elderly gentleman and made my way into the entry hall, my large piece of luggage hindering my steps. "Now don't go looking at us like that. We're moving in here while we do the work at hand. It'll be easier on us. Not so much back and forth. I'm sure Miss Marge won't mind." I sat my heavy load down and took Mama's suitcase from her. Mama's, I noted, was a great deal lighter than mine. Mama had no choice but to follow me into the home.

George stood, wide-eyed with surprise, but a smile crept onto his lips as he closed the door. "Margie's in the kitchen. I'll run fetch her. Just stay put 'til we get back." He walked away.

"Charlotte Graves, you didn't ask. I knew you hadn't." Mama turned her eyes heavenward. "Lord, where did I go wrong?"

"It'll be okay, Mama. Wait and see." I tapped the toe of my Keds as we waited.

"Mary. Charlotte. What's this about moving in here?" Miss Marge had obviously been baking again. Flour covered her apron and smudges dappled both cheeks.

Mama grabbed her suitcase and turned to leave. "Miss Marge,

please forgive us for being so presumptuous. I thought Charlotte had asked you. But apparently, she did not."

But Miss Marge's face shared delight with my concern. "Why, this is the most splendid idea I have heard in ages. Young people living beneath my roof again." She clapped her hands, sending a cloud of white dust into the air as George returned. "George, help them with their bags. You know where to put Mary." She nodded at George who returned, in kind. "Charlotte can go across the hall."

***

Per my arrangements with Miss Marge, Fee and Aunt Becky arrived later that morning while Mama and I rummaged through a couple of boxes in the parlor, and Miss Marge puttered in the kitchen, sending us an occasional line from a bygone song, namely Billie Holiday's "God Bless the Child," and Doris Day's "Sentimental Journey."

"Hey, y'all," Aunt Becky called from the entry hall. "Can we come in?"

"Come on in," I yelled back.

"How did y'all get out here so quickly?" Fee said just as another tune skipped from the kitchen to the parlor. Fee looked toward the back of the house. "Hey. Miss Marge has a sweet set of pipes on her."

I nodded. "She's in a great mood, I'm thinking." I looked at Mama, took a deep breath and answered Fee. "To answer your question, we brought things with us to stay for a few days. I wanted us to get here early enough to talk Miss Marge into it, if it came to that. At least until we find this murderer. Once Roan told me about the strange things happening out this way, I just couldn't leave Miss Marge and George out here alone."

Mama lifted a brow. "Someone broke into Charlotte's car last night."

"When did that happen? Where?" Aunt Becky looked pointedly at me.

"Look, it's no big deal. Roan got there in no time. I'm sure it was just kids trying to find some money or something. Nothing was missing. Anything of value was in the store with me."

Fee bore down on me. "So, you went back to that store. Alone. Again."

"I have a job to do. Actually, three jobs," I defended myself.

"My point, Charlotte, is that you don't have to go there alone." Fee towered over me, looking for all the world like Mrs. Henderson from eighth grade. The thought of that woman still gave me the heebie-jeebies.

"I can't wait around for help to arrive, Fee. I have to go when I can." I rubbed the back of my neck, an outward sign of my inward stress.

Fiona put her arms around me. "I wasn't fussing at you. I'm merely pointing out that I'm here to help you, with the store *and* with this mess." She indicated the things in the room. "With anything you need. And that includes helping you take care of Miss Marge."

Miss Marge chose that moment to arrive with trays of freshly baked biscuits. Following closely on her heels was George with a tray laden with coffee cups and a pot of steaming coffee.

"Now, what about Miss Marge?" she asked as she placed her tray on a sofa table now located against a wall.

"I think we just forgot anything that was on our minds, Miss Marge." I hurried over to George and removed the coffee pot from his tray to lighten the load.

"I distinctly heard someone say they were going to take care of me. Mary and Charlotte are planning to move into my home while they work on all of this," she indicated the music littering the floor and tabletops. "If you and Fiona are going to be coming out every day, Rebecca, why don't you both plan to move out here for a while, too? We'll make a ladies' party of it." She beamed as she passed around plates filled with hot biscuits and jam.

Fee looked at George as she accepted a plate from Miss Marge. "What does George have to say about that?"

"Pshaw," George said with a blush. "George don't mind having a whole bunch of purty women surrounding him, is what George has to say."

"Rebecca?" Miss Marge looked expectantly at Mama's younger sister as she took a plate to her.

"I guess I could come for a night or two. I have Angus to take care of. He's not much of a cook."

"Oh, splendid. I'll get right on preparing two more rooms while you all get back to your business." She took a step to leave but turned back to us. "Remember, there's more of everything in the kitchen and you are to make yourselves at home." She smiled. "George, I'll need your help, please."

There was Mama's telltale throat clearing again. I rushed to Miss Marge's side and motioned for Fee to follow me. "You go do what you normally do, Miss Marge. Fee and I will take care of the rooms if George will show us where to go."

"Well, if you want to do that, fine, but do enjoy your biscuits first. I'll attend to the mess I made in the kitchen and George can help you young ladies. Come and get him when you've finished eating." She reached up and patted me on the cheek before heading toward the kitchen. George followed close behind, munching on a buttery, jam-slathered biscuit as he went.

***

George had long since helped Aunt Becky and Fee carry their bags upstairs once they'd returned with them. He retired to his little cottage, leaving us ladies gathered in the conservatory where a soft glow from the few lamps on glass-topped iron tables made the space even cozier at night. The light reflected off the glass panes of the unadorned windows, casting shadows here and there.

"Did you ladies find your rooms to be satisfactory?" Miss Marge rubbed her hands over Oreo's black-and-white fur. Clearly, Miss Oreo had her run of the household.

"Oh, yes," we all answered at once.

"The room I'm in," Mama hesitated. "Is it the one I stayed in as a child?"

"Why, yes, Mary. It is exactly the same now as then. Rose Haven could use some updating, as you young people call it." Oreo purred beneath the soft, repeated touch of Miss Marge's hands. "I'm from the generation that lives with things until they wear out."

"I thought it looked familiar." Mama chewed on her bottom lip as she pulled her legs beneath her. She settled into a corner of a flower-print club chair.

"Miss Marge? Why do you call Mama *Mary*, and not *Polly* like everyone else?"

Fee shifted on her end of the sofa. "Good question. I've wondered that same thing."

"Oh, habit, I suppose." The older woman said. "In my generation, and in the manner in which I was reared, we addressed one another with our given names. I've always called her *Mary*. I'm rather fond of that name." She looked around at each woman in kind. "And Rebecca and Fiona, and dear Charlotte."

"Yet, we all call you *Miss Marge*. Why not Miss Marjorie?" Fee said.

"Oh, that would be my Papa's doing. I was always his *Little Margie*, but as I got older, people took to calling me Miss Marge. It just stuck, I guess you could say."

I spoke up. "And George calls you Margie."

"Yes, dear, sweet Georgie, as I used to call him. He's the only one who can get away with that these days." Her eyes twinkled as a Mona Lisa smile spread across her lips.

Aunt Becky smiled at Miss Marge. "I rather like being called *Rebecca*. No one has called me that since Mama and Daddy passed away."

"I'm recalling bits and pieces from my time spent here as a child." Mama walked to the rear windows which overlooked the deep forest, then turned and faced the other women. "I remember playing with Nina, Boopsie's mother, when I was a child." She walked to the green-and-white-checked sofa where I sat wedged into a corner. Mama eased down beside me.

"That's right, dear. You two had such a great time playing in the playhouse. Do you remember that? George turned one of the old cabins into a place for the two of you. It was spectacular." Marge closed her eyes then shifted in her seat, unsettling Oreo. "Did you keep in touch with Nina, Mary?"

"Oh, no, ma'am. It was just a natural split, I suppose. We remained friends throughout grade school, but we drifted apart after that. Then I met John, of course, and we opened our store. We just lived different lives."

"No wonder, Polly," Aunt Becky said. "She married that no-count Jeb Sweets who loved the bottle more than he loved his family."

"I remember Boopsie coming to school more than once looking as if she'd been up all night. Like she hadn't gotten a wink of sleep," Fee said. "Maybe that was the reason. We wouldn't have known that because children have always been shielded from such. It will probably take this more—shall we call it—modern generation to start calling things what they are."

I cocked my head to one side as I looked at my cousin. Between the war in Vietnam, the civil rights movement which had led to Dr. King's untimely death, the hippie movement, the recent death of RFK, and the whole "make love not war" sentiment ... the world as we'd known it when we were innocent children of the '50s was over. Boopsie's death, to me, seemed like the proverbial cherry on a melting bowl of ice cream. "Mmmm. With the way things are, I guess that makes sense. But still ... poor Boopsie. No wonder she was always so mean. I bet she was jealous of the way we were rai—reared." I leaned against Mama, taking her hand, hoping Miss Marge hadn't caught my near faux pas. *In the South, we raise our cattle and rear our children,* Mama always said. "I can't imagine Papa treating us like that, Mama," I said with a gentle smile. "He was such a good man."

Mama kissed the top of my head. "Yes. He was."

Here came the old memories again. Not just of Papa, but of moments with Roan. I couldn't think of Papa and Mama and the life they'd shared without thinking of the man I'd thought—for too long—I'd spend my life with. If I hadn't retreated from the pain—if I'd stayed and hashed things out with him—would I be married now and sharing the little cottage we'd dreamed about? Would I be a mother, too?

I'd had too many of those thoughts lately. I snuggled closer to Mama and willed myself not to cry.

Chapter Seventeen

Miss Marge broke the silence surrounding us in the conservatory. "I know I had a nap and should not be this sleepy, but I do get up with the chickens, as the old saying goes." The elderly woman rose from the chair, sending Oreo to the floor. "I'll just bid you all a good night. Do stay up as long as you wish. I really don't hear anything once I'm asleep." She walked to the door leading to the hallway, then stopped and turned back to us. "Good night all. Goodnight, Mary and dear Charlotte." With that, she exited the room, Oreo hot on her heels.

I noted that Miss Marge had taken to calling me *dear Charlotte*. Maybe she felt a connection to me because I'd come to her rescue, so to speak. But who wouldn't want to protect Miss Marge? I was becoming quite fond of her. She was sweet *and* a fabulous cook. Besides, I had a sense that, somehow, I knew her beyond knowing of her. That wasn't possible, but still, it niggled at the back of my mind. She definitely reminded me of someone I knew. I just wished I could remember who.

Mama rose from the sofa. "I think we should all head up, too. We need to get settled in for the next few days. I haven't unpacked, only peeked in." She glanced around at each of us.

Aunt Becky joined her sister in the middle of the room. "I agree. Besides, this old body needs to be in a reclining position. My bones can't take too much of sitting on the floor. Even with a thick, wool rug beneath me." She rubbed her right hip.

We followed one another up the stairs, each of us stopping at our assigned quarters.

I bid my family goodnight, and kissed Mama before she entered her room. I hadn't explored my surroundings this morning either. My gaze rested on each aspect of the enormous bedchamber. No other word would do. This wasn't just a bed*room*, this qualified as a bed*chamber* which boasted exceptionally tall ceilings for the current era. When was this home built? I'd read about it recently, but my mind was filled with so many other things. Let me see. Alabama became a state in 1819, this home was at least a couple of years older than that. Goodness. Why hadn't I remembered that? Brain overload, for sure. I tucked that tidbit away for later and headed for the bed.

The bed stood way too high for me to simply climb into it. I looked beneath and discovered a lovely mahogany stepstool. An old china chamber pot. "Please tell me there's a bathroom," I said to no one. Miss Marge had mentioned that each bedroom had its own bath, so ... I took one more trip around the room, opening every door, all of which squeaked as I opened them. The first two were small closets that, upon stepping back, looked as if they'd been added after the house had been built. It wasn't fancy but it would do. The old black-and-white marble floors boasting of the 1930s at their best lay beneath a clawfoot tub and a vitreous china basin held up by metal legs. The toilet had one of those overhead pull chains I'd only seen in the movies. I tugged it. Yep. It worked. A very good thing.

I exited the bath and heard a light knock on the door. Of course, Fee stood on the other side.

"Hey, just making sure you're still up. Wanna talk?" Fee climbed upon the bed without benefit of the stool.

"Sometimes I wish I were tall. Just sometimes." I pulled out the little stool and climbed up the three steps, tumbling into the bed, the mattress sagging beneath me.

"Mmm. You smell good." The curl I wrapped around my finger felt damp. "Wash your hair?"

"I did. It's that new stuff that has herbs in it. Makes me hungry." She pushed back against the headboard. "Think we could go raid the fridge?"

"I'm sure Miss Marge won't care, and Mama is probably out like a light." I eased to the edge of the bed and placed my feet on the top step of the little stool. "You couldn't have told me this before I climbed up here, could you?"

"Sorry. I didn't know I was hungry until you mentioned the smell." Fee scrambled off the far side of the bed.

We made our way down the stairs as quietly as possible. I cringed at each creak, thankful to have passed through the teen years without such a warning system in our home. I'd sneaked out but a time or two when Roan had come by for homework or study notes. When that happened, we'd sat on the front steps and talked for a while.

Pickled bricks. Too many old memories of Roan these days. We'd have to talk, for sure. But right now, too many other things demanded my attention. Roan would have to wait.

Downstairs, to our surprise, we found our mothers and Miss Marge sitting at the kitchen table, big bowls of peach cobbler topped with mounds of ice cream before them.

Fee stood with her fists on her hips. She glared at the three women. "Well now, isn't this a pretty sight? Do you see this, Charlotte?" She indicated the group at the table with a wave of her right hand. "Our moms hitting the caramel sauce at this hour of the night." She picked up the jar of caramel topping, still warm.

I shook my head. "Unseemly, that's what it is." I feigned shock, then Fee and I burst into laughter.

"Did you leave us any?" Fee said.

Miss Marge pushed back her chair, its legs scraping against the old wooden floors.

Mama laid her hand on Miss Marge's. "Stay there. I can get it for them." She stood, her hand patting Miss Marge's shoulder as she went to the freezer for the treats. "Y'all want cobbler? Just ice cream? Both?"

"Yes, please." We answered in unison.

***

After finishing off our late-night snack, we moved back to the conservatory. It seemed the natural place to settle in for a rest rather than retiring on a full stomach.

"So, Charlotte. How is your investigation going?" Like Fee, Aunt Becky was always to the point. "Have you learned anything yet? Any suspects?"

"Well, I know *I* didn't do it, in spite of what Mrs. Sweets may think." I grimaced. "She sure doesn't like me very much." I played with the fringe of the afghan folded on the back of the sofa.

"She doesn't know you, dear. If she did, she'd adore you." Miss Marge's smile spread across her countenance.

"What about the hidden grave? Have you girls had a chance to look for it?" Aunt Becky again. Ever the curious one.

Fee and I exchanged glances before I answered, "Uh, we've looked, but we haven't found anything yet."

"Mary, do you remember Papa ever mentioning a hidden grave?" Miss Marge asked.

My head cocked at the question. Why would Miss Marge think Mama would have been told about a missing grave? Then, Miss Marge had said her father doted on Mama. And what was *that* all about? I sure had more questions than answers. My brain overflowed with question marks while I longed for a few exclamation points.

***

Sleep hadn't brought dreams with answers. That would have been too much to hope for. Still…

After a much-too-large breakfast, Fee and I headed to the back of the property to browse through the outbuildings. Besides George's little cottage, there were ten cabin-like structures. Miss Marge had already told me that each had a living area, a small but adequate kitchen, one small bedroom downstairs, and a loft above.

Fee stumbled as we entered the first of the buildings. "I never thought about our hometown having slave quarters. Did you?"

"Oh. These weren't slave quarters." I moved an object out of the way as I tried to maneuver around the cramped space. "Rose Haven never had slaves."

"For real?" Fee jerked her head back. Her eyes grew wide.

"Nope. Not a single one. The original owner was an abolitionist. Hated slavery. He paid good wages and built these for his employees.

Lots of folks moved here when the territory was opening up. He brought many along with him when he came. And don't forget, at least a few, if not most, were likely kin of some kind." I shoved aside an old chair. "I did a bit of research, but not much. This place was built way back. When the first owners came here, before Alabama was a state, they were promised homes and jobs. I guess the jobs included building all this. Don't know how he afforded it, but wages were different back then. Who knows? A question for another day. And I have no clue how Miss Marge wound up with Rose Haven."

"Holy cow! Who would've thought that?" Fee stepped around an old trunk and other odds and ends to get to the far side of the room. "Spiders." She shivered and swatted at a cobweb. "I hate spiders."

"Hmmm. There's too many to save. I'll ask George to come out with us when we really go through all this stuff. Maybe get him to spray or something beforehand." I stopped in front of the trunk Fee had passed by. "Hmmm. That could hold a lot of treasures."

"Or just air."

"Thanks, Fee. I'm trying to picture artifacts and you're envisioning nothing." I pulled at the rusted latch. How long had this thing been in here? Evidently, quite a while. The room smelled musty. Very musty. "I'm thinking we need to cover our noses for this job. No telling what we'll encounter. Yukky stuff."

"I totally agree. So why don't we just let George do his thing then we can come back."

Fee headed for the door, careful not to knock me down.

I joined her outside the second building. "If all of these are as full as that first one, this is going to be a huge job. Think we may need some help?"

Fee nodded. "Yep. Big and dirty and lots of heavy furniture. I hope it hasn't been out here so long that it's all ruined."

"Me, too. That would be a shame." I stopped. "Mama mentioned the Cecil boy a few times. He's the one who helped with the boxes from Allegro. He has a truck *and* muscles." She looked at Fee. "You know him?"

"Who?"

"The Cecil boy." I looked at Fee. Where was her mind?

"Oh, him. Well, kind of. Depends on which one she means. There are four or five of them, I think."

"Well, I'll get the number from Mama since she knows which Cecil she's thinking of." I looked around at all the buildings. "I don't remember what she said his name is. Maybe he'd like some extra cash this summer. Gas money. Clothes. School supplies."

"I like that idea. Less work for us and a built-in bug killer." Fee shot me a lopsided grin.

Goofy girl. If I had to do a job like this in addition to the store and finding Boopsie's killer, then I was blessedly relieved to have such a pleasant sidekick. Things felt less threatening all of a sudden.

Except for the spiders. I needed to find George.

And call the Cecil boy.

Chapter Eighteen

After getting the number from Mama, I called Ned Cecil. He wasn't available, so I talked to his mama who assured me she'd have him meet me at Rose Haven later that morning. Glad to finally have some much-needed muscle power and a pick-up truck to boot, Fee and I headed to the outbuildings.

Fee pulled her long red curls into a hippie-cool head scarf. I'd secured mine earlier with a headband. I'd also come armed with two pairs of heavy-duty yard gloves and a can of bug-killer. "When is he supposed to be here?"

"I didn't want to make it too early. I told him nine. High-school kids like to sleep in, especially during summer break. I figured that was late enough, even if his summer break is almost over."

Both of us wore old jeans and tees. This was dirty, heavy work, so I'd chosen my cemetery-hopping Army boots. At least Fee hadn't worn fancy sandals. Instead, sensible, but fashionable tennis shoes donned her feet. We arrived at the first building at the same time as a mud-splattered, late-model pick-up truck pulled into the yard, Roy Acuff's "The Wabash Cannonball" blaring out of the opened windows. Figuring it to be the Cecil boy, I waved him over.

"Glad to know he's punctual." I pulled on the door of the first building and heard the truck door slam behind me.

"Yeah. That's niiiiii—yai-yai."

"Good mornin' ladies. I'm Ned Cecil." He touched his hand to the brim of his western-style hat.

Cecil *boy*, indeed. No wonder Fee suddenly found herself speechless. This certainly was no boy. Nope, this was a full-grown Viking. Broad shoulders. Long reddish-blond hair. Tall. Taller than Uncle Angus. And that was saying something.

Have mercy.

His blue eyes seemed to bore straight into Fee. Had he even noticed me? No way. He was lost in Fiona and vice versa. Well . . . it was about time.

Fee extended her hand and Ned took it in his. "Fiona Campbell." She grinned like a silly schoolgirl carrying her first crush. Then, she indicated me. "This is my cousin ... uh, Charlotte—umm—Charlotte Graves." Her hand remained within Ned's grasp.

He acknowledged me with a "Ma'am," but his eyes never left Fee's face.

Never, ever had Fee reacted to a man like this. Never. Always wrapped up in being that rare breed—a businesswoman—she seldom dated. I calculated, and to the best of my knowledge, Fee had been on only one date since I'd come back home.

I hated to break this up. . . this whatever it was, but we had work to do. I walked over and extended my hand. "Charlotte Graves."

Fee pulled her hand free of Ned's. He took mine, shaking it quickly. "Sorry to be a bit late. I had to help with feeding the livestock. It won't happen again."

"No worries. In fact, I'd say you're right on time." I glanced at Fee and spread my mouth into a huge grin. "If you'll follow me, I'll show you what I have in mind getting done around here."

***

By the end of the day, we'd cleared out two of the buildings, loaded Ned's truck and had a start on the inventory, which left me shocked at the finds. I hoped Miss Marge didn't want to sell all of this. It would be a great start for a museum.

Later that evening, Miss Marge, along with her guests, gathered around the kitchen table for another homecooked meal. Once again, the three older ladies outdid themselves. Baked ham, sweet potato soufflé, baby butter beans, and freshly made fried cornbread lined the center of the table. And Mama mentioned something about an egg custard pie for dessert. Oh, my. If I kept eating like this, I'd soon be as big as the side of Miss Marge's big red barn. My body obviously missed digging through cemeteries. That activity burned a far-out number of calories. Besides, I loved being out in the middle of nowhere, searching for someone's long-lost relative. To me, the hunt was more fun than the find. Well, maybe just as good, if I were honest.

The scene which lay beyond the windows grabbed my attention. Where could that grave be? Locating it was paramount. A mystery remained unsolved. And a murder. Someone had wanted Boopsie silenced. Why?

"Did you hear me, Charlotte?" Mama called from the other side of the table.

I looked at Mama. "What? I mean, yes, ma'am?"

"I asked if the Cecil boy showed up today. We were so busy, we felt we shouldn't stop to peek in on your work."

With a waggle of my eyebrows, I looked sideways at my cousin. "I think I'll let Fiona answer that."

Poor Fee. She blushed beneath her freckled face. "Oh, yes, ma'am. He showed up. He put in a full day's work. Took a load of things off to the charity." Fee turned her attention to her food, filling her mouth, chewing slowly and carefully.

"What on earth is the matter with you, Fiona?" her mother said. "Where are your manners?"

"Aww. Leave her be, Aunt Becky." I tried, I really did, but I couldn't stifle my laughter. "I do believe our Fee has met her match. And I do mean that literally. As in—*her match*."

"The Cecil boy?" Mama's hand flew to her chest. "But he's just a *child.*"

"Apparently, there's more than one Cecil boy," I said.

Mama's face changed from shocked to relieved. "Oh. Thank goodness. The boy who helped me was barely old enough to drive unassisted."

"Who is this young man, Fiona?" Aunt Becky meant business any time she called her daughter by her given name.

"He's . . . well, he's … perfection." Fee sighed and sank back in her chair, a dreamy look on her face. "All that and a bag of cherries."

Miss Marge joined in the fun. "It would seem that our Fiona finds herself taken with the Cecil boy."

Fee broke into the brogue of her Scottish grandmother. "He is right fine, for sure, Miss Marge. Fairly a Viking of the highest order. Worthy of a maiden of the Highlands."

"Fiona Campbell," her mother admonished. "You have just met this young man. What has gotten into you?"

I had to come to Fee's rescue. "Aunt Becky, he really is a nice guy. And he is a Viking. At least, he looks like one." Rescue complete, I needed to get Fee away from this. "Come on. We have work to do." I stood and waited for Fee by the back door.

"Indeed, we do, Cuz."

***

An hour later, we'd gone through about five of the boxes in the first building. The books alone were worth a fortune. My head spun with ideas of how to display all this, and I hoped Miss Marge would go along with my formulating idea of creating a museum. First, I needed to get this inventoried, clean the place up, and put plans on paper.

"Whew. This is not easy, is it?" Fee said. She found an old milking stool and sat.

"No. It never is. Linden and I used to do stuff like this all the time in Savannah. People would clean out old barns or find things in their attics. You'd be surprised at what people don't want to keep these days. Even when you tell them the value of it. To them, it's just junk." I leaned against one of the log walls, noting that the spider webs had been cleared by Fee's Viking.

"I don't think I'd want to keep much of this. It isn't my style." Fee looked around the room at the contents, now neatly organized by category. "Do you miss him?"

"Miss who?"

"Linden."

"Oh. Him. No, not really. To tell you the truth, Mama said the other day she thinks he did me a favor. I dodged a bullet. She's probably right." I kicked at an overlooked pebble on the floor.

"No regrets?"

"Nope. Wouldn't do me any good even if I had any." I looked pointedly at my cousin. "Let me remind you that he is the one who eloped with Sissy Jo, even though he was engaged to be married to me." Bitterness dripped from my words. I stood, held out my hand, then pulled Fee to her feet. "Come on. Let's stop talking about something that doesn't matter anymore and go sit on the front porch so I can tell you a couple of ideas I've had today."

***

I considered the idea that all the missing pieces came together at Rose Haven. If I could compile Miss Marge's family tree, compare it to the trees of other key players in Boopsie's murder, I may be able to link all the characters together in some way.

Many of the people in Loblolly were from old stock, people who were in the area prior to Alabama becoming a state in 1819. And many of those people were related, even if only distantly, in one way or another. That was the way it was back then—families and good friends all moved together from place to place. When the South opened up after the Trail of Tears, the land lottery drew even more people to the area. Of course, Miss Marge's family settled here long before the lottery.

The idea would mean a bit more digging, but it made as much sense as anything else at this point. I didn't like the idea of displacing indigenous people to make way for newcomers, but that had been the way of things back in those days. The thought tugged at my heart and I knew more research was in my future. Who knew what kinds of relationships that would reveal?

Another idea I'd contemplated was turning the Rose Haven outbuildings into a museum. But would Miss Marge go along with that? I wouldn't know if I didn't ask, but I'd have to have a written plan before I could even broach the subject.

But first things first. And first was solving Boopsie's murder. I relayed my thoughts to Fee.

"So, what do you think?" I rocked and the porch responded with a creak. Oreo curled at my feet, her soft purr warming my heart.

Fee rocked beside me with her long legs stretched out in front of her. "I say we begin on that tonight. Personally, I think the idea of a museum is a good one. But you'll have to convince Miss Marge. She seems to like you very much, so she may agree to it. But as you said, first things first, and that's Boopsie's murder." She paused long enough to swat at an insect. "Miss Marge'll probably have her family tree in the old family Bible, wouldn't you think?"

"Uh-huh. Probably. I'll have to spend some time in the library and the courthouse looking for records. If we can make a connection somewhere, I think we may be able to make some progress on this case. I'm not sure what or whom I'm looking for, but I can feel that it's just at my fingertips." I reached down and picked up Oreo. "Hey girl. You want to sleep in my room tonight?" I stroked the black-and-white cat, who purred even more loudly, as if in agreement.

Fee sniffed the air. "Smell that honeysuckle. Reminds me of summer every time. That and watermelons. Freshly cut grass."

My mind settled on those things for a moment. Tomorrow it would be back to searching for a murderer and digging up dirt on Loblolly's good or not-so-good citizens. For now, I savored my newfound furry friend and the quiet of a late summer's eve.

Chapter Nineteen

I floated into the kitchen, following the aroma of freshly brewed coffee and bacon sizzling in the pan. Bacon got me every time. Pulled me right in like the losing side in a game of tug-of-war. And this was one game I didn't mind losing.

"Mmmm. Smells so yummy." I stopped at the counter and poured myself a cup of coffee, stirring in two tablespoons of sugar and a good quarter cup of cream. I leaned against the counter and sipped at the warm liquid.

Mama and Miss Marge stood side by side at the stove. Miss Marge stirred scrambled eggs while Mama poured grits into a pan of boiling water. I narrowed my eyes at the two women. Funny how much they looked alike. Both were short, like me, making me wonder if they shared a common ancestor. I made a mental note to check that.

When I had time.

"Grab a plate there on the end of the counter. These eggs will be done in a jiffy." Miss Marge turned and grinned at me. "Anyone else up yet?"

"Yes, ma'am. I'm sure they'll be down in a minute. Anything I can do?"

Mama turned and smiled. "No, dear. I'll get the biscuits from the oven as soon as the grits are done. Won't be long now. The others will be in by then, I'm sure." Mama stirred the grits while adding a bit of cream from a bottle.

Just the way I liked them.

George sauntered into the kitchen followed by another man. I did a double take when I realized it was Max, Olivia's husband.

"Morning, ladies," he said. He walked to the stove, Aqua Velva wafting behind him, and placed a kiss on Miss Marge's cheek. "Aunt

Margie, you're still as good a cook as ever, if the smells wafting through this home are any indicator." His syrupy-sweet accent seemed overdone.

The elderly woman blushed and swatted her potholder at him. "Maxwell, you do go on so."

"Just stating the facts." He went to the coffee pot, removed a mug from the overhead cabinet and poured, but passed on sugar and creamer.

"You know Maxwell Lawrence, don't you? Olivia's husband," Miss Marge said as she ladled the eggs into a large speckled bowl.

"I'll get the biscuits." Mama leaned down and pulled the baking pan from the belly of the stove. "Charlotte, will you please go call your aunt and cousin?"

Whoa. Mama didn't even acknowledge Maxwell Lawrence. Was she deliberately being rude?

"Mary, good to see you. Charlotte, I enjoyed your presentation the other evening." Maxwell sipped his coffee, peering over the rim of his cup.

He'd been there while I was speaking? I thought he'd come in just before Olivia pointed out his presence. Hmm.

"What brings you out this way today, Max?" George stood sentry by the door, his eyes boring into the man who stood sipping coffee.

"Just banking business. Takes a lot of decisions to keep this place running. All that timberland." He indicated the woods behind Marge's home.

Before I could call them, Aunt Becky and Fee met me in the hallway outside the kitchen. "Look who's here." With my thumb and a nod, I indicated the room behind me.

Aunt Becky craned around Fee, who stood just outside the door. "Max Lawrence," she said, keeping her voice low. "What's he want?"

Fee turned toward her mother and shushed her. "Hush, Mama. He'll hear you."

"I kept my voice low," Aunt Becky said, now loud enough to be heard.

I raised a finger to my lips.

"Money'd be my guess," Aunt Becky said. "Seems he can't ever get enough of it from the good folks of this town."

What did that mean? Max Lawrence had to be the Max who grew up here. The one from Boopsie's diary. How many Max's could be in little Loblolly? Especially one who'd just show up out of the blue, and at this early hour. I hadn't liked him in the diner, and this certainly hadn't raised my opinion of him—not in the slightest. I pushed past Fee and entered the kitchen. "I found 'em, Mama. They're as hungry as we are."

"Rebecca ... Fiona," Max said.

I hated hearing their names coming out of his mouth like that. It sounded too . . . *wicked*? I wasn't sure what descriptor to use, but I didn't like it one little bit. It made my skin crawl. And I couldn't stand that fake southern accent. I knew a real one when I heard it. I wedged myself between Max and Mama. "Here, Mama, you go sit by Aunt Becky and Fee. I'll get this." I took the plate of biscuits from her and watched as Mama went to the table, a puzzled look on her face.

"And here are the eggs. The gravy and bacon are already on the table." Miss Marge looked over the spread, her finger pointing to each item. "Looks like everything's here." She took her usual seat at the head of the table. Max moved to the other end.

Odd ... he didn't even ask where he should sit. Yep, definitely the Maxwell who grew up here.

I unfolded my napkin and laid it across my lap, then sent a sideward glance to Max. He certainly was making himself right at home. And Mama had yet to speak to him. For sure something was up. I'd have to ask once I had a moment alone with her.

George stood over Max, looking down at him. He gazed over the top of his glasses, but Max ignored him, just took his napkin, opened it, and placed it on his lap. George glanced from Max to Miss Marge, who shook her head slightly, leaving him to walk to an empty chair near Miss Marge, pull it out, and sit.

***

Mama, Aunt Becky, Fee and I gathered in the parlor, and all whispered at once.

"Shhh. He'll hear us," Mama said.

"What on earth is going on? Mama? Aunt Becky?" My curiosity was getting the better of me.

"Close the door, Fee," Aunt Becky whispered.

Fee was halfway there before her mother got all the words out. Fee closed the heavy double doors after peering across the entry hall toward the dining room. "Okay, what gives?"

"It's Maxwell. He's always given me the creeps." Mama shuddered.

I went to Mama, who sat on the floor with her housedress spread out around her, flipping through the pages of another music book. "Is he the boy who was here when you were a girl, Mama?"

"One and the same." She placed the book in a labeled box and picked up another.

"Polly Graves. You tell me right now what went on between you and that boy," Aunt Becky said. She stood over her sister, hands on her hips, looking madder than a wet cat.

Mama shook her head, a look of disgust on her face. "Nothing. Honest. Nothing happened. Ever. He just always gave me the creeps."

In all the times we'd been in the same social settings, I didn't remember my mother ever carrying on a conversation with Maxwell Lawrence. Not even so much as a how-do-you-do. "In what way?" I said.

Mama stood, went to the sofa, and sank into its softness. "He was always here when I came. He clung to Sarah Harkins, his aunt. She was Norah's twin sister. I do remember that. Norah was Boopsie's grandmother. I always thought it odd that he was so clingy with Sarah and called her 'Mama' rather than Norah, his mother." She picked up a fringed pillow and held it to her chest.

"What on earth?" Aunt Becky sat beside her sister. "Polly, that doesn't make a lick of sense. Whoever heard of such a thing? Did you tell Mama that?"

"I'm only telling you what I know. I remember that because, even as a child I found it peculiar. And, no. I didn't tell Mama. She … well, she wouldn't have cared."

Fee spoke up. "I agree with Mama. It doesn't make sense."

"He seems mighty at home, too," I noted. "Did he live here, Mama?"

"I think so." Mama scrunched her face up in thought. "Oh, I remember. The little cottage where George now lives was where he lived with Norah."

"What was Sarah doing here, Polly? You said Maxwell clung to her. And why would you say that Mama wouldn't have cared?" Aunt Becky drew her brows together. "That's just not so, Polly."

"I said it because it's true, Becky, whether or not you choose to believe it." She turned to me. "I only know what I saw, but wish I knew the story. I didn't overhear conversations, if you're asking me that." She picked at the fringe on the pillow. "The majority of my time was spent here in the conservatory with Miss Marge and her father. But Sarah was here, too, now that I think about it."

"This whole mess stinks to high heaven, if you ask me." Aunt Becky didn't look or sound too pleased. "It just doesn't sound like something our mother would have put up with in the first place, Polly." She grabbed her sister's hand. "Why would she let you come here to a house full of strangers and not let me come? Ever. It doesn't make any sense."

"I know, Becky. I've often wondered. I used to think it was because she wanted to get rid of me once you came along."

"Mary Jones Graves. You know that's not so. Mama loved you. I always thought you got to come because she loved you more."

I looked at Fee, who shrugged and shook her head. "Well, there has to be a story here somewhere," I said. "It's all too weird and too unconventional, no matter how you look at it." I wasn't often confused by relationships, but this one had me scratching my head. Something definitely wasn't right here.

***

After a full day of working on the contents of the outbuildings, we were ready to call it a day. Max had long since left, a very good thing. But so many questions remained. I could feel that the floodgates were about to burst wide open.

But with what?

I needed time to think. Problem was, I did my best thinking while driving, and my car was in the shop, having its broken windows repaired.

After dinner Fee and I joined our mothers in the parlor to help with the boxes from the music store. It was after midnight when we climbed the stairs for bed. Oreo had obviously taken a liking to me and followed me into my room.

"Miss Oreo, welcome to my home away from home." I reached down and rubbed the cat from her head all the way to her tail. In return, Oreo purred her approval and jumped up on the bed. "Now, I don't know about you sleeping in my bed. Does Miss Marge let you do that?" I picked up the cat, gave her one last hug and placed her on the floor.

I pulled down the covers then went into the bathroom for my nighttime routine. When I exited the bathroom, Oreo was sitting on top of the bag I'd brought up earlier. "Hey girl. I don't think there's anything in there you'd want." I returned the cat to the floor and peeked inside the bag to the two old hymnals Mama had set aside for me. I pulled them out and showed them to Oreo. "Shall we have a look-see at these?"

Oreo meowed her agreement.

I pulled out the little stepstool and climbed into bed but, this time, didn't protest when Oreo joined me. "Okay, silly kitty. This can be our little secret." Oreo settled on the pillow next to me as I scooted around and down to look over the books.

The first few pages had me intrigued. Mama indeed had a good eye for antiques. Maybe she'd help with Miss Marge's things when she and Aunt Becky finished with the store's business. This book was like nothing I'd ever seen. A very old hymnal. Some of the titles I recognized. Some I didn't. I turned through the pages one by one. When I reached the last page, there, tucked inside the back cover were a few folded papers, yellowed and smashed flat over the years. I removed them, gently unfolded them, then began reading.

My heart raced. "Oh. My goodness." I couldn't get out of bed fast enough. I tore open the bedroom door and flew down the hall to Fee's room. I took a deep breath, blew it out, and made myself knock lightly. "Fiona?" I backed up and bounced on the balls of my feet as I waited. There was no light coming from beneath the door. "Fiona?" I called again. The knob turned with only a slight squeak beneath my grasp. Silently, I tiptoed to the side of Fee's bed, then pushed against her arm with the tip of one finger. "Fee. Wake up."

"What?" Fee opened her eyes. "Charlotte? What's wrong? Mama?" She sat up and threw back the covers to reveal her choice for bedclothes: adorable, right-off-the-rack, lace-enhanced baby doll pajamas. Me? I typically wore men-styled pajamas. Comfort. My choice in fashion was all about comfort.

"No, it's not your mother. Hush. You'll wake the whole house." I motioned for her to move over. "Scoot. I've got something to show you."

Fee moved to the far side of the bed, making room for me. She rubbed at her sleepy eyes. "What time is it?" Fee reached for her clock, but I was in the way.

"It's late. If you'll be quiet, I'll show you." I climbed in next to her and opened the hymnal to the back. I pulled out the yellowed pages.

"What is it?" Fee reached for the paper.

"Careful. It's old. And you won't believe it."

Fiona carefully opened the pages. "I can barely read this. I'm half asleep and you know I can't decipher that old handwriting. Just tell me what it is." She handed the yellowed pages to me and settled back with her own pillows.

"I'll read. You listen." After adjusting the pillows one last time, I leaned back and began:

December 1869

I am not one to write down my personal thoughts and actions, but I feel that my story will be told so frightfully altered that future generations born of my two dear sons will never know the truth without me putting ink to paper.

My dear sons, Daniel Evan Lanier and Bray Jones Lanier, you need to know how much this mother's heart loved each of you. I dare to hope that you will both forgive me for leaving you far too soon. It is my earnest prayer that you remain, for the duration of your lives, true and loving brothers.

Fee placed her hand on my arm. "Wait a minute. Daniel Evan Lanier. Isn't that Miss Marge's great-grandfather?"

I lowered the paper to the bed. "Let me think. Her great-great maybe? I remember the name. I just don't remember the degree."

"This is just too convoluted for my brain to sort out. I'm going to need your help in understanding all this. Go ahead and keep reading. I'll try not to interrupt you again."

"Where was I?" I scanned the page. "Oh, yeah. Here we go…"

It is my earnest prayer that you remain for the duration of your lives true and loving brothers.

What I am about to tell you is the truth. Anything you may be told which does not accurately repeat this account is a bold falsehood. Believe only my words.

I have loved two men in my lifetime. These men, uncle and nephew to one another, are the fathers of my two sons, Evan and Bray Lanier.

I came to marriage with Daniel Lanier at the age of fifteen. It was not a love match at first. My mother had died, and my father wanted to move out west as the country expanded. My father offered my hand to our neighbor's son, Daniel Lanier. I did not love Daniel then, but I came to be quite fond of him in the weeks before we were joined in holy matrimony. One thing my father did for me was to find a God-fearing man who had no qualms about marrying within the walls of the church house. Daniel was only eighteen, but a grown man with responsibilities for land and hired hands. He was from a prominent Virginia family with roots running deep in the South. During the brief years of our marriage, I came to respect and to truly love Daniel. With the birth of our son, Daniel Evan, I felt my life would be very rewarding for the rest of my days. But that was not to be.

My husband took ill and died in 1859, taking with him most investments and monies Daniel Evan and I would need to survive. I had no choice but to move into the home of my husband's oldest brother, Richard Parker Bray Lanier, who offered to take over his brother's estate and give my son and me a place to live in return. Daniel Evan was six. Richard's oldest son, Parker Bray Lanier, was nine.

Do not ask me to give you the details. I can only tell you that Parker Bray and I, somehow came into a very deep love for one another, a love that resulted in the birth of my second dear son, Bray Jones Lanier.

Fee sat up. "Wait, wait. She fell in love with a boy who was essentially her nephew. What kind of woman does that?"

"Apparently this kind." I pointed to the letter. "I'm as puzzled as you, but we have to remember, times were very different back in those days. And he was her husband's nephew. Hers because she married Daniel. And … who can explain love? Look how quickly you reacted to the Cecil boy."

"I did not," Fee said, her back suddenly straight.

I couldn't help but laugh. "Okay. Let me keep reading and maybe it will explain some of this."

Parker Bray and I escaped into the adjacent county under the cover of darkness to join our lives in matrimony. Again, performed by a minister of the Gospel.

When we announced our marital state to Richard and his family, they were outraged that I, at the age of thirty-nine years, would marry their son who was so near the age of my own. All I can do is to ask God to forgive me if this was a sin. I tell you, my sons, that I loved both of your fathers. Each man followed the teachings of the scriptures and were good men.

I am now very ill, and I have asked Parker to remarry as quickly as possible so that you, my son, Bray, will have the love and the touch of a mother upon your life. Give your young heart to her as your true mother.

Evan, I beg you to forgive me for any shame you have had to endure because of my actions. Please try to understand that the heart loves, often without our understanding. I also beg of you to be kind to your young brother. I love both of you equally and for all of time.

I have done all that is in my power to protect you, my dear son, Bray. I entrust you into the hands of my Heavenly Father, your earthly father and his new wife, your true mother.

May God forgive me for all my sins. I leave you forever—
Your Affectionate Mother, Josephine Jones Lanier Lanier

I held the letter as I leaned against the headboard. "Wow. I didn't expect any of this."

Fee raised her eyebrows. "Well, I guess not. So, this . . . this Josephine Lanier woman, married her first husband who died. She moved in with her brother-in-law and his family, and subsequently fell in love with *his* son and married him." Fee twirled red curls around her fingers.

I folded the letter. "Seems that way."

"Charlotte, the woman was twenty years older than her second husband."

"True, but if she had been a man and did that, no one would have thought a thing about it." I slipped the letter into the back of the hymnal.

"What was it Bob Dylan sang in his song? The times they are a-changing? Well, they aren't changing *that* fast."

"There's a second letter. Want to read it tonight or wait until tomorrow?"

"By all means read it tonight. Hopefully it will explain some of this craziness." Fee crossed her arms over her chest. "Because these people aren't just far out, they're far-far out is all I've got to say."

I looked at Fee. "You ready?"

"Ready."

Chapter Twenty

"This one is dated 1870. So, it was written pretty close to the first one." I carefully unfolded the second set of papers and studied them. "Different handwriting." I turned to the last page. "Yeah ... yeah ... different writer ..." I cleared my throat and began reading.

I am so overwhelmed by the events of the past few weeks. My mind can scarcely comprehend the turns my life has taken. I feel as though I am a lifetime away from all that has been familiar to me.

Only a short while ago, I became the second wife of Parker Bray Lanier. In marrying Parker, I became the mother to his infant son, Bray Jones Lanier. May God be forever in the midst of our lives as I know I have entered into an uncertain future. I have been entrusted with the pages written here in the hand of Josie Jones Lanier Lanier. She is the mother of my son, Bray, by right of having given birth to him just three short weeks ago. Parker came to me, Josie's closest friend on this earth, to ask me to marry him and to raise Josie's son as my own as this was her last request. I had no other choice but to readily accept Parker's proposal. We were married in my father's home the day after Josie's passing, by the Rev. Caleb Hughes. My father was in the most controlled state ever witnessed by me. Parker and I left his home that night and returned six months later with our son, Bray, now almost seven months old. I cared not what anyone thought of me. I cared only about protecting this child of my friend. This child, my son.

You may ask how I, at age seventeen, could be so close to Josie who was several years my elder. She was like a mother to me, but she was also my dearest friend. I confided in her and trusted her with my secrets as I kept hers hidden within my heart.

By the time Parker and I returned to his home, Josie had been safe with Jesus for six months. Parker's family buried Josie, not in the family plot behind the church near their large home, Rose Haven. No, they took her far into the woods, burying her without the aid of anyone save Old Hiram and his son, Moses, whose task it was to dig her grave.

Fee sat straight up. "What? Is *this* the grave we've been looking for?"

"It has to be. Anyone else would be buried in the family plot." I shook my head. "Unbelievable. What kind of people would do that?"

"I have no clue. Keep reading. Maybe she'll tell us." Fee crossed her arms over her chest.

"Okay. So, where was I?" I scanned the old handwriting and found where I'd left off.

I know of Josie's resting place because of Missy, a trusted servant. I begged her to take me to Josie's final resting place. Missy was so afraid to tell me. Afraid my husband's family would send her away. I was not about to allow that. No stones or a marker of any kind adorned and marked Josie's grave. They had placed her in the earth to be forgotten. But I didn't forget. I will never forget. Missy and I hauled stones in a wagon as close as we could get, then we carried them until we thought our arms would fall from our bodies. A decent burial place is what my friend deserved. Moses made an iron cross in the livery. That was the best we could do. It was fashioned in a French style, honoring her husband's roots.

As I placed the iron cross on Josie's grave, Missy pulled from deep within her apron pockets, a sheaf of papers. Josie's final letter was now entrusted to me.

"Holy Hannah, Batman," Fee said. "This is unbelievable. So, she *is* buried in those woods somewhere."

I sat forward, pulled up my knees, then leaned on them. "Now we know who we're looking for, Fee. Josie."

"Yeah. And I bet you anything that Boopsie knew this. She heard way too many conversations not to have overheard." Fee pulled a tissue from the box on the bedside table and wiped at her eyes. "This is so sad."

I nodded, then continued reading.

I tell you, Daniel Evan Lanier and Bray Jones Lanier are brothers. Sons of Josie Jones. Daniel Lanier is the father of Daniel Evan. Evan's cousin, Parker Bray Lanier, is the father of Bray Jones Lanier.

I have loved Bray as my own since the day Parker laid him in my arms and told me that Josie asked that we marry and raise him together. I do not know what the future will hold for any of us. I can only ask God for His blessings and ask Him to soften the hearts of Parker's family. Please help them to forgive Parker for loving Josie, and above all, help them to love this innocent child.

Signed by my hand.

Anna Mayhew Lanier.

Fee almost jumped off the bed. "What? She was a Mayhew? Lord, have mercy. This is getting more complicated by the minute."

"You're not kidding." I folded the letter and placed it in the back of the book with the other one. "It would explain how Miss Marge came into possession of Rose Haven, too. I wonder how they're related."

"I have no idea, but Anna was certainly a good woman. And so young. I'm not sure I could have been that strong and done that. Just get married out of the blue and raise someone else's child as my own?"

"That's for sure. There were plenty of strong women around back in those days. I guess they had to be." I closed the hymnal. "Mama has no clue what she found. I can't wait to tell her."

Fee placed her hand on my arm. "Do you think that's wise? I mean, Boopsie was killed because she knew stuff. What if this is the information they didn't want her to spread around?"

"Yeah. I guess you're right. I certainly don't want to put Mama or anyone else in danger." I chewed my bottom lip. "But how do we go about finding that grave?"

"Well, now that you know whose it is, do you really need to find it?" Fee scrunched down beneath the covers. "I'm too sleepy to think about this anymore tonight. Let's sleep on it, okay?"

I rose from the bed and went to the door. "Okay. I'll try to figure out something, then I'll turn in too." I opened the door, flipped off

Fee's light, then went to my own room. I had a lot of thinking to do. This case was getting more convoluted by the minute. Should I share this with Roan and the sheriff? Just my luck, I may need their help.

Tomorrow.

Chapter Twenty-one

Sleepless nights made for bad mornings. But work called me. How on earth to keep all this new information a secret? But, did it really matter to anyone besides me?

I hurried to get to the courthouse to search through some old documents. Until I had a paper trail and proof of who these people were and their relationships, I'd say nothing. I agreed with Fee—it remained best to keep this a secret for now. Thankful I could use the music store as an excuse to go to town, I bummed a ride in with Fee.

"I cannot believe you found those letters last night." Fee slammed the door, inserted the key, and cranked her car.

I pulled my door shut and settled into the seat. "You didn't say anything about this, did you?" I wanted to hear Fee say so.

Fee glared at me as she pulled out of the circular drive. "Of course not. Let me remind you that I'm the one who suggested we might not want to share this with anyone. Not even our mothers."

"Sorry. I'm just nervous over all this." I reached down and took the hymnal from the canvas bag I'd brought along.

"So, what's your next step?" Fee looked both ways then pulled onto the country road leading into town.

"Courthouse. Research. Ask questions very carefully."

"I wish I could come with you today, but I have to go check on things at the boutique. I can't leave Iris to run things alone forever." She shifted gears and pressed down on the gas pedal. The engine roared to life.

Fee parked in her usual spot behind Soilse, then we entered through the rear of the boutique. She plunked her pink-patent purse that so perfectly matched one of the swirling colors in her pantsuit, not to mention her strappy sandals, on top of her desk. "So, I'll see you later this morning?"

"That should be plenty of time. If I get stuck, it could be a bit longer. I'll call you." I bid my cousin good-bye then walked the few short blocks to the courthouse, situated on one end of the town square.

I made my way to the records room. I'd have to go to the archives for some of the files. They could be stored in back or even downstairs. I spotted a woman I knew working behind the counter, a member of the WHS. Martha Ann Foster was a couple of years older than Fee and me. We hadn't been close friends in high school, but we did run around in the same circle of people.

"Hey, Martha Ann. How are you?" I looked around, noting she was the only person in the vicinity.

Martha Ann looked up from her work. "Hey, Charlotte. You need something for the upcoming meeting?"

"Could be. Just some information. I'm not sure what I'll do with it at this point, but I want to look through some old census records and land deeds. I think a couple of people in the group could use the info I thought about. It's a good starting place, for sure." I flashed a smile. I hated the deception, but how else could I gather the needed papers without the entire town knowing about it before nightfall? Some things required . . . well, not *lying*, I don't agree with that, but . . . leaving out information. Worded in that manner that I could live with myself.

Martha Ann motioned for me to follow her to a back room. "You need to set up in here. These books can't be removed from the area, and they're heavy, even if you could move them." She patted the top of a massive old oak table. "See. We have tables back here, too. Most people don't do the in-depth research you do. Mostly they ask us to look it up for them."

"Well, I'm not *really* a professional, so don't give me too much credit." I laid my tote-bag on the table, took a deep breath, then looked around at the room's contents. "Wow. For such a small town, there are a lot of record books here."

"Well, now, don't forget that we're the county seat. That's where the records were filed for all of Woodville County." Martha Ann cocked her head and looked at me. "You haven't been back here—in this room—before now?"

"Nope. First time." I wasn't about to tell Martha Ann that I hadn't given two figs for genealogy when I lived here before. It wasn't until I moved to Savannah and had gotten involved with Linden that I'd gained an interest in finding people's roots. He'd taught me a few things about records and where to look for certain items, but my forte had been in finding graves. I loved the outdoor parts of doing genealogy. Give me a map, a name, and an area, and I'd look through cemeteries until I found buried treasures. Nothing quite like digging up dirt.

There was no time like the present to educate myself on the fine art of record-searching. Not my favorite, but I could do it. Linden may be a rat, but he was a good teacher when it came to all things related to family histories and genealogies. I wasn't the best of students. I liked searching for those graves and the lost artifacts, family heirlooms. I'd just begun my art history studies when Linden suddenly announced his elopement. That put a quick end to my dreams of pursuing that. Oh, well. I reckon it wasn't in the plans for my life. Not now, anyway.

I reverently turned the pages and searched for insight into the lives of the people named in the papers inside the hymnal. Each time I found even the slightest of clues, I made an entry in my notebook, careful to record the book number and other pertinent information. I wondered if we'd still be doing research this way in the next decade or two, or if modern marvels would be the rule of the day. Searching through the original documents gave me goosebumps. Touching things that hadn't been touched in decades. I was beginning to feel like a real genealogist. The only problem I had was several pages with information I needed appeared to be torn from the record books. Would those records be in the state archives? I'd have to alert Martha Ann and ask her.

***

The rumblings of my stomach demanded I check the time. Just past noon. No wonder. I returned the books to the proper shelves then gathered my things before heading for Soilse. Fee would definitely have an opinion about my discoveries.

But was I ready to act on them?

The information I'd gathered was going to be life-altering for quite a few people. And those were the ones I knew of. What about all the ones who would inevitably come out of hiding?

The walk from the courthouse to Fee's boutique wasn't a long one, but my heavy bag made the trip uncomfortable. I opened the door of Soilse and stepped inside. The blast of cool air brought blessed relief. Fall may have been just around the corner, but summer hadn't bid Loblolly farewell yet. I gazed about, searching for Fee, who looked up as I closed the door behind me.

"Hey, Cuz." Fee placed a customer's purchases into a bag with the Soilse logo, the name of the store printed on top of a rising sun. She motioned for me to join her. "Come on back. I'm almost finished here."

"I don't want to interfere. I'll just browse a bit."

"Be sure to take a look at the new dresses. There's a sapphire one that would be gorgeous with your eyes." Once her customer left the store, Fee walked to the rack and pulled the dress from it. "Here." She held it up in front of me. "Very Marlo Thomas as Ann Marie. Go into the dressing room and do not come out without this dress on your body."

I knew this drill. We'd been through it many times in the six months I'd been back in Loblolly. Fee knew I didn't wear dresses. Well, rarely wore dresses "Really, Fee. We've been through this same thing countless times. I don't like dresses. They make me feel . . . funny."

"They make you look fabulous." She held the dress out again, a look of determination on her face. "And I've got some groovy earrings and shoes that will go great with it."

Resigned to my fate, I took the dress along with a pair of dark stockings, the shoes, and earrings and headed to the fitting room. In five minutes, I was out front, standing before the three-sided mirror.

"Oh, my." Fee walked a circle around me, looking at me from every angle. "It's even better than I imagined." Fee's hands went to her mouth. "Charlotte Graves, this dress was made for you. Do you hear me? You have to buy it."

"I don't wear dre—"

Fee held up her hand in a *stop* motion, as if she were singing the Supremes' hit. "Not another word. I'm giving you my discount, so there is to be no arguing about how you don't wear dresses, or that you can't afford it. Nothing."

I gazed at my reflection. This was three times Fee had gotten me into dresses in the last two months. I hated to admit it, but I really did look good in dresses. All those treks through cemeteries, climbing over fallen logs in hidden country graveyards, not to mention all the running around with Linden when I'd been in Savannah, had done wonders for my figure. I'd left eight years ago, a somewhat pudgy teen. Now, thanks in part to Fee, I was beginning to see myself as an attractive woman, for all the good that would do me.

"Do you want to tell me where I'm supposed to wear this?" I managed to pinch a bit of the fabric at the sides of the dress. It clung to my figure. When had I gotten . . . skinny? Not a word I'd ever used to describe myself. I'd hidden beneath jeans, tees, and baggy flannels for so long, I had no clue I'd gotten thin. I'd always been like Mama, a bit *pleasingly plump,* as Grandpa had always called us.

"Well, there's bound to be a wedding or a bridal shower. A dinner out or a dance or how about ... church?" Fee shrugged, holding her hands palms up.

"Mmmm. We'll see." I made my way to the fitting room where I removed the dress and put on my daily jeans and tee. I bent and tied my boots, then returned to the front of the store where Fee was waiting behind the counter, then handed her the dress.

"Good choice. You'll see. There will be some occasion for you to wear this. I can almost guarantee it." She rang up the sale and placed the dress in a plastic hanging bag, also printed with the Soilse sunrise.

"I haven't even had a chance to share what I found at the courthouse. I'm starving now and I don't have time for lunch if I'm going by the library before we head back to Rose Haven."

"Sure, you do. Walk over to Serena's with me and we'll grab whatever her special is. I can work late so you'll have plenty of time in the library."

***

The Copper Pot was crowded, even at this hour. That was because Serena served the best food in town and her prices were light on the wallet. We had to wait for the busboy to clear a table. Instead of getting our usual in the back, we were seated across from Cam Lawrence and the two men who'd been with him at the cabin behind Miss Marge's home.

I stared at the men and hesitated a second too long before sliding into the booth in the center of the restaurant. One of the men kicked Cam beneath the table and cocked his head toward Fee and me.

Cam looked up at us. "Well, I do know," he said, his face screwed up in a sneer. "Look what just strolled into my little corner of the world." His slow southern drawl always bothered me. He sounded too much like his father. I wasn't sure if either accent was real or an affectation to garner attention. At any rate, they made my skin crawl.

Cam got up and slid into the booth sitting next to me, far too close. He leaned into my side, almost resting his head on my shoulder. "You not speakin' to me today?" He looked over at his goons, who shook with suppressed laughter.

"I don't recall asking you to join us. And if you don't mind . . ." I shoved him away from me. The men across the aisle burst into laughter this time.

"You'd best be thinking about who you're pushing around, Miss High and Mighty. He might not take to being treated so unkindly." He grabbed one of my curls and yanked it before he left our booth.

Fiona opened her mouth to speak, but I kicked her beneath the table before she could say anything. She looked at me with a tilt of her head and her eyes narrowed.

Ignoring the dunces across the aisle was the best way I knew to deal with them. I picked up the menu. "So, what shall we order today?"

Cam hadn't hurt me in the slightest when he pulled my hair. Had he intended to hurt or, or had he intentionally not hurt me? This wasn't the place to go into that. I figured the best plan of action was to act normal. Just order, eat, and get out of there. We both breathed a sigh of relief when, two minutes later, Cam and his friends left.

"Has the morning been productive?" she asked after we placed our order.

"It has ... but ..." I glanced around the busy restaurant. "Not here."

Fee nodded once. "Got it."

***

I managed a few more hours in the library then walked back to Soilse where I joined Fee for the ride back to the country estate. The sun was about to set and there was a definite chill in the air. Not much of one, but it was there.

"So," Fee asked after only a few minutes. "Are you going to tell me or not?"

"I will," I said, "but I need to sort some things out first. Give me until after dinner, okay?"

Fee rolled her eyes, but nodded.

The countryside rolled by unnoticed this close to dark so I let my mind wander, pouring over the things I'd learned in the past few days. We arrived at Rose Haven before I knew we'd even turned onto the shell drive.

Things were relatively quiet and the peaceful evening felt like a blessing. After a light dinner of tomato sandwiches, assorted pickles, chips, and homemade cookies, we settled in the parlor once again. Mama and Aunt Becky had made great progress on the music store items. There were at least a dozen boxes of old music books or sheet music they felt we could sell. The fixtures, which of course we hadn't brought to Rose Haven, Mama would sell to the new owner of the store should they want those. Otherwise, we'd salvage what we could and donate the rest. Many of the fixtures consisted of racks for the music or bins for instrument parts or reeds. The bins would make good storage for Mama's sewing supplies. We figured we'd make a trip down to Allegro and look over things and see if there was anything else worth keeping. But not tonight.

I was glad when the older women announced they were heading to bed. I'd finally get a chance to talk to Fee, who'd been antsy all night.

***

Less than fifteen minutes after climbing the stairs, a fashionably pajama-clad Fee (and not the same baby doll pjs as the night before) bound into my room and waved her hands. "Okay. I've waited long enough. Tell me, tell me."

"Hey, I haven't even had a chance to brush my teeth." I walked into the adjoining bathroom. A couple seconds later, toothbrush in hand, I poked my head out the door. "See if you can find Oreo. She came up with me but didn't follow me into the bedroom. I'll be out in just a sec." I closed the bathroom door and heard Fee calling for Oreo on the other side.

I came out of the bathroom, leaned over the bed, and pulled back the covers. "No luck?"

Fee lifted the eyelet dust ruffle and peered beneath the bed. She opened the closet and looked inside. "Not yet. The last time I saw her, she was running past us on the stairs. I figured she'd come in here with you." She closed the closet and leaned against the oak door.

"Hmmm. Maybe she sneaked back down without our noticing. I'll go back downstairs and see if I can find her. Glad I didn't change yet." I opened the door and headed down the stairs. When I didn't find Oreo, I returned to my bedroom. "I didn't find her. Did you keep looking up here?"

Fee shook her head. "Nope. I figured you'd find her. But I'll help you look." She hopped off the bed and slipped her feet into a pair of slippers, then grabbed a flashlight from my bag. "Where to begin? This is a big place."

"How 'bout we just call her? Maybe she'll come out." I pushed up the dust ruffle and looked beneath the bed, then in the closet one more time. "Here, Oreo. Kitty, Kitty."

We went into the hall and walked from room to room, softly calling. Still, no Oreo. We moved from one end of the hall to the other, noting the lack of light beneath our mothers' doors, which we moved as quietly as possible

Fee glanced sideways at me. "Do you think she could get into those secret rooms? You know, the ones Boopsie mentioned?"

"She's a cat. She can get in just about any place that's left open. Probably some that aren't, too." We entered every room except our mothers' bedrooms. "She wouldn't be in there. Mama would have gotten me if a cat followed her to bed. And I'm sure Aunt Becky would do the same."

"You're not kidding." We closed the last door behind us. "Is that Miss Marge's father's room at the end of the hall? Do you think Oreo would go in there?"

I looked at my cousin. "Isn't it locked? Miss Marge probably doesn't want it to be disturbed in honor of her father's memory."

"Well, we have a lost cat—one we know was in here just after dinner as she followed us up the stairs. Did *you* see her leave?"

"No, I didn't." I raised my brows. "We've got to get into that room."

"Agreed. You first." Fee held out one hand, ushering me in front of her. She was always ushering me in first. I wasn't sure I liked that. But now wasn't the time.

"Oreo. Here, kitty. Come out, kitty." I called softly, then waited for a response. "Oreo?" I put my ear to the door and shifted my eyes toward Fee. "Did you hear that?"

"No, let me." I made room for Fee who put her own ear to the door. "Oreo. Sweet kitty?" She listened, then nodded. "Yes. I think I hear her, too."

"So, how do we get into a locked room?" Hands on my hips I thought for a minute. "How did *she* get into a locked room?"

"The key on the hook in the kitchen? It's a skeleton key. Shouldn't it fit all the locks?"

"Fee, you think the cat used a key?"

"No, silly ... I'm saying we can get in with the key."

"One would think."

Fee stopped me as I turned toward the stairs. "Let me. My legs are longer. Be back in a flash."

Fee left me standing in the dark, but returned in less than five minutes and, sure enough, the key fit and we entered the locked room. But it wasn't just a room. It appeared to be a suite with a hall leading to adjoining baths and closets between two bedrooms.

"Should we turn on the lights?" Fee asked.

"Better not," I answered as she scanned the room with the flashlight's beam. "And I thought the rest of the house was spectacular." A quick tour told us one suite had to have been Miss Marge's father's and the other her mother's. "I'm speechless. Who knew Loblolly had this kind of opulence?" I ran my hand over the mahogany footboard. "Kitty?"

"Listen, Charlotte. It's coming from the closet." Fee pointed the flashlight to her right.

I rushed to the door and opened it, then called into the dark, "Oreo. Here kitty." I bent and looked beneath the outdated clothing which hung from wooden hangers. "Kitty, kitty."

"She'd come out if she could. She's stuck somewhere." Fee pushed back dresses and coats. "Come on, Oreo. Tell us where you are."

As I pushed back clothing on the opposite side of the huge closet, I lost my footing and bumped against the back of the closet. A panel gave way and I tumbled into another room. I rolled onto my back as Oreo bounded out, running across my chest, before leaving the room.

"Where are you?" Fee called out.

"In here. Some sort of a hidden room," I said. Darkness completely engulfed me. "Move those clothes and come on in. And bring the flashlight. It's so dark I can barely see."

Fiona joined me in the inner chamber. She shone the light along the walls in search of an electrical switch. "We're turning on a light," she said. When the beam found one, she flipped it on. Dim light fell upon what looked like a nursery. A bassinet stood in one corner. A crib against one wall. White netting hung from a golden crown at the ceiling and draped around the back and two ends of the crib. The walls were painted a soft pink. A short bookcase housed a variety of children's books, all well-worn. A little girl had slept here. But who? And whose? Were they Miss Marge's when she was a child? But who would put a baby in a secret room? Had it always been a secret? Still more questions and nothing about any of them felt right. My female intuition was beginning to kick in.

I made my way around the space, realizing it smelled fresh, as if the windows had recently been opened. I walked to the row of windows and tested one. It was unlocked and rose easily, allowing me to peer into the yard below. So, this was on the back side of the home. Maybe near or above the conservatory? I made note to check that out tomorrow, then turned back to the room.

The style of the furnishings had to be from the early twentieth century. Maybe even late nineteenth century. On one dresser was a framed photograph of a woman holding a baby. I picked it up and drew my brows together. "Fee?" Fee came up behind me, then leaned over my shoulder. "What's a photo of Mama doing in here?" I pointed. "And who is this baby? That's not me."

"Uh . . . Charlotte? That's not Aunt Polly. Look at her dress and that hairdo. This is a much earlier do if ever I saw one." She pointed at the photograph. "Look at her necklace. That's like the cross you wear all the time. Didn't you call it a Huguenot cross?"

Sure enough, the woman in the photo wore a cross identical to the blue-and-white enameled one I often wore. "It is just like it. The one I wear was Mama's. It was a baby gift from someone. She's never known who."

"Let's take the pic and show it to our mothers tomorrow."

"We can't just take this out of a secret room. It's secret for a reason." I set the photo back on the dresser, wiping my fingers across the top as I did so. "Fee ... this place is clean as a whistle." My fingers told the tale. "Not a speck of dust. That must be how Oreo got in here. Someone comes in to clean this place, and Oreo knows how to get in." I sniffed the air. "And smell that."

"You're right. Miss Marge." Fee sniffed the air. "That's her scent. Youth Dew. Only older women wear that."

"I agree. But we still can't take the picture. We'll have to think about this. After the records I found today, I think things are adding up, and I know some people who are not going to be happy with what I believe is going on." I tried to memorize the photo, then turned toward the secret door. "Come on. Let's get out of here. I have lots to tell you."

Chapter Twenty-two

I joined Fee in the middle of the big bed, plopping my tote bag beside me. I sat with legs crossed as I pulled my notebook from the bag. "Do you remember Martha Ann?"

"A couple grades ahead of us? That Martha Ann?" Fee turned her head to the side. "Wasn't she a Foster?"

"Yes, she was. I saw her at the courthouse today. She helped me with some records." I opened my notebook to the page with my latest entries. "I made a few notes in here and took some photos of records. I make all these notes, but I think I prefer having the photos to remind me of what I saw. I'll get these to the camera shop as soon as I can."

"Okay. So, talk. I'll listen."

"I wasn't sure who I was looking for, but Martha Ann is a fountain of information. She's been helping folks with their genealogies for years ... since she was in high school and worked at the courthouse as a student assistant." I scooted up in the bed, adjusting the pillows behind me and stretching out my legs, which were well on their way to being asleep. "I asked about land records and such. She sent me to the library for the things I couldn't find in the courthouse."

Fee wiggled her feet. "Like what?"

"History books on the area. A lot of people, not just Hiram Moore, wrote about the history. It was a happening place early on, even before Alabama became a state."

"What about the Indian population?"

"Well, I wasn't looking for that in particular, but there is a deep history connected to them around here. Lots over in the panhandle of Florida. I'd like to study that some more. I'm sure many of the people who live around here are descended from local tribes, even if we don't talk so much about that anymore."

"That would make a good talk at our society."

"I was looking for land grants and things like that with the Lanier name."

"And?"

"Well, the land on which Rose Haven was built was purchased in the early 1800s. It was originally bought by the Woodvilles." I waited for Fee's response and wasn't disappointed when she raised her eyebrows in surprise.

"Olivia's family? The one she's so proud of?"

I nodded. "One and the same." I pulled up my notes from a record and showed it to Fee. "And it was passed down until a Woodville married a Lanier and the Laniers inherited and it got passed down eventually to Miss Marge."

"So, Miss Marge is related to the Laniers and the Woodvilles and thereby to Olivia." Fee scrunched her face in thought.

"That's right."

Fee sat up and put her hand on my arm. "But wait a minute. I remember that the one woman, the one who married the two Lanier men, was a Jones. Is she any relation to us?"

"Well, not that I've found. Maybe distantly. I haven't gotten that far yet." I ran fingers through my hair and chewed my bottom lip. "But Constance Lanier, who died after falling down a flight of stairs—"

"How do you know that?"

I had to think for a moment. "I believe Miss Marge told me. Otherwise I wouldn't know. Anyway … she and Jackson Mayhew were Miss Marge's parents. That's about as far as I've figured out at this point."

"You're doing a great job, Cuz. I have every confidence in your abilities to solve not only Boopsie's murder, but this tangled mess, as well."

"It's appreciated, but let me remind you again, I'm not a professional genealogist. I'm just doing the historical society for now, until Olivia can find someone who knows a lot more than I do to run things. My heart lies in a historical museum, the artifacts, family heirlooms, and out in the cemeteries."

***

The next morning, I rode into town with Fee, who dropped me off at the car repair shop. The windows finally arrived and were now securely installed in my faithful old Chevy. It was nice to have my own wheels again. Relying on others for transportation was highly unreliable.

I stopped at the hardware store on the town square to purchase supplies for a project I'd thought of in the night. Once I told Fee of my discoveries, we planned on heading out to explore and investigate further. But first I needed those supplies.

It seemed that every store in Loblolly had a bell on the door. The hardware store was no exception. Inside was just as I remembered. The dark-stained oak floors still creaked beneath my feet as I approached the back counter. It had been a while since I'd been here, but it looked pretty much the same. Still, it was better to ask for help. Besides, I might learn something about the people associated with Boopsie if I could steer the conversation that way.

George perched on a stool behind the counter, surprised me. "George? I didn't know you worked here." I placed my heavy bag on the counter.

"Miss Charlotte. Howdy do." He came around to stand in front of me. "Only sometimes if Lem needs a little help. His wife's mighty sick and he tends to her. I come when I can just to lend a hand to an old friend."

"You are one nice man, George." I reached up on my tiptoes and gave him a quick peck on his cheek. He blushed, his red face matching the old Coke sign hanging on the side wall.

"What can I do ye for? Anything partic'lar in mind?" He walked to a nearby display and straightened the already straight contents.

"I need something thin . . . I'm thinking maybe copper. I need to do some headstone rubbings. I've seen a few done in copper and they're gorgeous."

"Out genealogin' again, huh?" He rubbed his chin. "Well, let me ask you, you gonna keep this or frame it like some do, or is it just for information gathering?"

"A bit of both. Some for framing, some for information."

"Well, I'd say you'd be best off going over to the five-and-dime and getting one of those big ole drawing pads for the genealogy stuff. Be a lot less money than a bunch of copper." He headed down one of the aisles and motioned for me to follow. "Now, this here is good copper for your rubbings. It's not too thick to work with. Not as pricey as it could be. Seen a few folks doing those rubbing things you mentioned. Didn't know that's what it was, but I seen 'em with copper even out at Margie's place."

Now who might have been at Rose Haven doing rubbings? "Not only are you a nice man, you are a wise man, George." I picked a couple of sheets of the copper and followed George to the register. They weren't cheap, but they weren't going to put me in the poor house, either. Besides, this was for a gift, if things worked out the way I figured they might.

"You doin' this to try to find Boopsie's killer, or you got a good client?" George followed me toward the front of the store.

"Well, kind of both, but in a roundabout way. I'm thinking that there are some pretty weird things and relationships that don't quite add up and if I can just get to the bottom of that, I may have a lead or two that will take me right to whoever killed Boopsie." I shifted my bag.

I didn't want to put too much information out there. But this was George. He was harmless and wouldn't go blabbing. He wasn't one of the town's known gossips. Still, changing the subject seemed like a good idea. "I love coming in here. It always smells as I remembered from when I came with Papa. Paint, wax . . . old. I think it's the old I like best. Some things don't need to change to still be good and useful." Soon, George had rung me up and walked me to the door. A quick wave and I headed next door. The bell tinkled a sweet goodbye as the door closed behind me.

***

Like the hardware store, the "dime store," as the locals called it, was another of the places I frequented with my daddy when I was a child. Here, too, the bell tinkled upon my entrance. The aroma of fresh-popped corn welcomed me, drawing me into the store. I wandered to the centrally located candy-and-nut-filled glass cases. That Loblolly had kept so many of the old ways of life was part of its charm. Progress was a good thing, but as the old saying goes, *if it ain't broke, don't fix it.*

I inwardly drooled over the treats inside the case. Hot nuts—pecans, peanuts, and my favorite, cashews—glistened beneath the heat of the lamps and took a carousel ride on the spinning central tray. Chocolate-covered peanuts and maple nougat pieces rested behind another glass panel. When I was a child, I always purchased a dime's worth of the goodies. Hopefully the price hadn't changed in eight short years. For sure, I couldn't come here and not buy something.

An elderly lady appeared behind the candy and nut counter. "Why, Charlotte. Is that you?" She pushed her glasses up with her index finger.

"Miss Ludie? You're still working here?" I could hardly believe the woman who had waited on me when I was a child was still here. She had to be older than dirt.

"Why, yes, dear. I'm such an institution around this store, they decided they'd best be keeping me. Besides, I'm the only one who knows how to work this contraption." She pointed to the carousel. "Still have a sweet tooth, huh?"

"Oh, yes, ma'am. I don't think I'll ever not have one. I'll take half a pound of the chocolate covered peanuts, please." I beamed my brightest smile at the elderly woman, who bagged the treat, came around the counter, then handed it to me. She was just as I remembered. Her hair was short and curly, and she wore an apron tied about her to protect her work dress. She also wore sensible shoes, like the ones Nana had worn, only Miss Ludie's were white. "Thank you, Miss Ludie."

Miss Ludie returned the smile. "I hear through the grapevine that you're investigating the murder of that poor girl."

"Oh, yes, ma'am, but not officially. I'm just trying to find out things that the sheriff and his deputies might not think about. You know I do genealogical research, so this doesn't feel a whole lot different to me."

"Well, I hope you can do some good. Her poor mama is so upset, bless her heart. And her brother, Bubba. Well, he's beside himself, they say."

"Oh? Who's *they*, Miss Ludie?"

"Oh, you know. Sarah Harkins likes to talk. She was going on about how you always messed with Boopsie when you were kids. Says she wouldn't be surprised to find out you'd actually done it and the fool of a sheriff let you go. Things like that." Miss Ludie took a feather duster from the deep pockets of her apron and began dusting the exterior of the glass cases.

I gasped, but quickly covered my shock. What was I supposed to say to that? Denial would only make me sound more guilty, especially if Miss Ludie had already made up her mind.

Getting out of that store was the best plan of action, with or without the paper. I 'd have to go to the discount store in the shopping center on the edge of town. "Thank you for your help. I'll just go pay for this and be on my way."

I couldn't get out of there fast enough.

Chapter Twenty-three

"Where have you been all day?" Mama greeted me as I entered Rose Haven through the kitchen door. Whatever Mama was cooking smelled mighty good. I laid my packages on the table and placed a kiss on her cheek. "Smells wonderful, Mama." I peered over her shoulders and spied chicken and dumplings bubbling away. That explained the mouth-watering aroma.

"Thank you, dear, but you didn't answer my question."

"Well, I went to the hardware store." I rummaged through my packages until I found the bag of chocolate peanuts. I popped two into my mouth, the velvety-smooth sweetness of the chocolate blending with the salty crunchiness of the peanuts encouraged me to burst into a rousing rendition of the "Hallelujah Chorus." I restrained myself. "Did you know George works there?"

"Mmmm. No. I didn't." Mama dropped a strip of dough into the boiling water and waited for it to cook before stirring and dropping in another. "Since when?"

"Since Mr. MacDougal's wife got sick, I guess." I ate two more peanuts then closed the bag. "Where are storage containers, Mama?" I rummaged through the pantry.

"Look in the bottom cabinet to the left of the fridge. You'll find the freezer bags there. Will that work?" She stirred the pot of dumplings. "That explains why I haven't seen George all day. I wondered where he'd gotten off to."

I found the bags, pulled out one and poured the peanuts into it, then twisted the tie. "Then I went to the dime store. Did you know that Miss Ludie is still working there?" I pulled out a chair. "Why don't you sit, Mama, and let me finish that?"

"Because you can barely find your way *to* the kitchen, is why. After working this hard, I'd like it to be edible." She shook her head at me as she continued to add strips of the dough.

"She said Miss Sarah thinks I killed Boopsie."

Mama turned as quick as a wink, hands on hips, and looked at me. "What on earth? Why would that silly woman say something so outrageous? Why, I've a good mind to go over there and give her a good talking to." Mother-bear mode reared its ugly head again, but I had to admire Mama's spunk.

"Would just make her madder. I didn't know Miss Ludie or Miss Sarah were gossips. Never heard anyone say so, anyway." Too funny— the women of Loblolly gossiping about gossips.

"Well, you've been gone a while and you were too young and too busy trying to get out of high school to take any notice of such."

"And way too wrapped up in Roan." Whoa. I said that out loud. But it was the truth. Maybe I shouldn't have been so deeply involved with him. If I'd guarded my heart, I wouldn't have been so hurt and then I'd never have left Loblolly. Then I could have helped Papa in the store more. Then he might still be here. But ... there was no changing the past, no matter how much I wanted to. "Where's Miss Marge and Aunt Becky?"

"Becky went home to take care of a few things there and to see to Uncle Angus. Miss Marge is out in the garden. She could probably use some help, if you don't mind. I think she's picking green peas to go with the dumplings."

"Okay. Let me take this stuff upstairs and I'll be right back down."

"What did you buy?"

"Just some stuff to do headstone rubbings. That's why I went to the hardware store, then the dime store. But after the revelation from Miss Ludie, I decided to go to that new store in the shopping center."

"Fee will want to help you with that. And let me know if Becky and I can do anything." She stirred the pot one last time and put a lid on it. "Better hurry. Miss Marge'll be done without you."

Up in my room, I threw the packages on the bed, then headed back downstairs and out the back door. What a day it had been. Picking peas would take my mind off the yucky unpleasantness. And I'd be outdoors—my favorite place, other than outdoors in a cemetery. I loved cemeteries. Seemed I had chosen my career wisely. Well, that was a change. Charlotte Graves doing something downright wise. Would wonders never cease?

"Hey, Miss Marge. I came to lend you a hand." I ambled to the row of peas where the older woman stooped, her right hand pulling at the pea pods as her left held the vine.

"Land sakes, child. I don't need help. Did your mama send you out here?" Miss Marge raised up and stretched a bit. She threw the pea pods into the basket at her feet as her right hand went to the small of her back. Clearly, this task wasn't easy on her.

"Tell me which end you started on so I don't go back that way." I looked up and down the rows of peas whose tendrils climbed up strings held up by a central pole. "Mama said she could use some help with supper, if you don't mind me finishing up here."

"I have a feeling that you and your mama are in cahoots to get an old woman out of doing her chores." She shook a short, pudgy finger at me, but a smile crept across her lips.

"Maybe. But it's a lot cooler inside and I need to do some thinking. This is as good a place as any."

"Well, I was heading that way." She pointed to her left. "Don't pick the thin ones. They aren't ready yet."

"No, ma'am. I won't." I bent to the vines and began my work. I pulled pod after pod, throwing them into the wooden basket and shoving it along with my foot as I went down the row.

The conversations from earlier in the day and the surprise of George working in the hardware store wouldn't leave me be. But Miss Ludie being behind the counter at the dime store and her remarks took center stage. And how did she know what Miss Sarah thought? Were they friends? Must be. I bet Miss Ludie might share a bit of information if I could get more time with her. Maybe Miss Marge knew her. Over dinner could be a good time to inquire.

This might be going someplace.

I pulled at another pod and dropped it into an almost-full basket. Looked like enough. Time to go inside.

***

"Here are the peas. Want me to shell 'em?" I placed the basket next to the sink.

"Why don't we all sit on the front porch and do that?" Mama took her hands from the dishwater and wiped them on a cloth hanging from the front of the cabinet.

"That sounds like a very good idea. Let's do that." Miss Marge steepled her hands, a delighted look spreading across her face. "These will be done in a jiffy with all of us working together." She reached into the cabinets and pulled out three chipped porcelain pans, one for each of us.

We trekked to the porch and settled into the rockers. Oreo slept away in one of them.

"Silly kitty. You had us looking all over for you last night," I scolded.

"She likes to hide in my room, I'm afraid. She sneaks in without me knowing it many nights." Miss Marge looked from the cat back to me.

Did Miss Marge mean her bedroom, or the hidden room? I dared not ask at this point. I'd need more information before I could bring up any of the revelations of the past couple of days. "Miss Marge, how well do you know Miss Ludie over at the dime store?" I picked up a fat pea, pulled the top down zipper-fashion, and released the round, green pearls with a swipe of my thumb.

"Oh, we were in school together. Her father owned the five-and-dime. Did you know that?" Miss Marge rocked as she shelled the peas in her dinged-up pan.

"I don't think I knew her daddy had owned the store. No wonder she's still there." I harrumphed. "Does she own it now?"

"Oh, no. That was a hot point of contention awhile back. It seems Ludie thought she'd inherit it upon her father's death, but he left it lock, stock, and barrel to Ludie's brother's boy, Frankie. Ludie was mad as a wet-setting hen, I tell you. After she'd helped her father all those years build up that business ... and then her lazy, good-for-nothing nephew got the store. Well, it just wasn't right." She shook her head. "I'm sorry. I shouldn't react in such an unladylike manner. Ludie was a friend and her family didn't do right by her."

Wow. This was a side of Miss Marge we hadn't seen. At least, I hadn't seen it. She always seemed so sweet and agreeable. It was nice to see some of Mama's spunk coming out.

Mama's? Now where had that come from?

"Miss Marge, you said that Miss Ludie *was* a friend. Does that mean something happened and you stopped being friends at some point?"

"Charlotte Graves," Mama said. She stopped shelling to send a pointed look my way. "You know better than to ask such personal questions. It's indecent."

"It's all right, Mary. I don't mind answering." Miss Marge smiled at Mama before turning her attention back to my question. "Yes, dear. Something did happen a long time ago." Miss Marge looked off into the distance. "That is all I can say."

I followed the direction of Miss Marge's gaze beyond the porch to the lawn around it. Moss dripping from the oak trees swayed with the gentle breeze as the sun sank lower in the sky and filled the blue with touches of pink and purple and so many shades of orange, I couldn't possibly number all of them.

But I doubted Miss Marge saw a speck of it.

Chapter Twenty-four

Since Aunt Becky and Fee decided to remain in town, Miss Marge, Mama, and I made an early night of it and retired to our own quarters at Rose Haven. Mama headed to her room with a new romance novel by one of her favorite authors. Miss Marge declared she was going straight to a shower, then to sleep. I climbed the stairs, followed by Oreo.

"Now don't you go scaring us half to death like you did last night," I said as Oreo jumped on the bed. I shook my finger at the cat, who meowed in agreement. I reached over, rubbed between her ears, then stepped back to prepare for bed. The shopping bags from my trek into town called to me. "Look, Oreo. Want to see what I bought today?" I opened the bags, removed the contents, and laid them on the bed.

"Shoot— should have brought up the peanuts." Oreo looked at me as if she understood every word I uttered. "Maybe I'll go get them in a bit." I thumbed through the drawing pad then picked up the package of charcoal pencils. "See. These are for doing headstone rubbings, and this . . ." I shook a box of white chalk at Oreo. "This, my dear kitty, is for rubbing on those gravestones that are so dark they can't be read." Off to the side was a roll of masking tape and some scrub brushes. I stood with one hand on my left hip and looked over my purchases. "Hmmm. Looks like everything I'll need. But I also need to call Fee. What do you say to that, Miss Oreo? Shall I call Cousin Fee?"

***

I rubbed Oreo behind the ears, then went to the kitchen to phone Fee. In three rings my cousin was on the line.

"Hey. What's up?"

"Just sitting here with Oreo, who didn't get lost in the shuffle

179

tonight. Wondering if you could come out tomorrow. Thought I'd do some headstone rubbings in the cemetery."

"Great idea. I'll call Iris and ask her to come in early. She never minds working extra hours."

Munching came from the speaker. "You're eating dinner. Sorry. I can let you go."

"Nun-uh. S'all right. Just having a snack in my room"

"Funny, I just came down to grab a snack, too." Now where had I put those peanuts? "And to call you."

"Hey, Charlotte … you know, we didn't know Nana long enough to know if she was like that. Do remember her being a bit . . . aloof."

"Ya think?" Sarcasm coated my tone like the thick, creamy chocolate on those peanuts. The ones now calling my name. Where had I put them? Maybe Mama had put them away. "I don't get Mama's relationship with her. She seems to think Nana didn't love or even like her."

"Yeah. It is odd that we . . . well, I've never heard this stuff before." Fee continued munching.

"Hey, you aren't the only one. I don't get it. Has to be more to it than just her mother didn't like her."

"All girls think their mother doesn't like them at some point. It's the natural progression of things."

"But to carry that with her all these years?" I wrapped the phone cord around my fingers and let it go again, all the while wondering about those peanuts

"That's a heavy burden, Cuz. Maybe you should talk to her about it."

"Uh-uh. I'm not going there. I've got enough on my plate." I opened the pantry, found the bag I'd thrown in there earlier, then undid the twist-tie on the freezer bag. Suddenly, the chocolate-covered peanuts didn't seem to be enough to satisfy my growing appetite. "Listen, you're making me hungry with all that chewing. I'm gonna go round up a snack. I'll see you tomorrow, 'k?"

I stood in front of the open fridge. Cold leftover dumplings had no appeal. Neither did much else in there. I pulled on the freezer and peered inside, pushing aside cartons of this and bags of that. Ah, ice cream. "Chocolate. My favorite."

"They're all your favorites."

I jumped and turned toward the voice. "Mama. Good night alive. You scared me half to death."

"Feelin' guilty about eating ice cream at this time of the night?" She pointed to the carton in my hand.

"I've never felt guilt over ice cream." I waggled my eyebrows at Mama, a grin spreading. "Want some?"

"How 'bout if you fix it and we go into the conservatory to eat it? I just love that room." Mama leaned on the countertop and watched me dish three heaping spoons of the cold yumminess into each of the two big bowls.

As an afterthought, I added a handful of the chocolate-covered peanuts to each bowl. "Here you go." I handed a bowl and a spoon to my mother. "I'll follow you."

The conservatory glowed warmly within the illumination cast by several table lamps as we sat in overstuffed club chairs, our feet propped on soft ottomans. It was so quiet we could hear the grandfather clock ticking away the time in the adjacent parlor.

"Miss Marge is very blessed to have gotten to live her life surrounded by such beauty." Mama gazed around the glassed-in room. Lights reflected off the panes like the sun on the duck pond.

"That's the truth. I can see why you love this room, Mama. It's something you would have done if you could've." I took in the furnishings. The chairs in which we sat were floral with shades of red on a cream background. They complemented the green-checked sofas perfectly. Then there were the plants we'd seen the first time we came to Rose Haven. Well, the first time I'd been. For Mama, it was one of many. "But I wonder if Miss Marge would agree that this big old place has been a blessing. She seems so lonely to me." We ate in silence for a few moments.

"Mama?"

"Mmmm?" She stirred the ice cream in her bowl and looked sideways at me.

"I know you find it odd that Aunt Becky never came here as a child, but you were a frequent guest."

Mama shrugged. "I guess. We've already talked about this, Charlotte. I really don't want to discuss it any further."

"But Mama, there *has* to be a reason." I placed my empty bowl on the glass-topped wrought-iron table between us. How had I eaten that so fast? I sat forward and leaned, elbows on knees. "I've been doing a lot of digging, Mama, and the things I've found are . . . well, they're baffling, to say the least."

"What on earth are you talking about, Charlotte? What have you been messing around in? Didn't people warn you not to dig into the past?" She turned back to her ice cream, stirring with intention.

"We have to figure out all this. At least, I do. Tank may have released me, but he told me I'm not out of the woods and people are still talking, saying I killed Boopsie."

Mama looked up from her bowl and stared pointedly at me. "You just need to let Tank and Roan do their jobs, Charlotte. Some crazy person has already killed one young woman. I do not want to lose my only child." Mama's voice strained against the thought, the sound of it nearly breaking my heart. "I couldn't bear it," she continued, tears now swimming along the rims of her eyes. "Do you hear me? I've already buried your daddy—I can't lose you, too." The tears slipped over the edge and trickled down Mama's cheeks.

I rose from the chair and kneeled, then placed my hands on Mama's knees. "You're not going to lose me, Mama. I'm careful. Fee is almost always with me."

Mama swiped at a tear. "It's the *almost* that has me worried. What about the times you just go off half-cocked and get yourself in a heap of trouble? I was hoping you'd changed in the years you've been away, Charlotte. But you haven't. You're still as reckless as you always were. At some point, you have to start thinking like an adult and face up to issues. You can't go running away from your troubles, and you certainly don't go running off creating *bigger* problems for the people you leave behind."

I tilted my head and furrowed my brow. Was that it? Had Mama resented me leaving that much? Maybe she even blamed me for Papa's untimely death. And if so, could we get past this? My heart shattered, just as surely as the glass panes in this room would shatter beneath a hurled rock. *I'm not reckless. I'm not.* I held my breath.

"Do you truly believe I'm *reckless*?" I searched Mama's face for a clue. That was . . . what? Fear? "I told you, you are not going to lose me. I may be a bit flighty and I may have run from my troubles years ago, but the past few months have been eye-opening for me." I fanned the air as I spoke.

"Charlotte, you've just always been such a free spirit, running to-and-fro, never paying attention to what you leave in your wake."

"I don't get it, Mama. First you tell me to use my skills to find Boopsie's killer, and now you don't want me to be involved at all. You even called me *reckless*. I know I did those things in the past, Mama, but I'm an adult now. I'd like to think I've moved beyond those days." I sat back on my heels and looked intently at my mother. "What's really going on, Mama? Talk to me."

Mama looked up. "It may not be right, but maybe I did blame you for John's early death." She placed her bowl on the tabletop, next to mine. She gazed down at her hands, now tightly gripped in her lap. "You weren't here to help when things got to be too much for him to handle on his own. I knew he needed you, but I couldn't call you to come home. You'd made a new life for yourself in Savannah. You finally sounded grown-up and settled. Happy. All the things we ever wanted for you."

My stomach quivered. The lightning bolt that struck my heart created an almost visible zigzag pattern across my chest. I bit into my lips. *Oh, Mama. You should have called me. Now it's too late.* "I would have come, Mama. Nothing is more important to me than you and Papa. It's just . . . it took me way too long to realize that." Tears now formed in my eyes. "I . . . I even knew that Linden wasn't that important to me. I told myself I was happy, but I wasn't. I missed you and Papa. I missed home. But I was too proud to admit how wrong I'd been about so many things." I leaned forward and laid my head in Mama's lap. "I'm so sorry, Mama. For everything. For running away. For staying so long. For . . . for being my silly, foolish self."

Mama unclenched her hands and stroked my hair, wrapping the curls around her fingers. She sniffled then hiccoughed on a sob.

I raised my head, forcing Mama to remove her fingers from my hair. "I'm sorry for my shortcomings. For always running away. I want you to know, Mama, I really have changed. I didn't realize how much until I returned to Loblolly, until I had to step up to the plate and take on Papa's work. Do the things he'd want me to do. Then, all these troubles fell upon us. I'm doing my best. I hope you know that. But I can't just let people think I killed Boopsie and not try to prove my innocence. Do you see that?"

Mama nodded. "I do. Just . . . just promise me you'll be extra careful." She put her hand beneath my chin, raising my head a tad more. She looked straight into my eyes. "Roan is a good man, Charlotte. Let him help you. Don't shut him out . . . please." Mama rose from her chair. "And Charlotte, maybe it's time you started running *to*."

I nodded then wiped at my tears. "Let me grab our dishes. You go on up. I'll turn off the lights and clean up the kitchen." If I could only clean up this mess I'd gotten myself into as easily as I could clean these dishes. I watched Mama leave, carried the ice-cream bowls into the kitchen where I washed them, then turned off the lights. I needed to figure out things and fast. Before someone else got hurt or killed. Should I call Roan? Could I run to him?

Sleep would be elusive tonight.

Chapter Twenty-five

Sure enough, sleep evaded me for most of the night as Mama's words echoed in my mind. I stretched across the bed and reached for the tick-tick-ticking alarm clock on the bedside table. Five a.m. Sleep wasn't forthcoming, that was a certainty, and hunger continued to call me. Seemed like I ate a lot more these days. Nerves? No idea.

I tiptoed down the stairs and crept into the kitchen, making as little noise as possible. I whipped up scrambled eggs, the only thing I was capable of cooking without ruining. My hastily made breakfast finished, I put the dishes in the sink to soak, then returned to my suite and dressed for the day. I grabbed the things set aside for the headstone rubbings. The sun would peek over the horizon soon and I wanted to see it from the vantage point of the little chapel.

On the exterior of the chapel, next to one of the doors, hung a historical marker plaque. Savannah had quite a few of these. I had no clue that any existed in Loblolly. I stood on the tiny covered porch and tugged on the handles of the double doors, which let out a loud groan when pulled toward me. Inside, the air was musty, much like the outbuildings, only not as much so. Perhaps either Miss Marge or George used this little chapel on a regular basis, giving it enough fresh air to stave off most of the stale odor. Another question. No surprise— the floors creaked like the ones in Miss Marge's home the second I made my first step inside.

Of course, the altar was located in front, but darkness stopped me. A search for a light switch proved fruitless. My faithful tote produced my handy flashlight. This would have to do. I pushed the sliding switch to the "on" position and the beam fanned out in the small space, throwing light in some corners, shadows in others.

A timid step took me to the aisle. I breathed in and out the familiarity. When had I last been inside a church? Years. The one I'd attended in downtown Loblolly with Mama and Daddy during my childhood was larger than this one. A sanctuary, not just a church. But this was tiny. Intimate. That was it. This was an intimate setting, perfect for one's closest family members or dearest friends. An even better place for just two. An unwanted picture of me with Roan standing before the altar appeared in my mind.

"Stop it, Charlotte. Those days have long since passed for you. Love doesn't want to claim your heart. Like you, it only wants to run away." I wandered down the short aisle, running my free hand along the arms of the pews on the way, the old oak wood cool beneath my fingers.

Who had sat here in the past, and who had filled the pulpit? Miss Marge's ancestors … who were they… what were they like? Research brought together a bigger picture, but I longed for details. The papers tucked away within the cover of the hymnal shed some light on the family who'd lived and worshiped here. But questions remained. Names on the papers were simply that—names. I longed to know the person behind each. That was the part of genealogy I loved. Getting to know the people on a personal level.

At the altar, I stopped and rested the beam on a semi-sturdy table in the center. On it lay a crocheted cloth and upon that an iron cross and an old Bible, open to the Gospel of John. I leaned in, the light shining against the yellowing of the paper and the black lettering. I ran my hand over the pages of the ancient text. How many generations had read from its pages? Was there was a family tree in the front? Dare I look?

Both hands were needed so that I didn't tear the delicate old volume. I propped the flashlight on its side, which cast an eerie oblong illumination on the Bible. Carefully, I turned the book, bringing the front cover to a close. Lifting it again, I turned first to the front pages, but found nothing, then to the middle of the sacred text, knowing that if not in the front, then—hopefully—in the center pages, knowing that most family records were located there. When I found the glossy pages, I blew out the breath I'd been holding.

There, in script likely from an old inkwell, someone had scrawled the names of those I supposed were Miss Marge's family. I picked up the light and directed it onto the page. I ran a finger down the list of names—husbands and wives, children, marriage dates, death dates. Carefully turning the page, I read on. How many generations were here, I couldn't know until I scrutinized the dates. I needed to snap some photos ... I found my camera in my tote, and after tucking the flashlight beneath my chin, its beam aimed on the pages, I snapped away.

Finished, I returned the book to its former state and packed up my things. As I exited the little chapel, the sun made its appearance above the horizon. It was going to be another hot day.

***

"So, did you find anything in the chapel?" Fee stood in Soilse, coffee mug in hand with the phrase *Flower Power* emblazoned across a field of daisies. She sipped from the cup.

"I did. I'm just not sure what at this point." I pulled the Coke I'd just purchased from the corner drugstore through a long straw shoved to the bottom of a large paper cup covered in red-and-white diamonds, each shape printed with the word COKE or HAVE A COKE in its center. I hit the bottom and made a slurping sound. "Sorry. Mama would be horrified." But I laughed, nonetheless.

"Yep. Same genes as Mama." Fee placed her cup on her desk and sat in the chair behind it. "So, what's next with our investigation? I've missed out the past couple of days. Anything new?"

"Other than finding those old letters and, oh—a family tree in an old Bible in the chapel. At least what I think will be a tree, no. Not much. Just trying to get finished with the store so we can sell it. Mama wants to be done with that part of her life." I threw my empty cup into the trash container at the side of Fee's desk.

The desk, like everything Fee touched, was totally, well . . . Fee. Ornate and French provincial with a touch of country was Fee's style. I always felt a bit out of place when in Soilse, especially when it came to the current fashions hanging from this hook and that one. Forever clad in jeans and a T-shirt or a flannel one, I couldn't hold a candle to Fee's style. Even now, a winter-white and elegant puffy-sleeved high-bodice gown hung behind her. When she caught me staring at it, she turned to glance at it, then said to me, "That's the latest for this year's Christmas season."

"Christmas? Already?"

"I'm always a season ahead." She stood, walked to the dress, and played with the laced sleeves. "Isn't it gorgeous?"

"Well ..."

"I know, not your style, but trust me, it feels like a million dollars once you put it on."

"I'll take your word for it," I countered, and she smiled. Thankfully, Fee always welcomed me into Soilse, no matter how I was dressed. Gotta love a cousin who accepts you as you are. "You still game to go do some headstone rubbings?"

"Mmm. Let me check with Iris. She did say she'd cover for me, but fall merchandise is *already* in and it all has to be tagged and checked against orders. You know the drill. It may still be hot in southeast Alabama, but fall will be here before we know it and I can't wait to don a couple of the new sweaters I got in." She waved her hand in the air. "You know what, Charlotte? I'd probably better pass this time."

"Uh-huh." I decided to hide my disappointment with another subject. "So ... heard from Ned?"

"Yeah. Met him for coffee twice over the past couple of days. No big deal."

Ah. Well, that would explain her absence. Couldn't blame her. I swung my feet from their draped-over-the-arm-of-the-sofa position to flat on the floor. "No big deal? Who are you trying to kid, Fiona Soilse Campbell?"

Fee waved in the air, indicating for me to relax. "It's just coffee. No lunch. No dinner. Just ... coffee."

I watched as my cousin turned crimson, all the way to the roots of her red hair. "Me thinks the lady doth protest too much." I quoted using my best imitation of Uncle Angus's Scottish brogue.

"Stop it." Fee chuckled. "You are so bad at that. Daddy's bad enough, but you are the worst." She returned to her desk, picked up a pencil and clipboard, and began making notes.

"It's true, though. You are just a bit too touchy for this not to be a big deal to you. So, come on, 'fess up. Tell good ole Charlie all about it."

"Have mercy. The sky is going to fall for sure. Charlotte Graves just called herself *Charlie*."

"I did, didn't I? Wonder where that came from and what it means?" I gazed into the distance. Surely, I was not getting used to the idea that I could be Roan's Charlie again. File that idea way back. Not back-burner back, but the-iron-ore-is-still-in-the-ground back. No time for such. I had to find a murderer . . . and a missing grave. Somehow, the two were related. I could feel it in my bones.

"Hello. Earth to Charlie. I think we both know what it means. You are finally lightening up on Roan a bit. At least, I hope that's what it means."

"I don't know. Maybe. I'll have to ponder it a while."

"May I ask what brought about this very sudden change of heart?"

"Not what. Who. Mama. Something she said last night. It just made me think about a lot of things. Roan was one of them." I breathed deeply. I didn't want to get into this right then. "I'm not ready to talk about it, but I'll let you know when I am. You can count on that."

I stood and gathered my things. "I'm heading back to Rose Haven. If you change your mind, that's where I'll be. More than likely in the cemetery. If I'm not there, I'll be in Outbuilding One, doing more research on the items we put in there." I headed for the door to Fee's office but turned before going out. "If you and Ned want to come out together, we can try to empty some more of the buildings." I smiled and left without waiting for an answer.

It was good to see Fee so happy.

Chapter Twenty-six

*B*rutally and *hot* were the only two words to describe Loblolly that day. If I 'd thought it through, I would have come straight to the cemetery from the chapel, but I missed Fee and wanted to share with her about finding what I hoped would be a family tree in the Bible. Not just any family tree, but Miss Marge's. Nothing else made sense. I only needed time to sit and study and tie all the loose ends together.

I barely refrained from going and reading the pages right then and there. But with so much to be done, things like that had to wait. My actual job was to help the members of WHS track their roots, and I'd been absent from the historical society far too long. I doubted Olivia would be patient much longer. What I really needed to do was pay her a visit. Finish out in the cemetery, clean up, head to Mama's for some decent clothes, and then go to the WLC offices.

I liked when plans came together.

***

I didn't recognize the thirty-something woman sitting behind the desk in the receptionist area. Not even by name. "Mrs. Lawrence wasn't expecting you, Miss Graves. Please have a seat and I'll see if she has time for you."

While the receptionist picked up the phone, presumably to call Olivia, I looked around the waiting room. Or anteroom. Or whatever-you-call-it room, which looked much as it had looked a few months ago when Olivia had interviewed me for the WHS position. A Persian rug lay on the wooden floors. Leather chairs sat side by side in front of the leather sofa where I sat. Ornately framed portraits of Olivia and her father hung on the wall. A well-stocked bar stood to the right of the receptionist.

"Mrs. Lawrence will see you now, Miss Graves. If you'll follow me, please."

Upon entering Olivia's office, I was relieved that I'd stopped at Mama's to change clothes. I'd left the sapphire blue dress there after the purchase and had quickly changed in to it before coming to WHS. Note to self: remember to thank Fee for insisting I purchase this dress.

"Charlotte, dear. How are you?" Olivia didn't bother to get up, but instead indicated a chair across from her desk—French provincial, much like Fee's but on a grander scale.

Unlike the other room, this one screamed Olivia Lawrence. She sat behind the heavily carved, off-white-and-gilded oversized desk, in its matching chair. I sat on a sofa that closely matched Olivia's chair, covered in cream-colored velvet. The Aubusson rug was thick and in shades of cream, camel, and soft grays with the slightest hint at pinks and blues. Olivia had to have searched all over to find one like it. Must have cost her a pretty penny, too, as Nana would have said. I'd seen my share of rugs, but never an Aubusson in so many elegant shades. It felt divine beneath my three-inch-heel-clad feet, which protested the audacity of my purchase. No, these feet were made for flip-flops, Keds, and boots, and not much else. Especially not such high heels.

"How may I help you today?" Olivia leaned back in the ornate chair, rested her elbows on the arms, and templed her fingers. "Are there issues with the historical society?"

"Oh, no. Not at all. At least, I hope not. I only want to apologize for not being as diligent as I had hoped to be in my duties at the society. This ... murder ... has me running all over the county. Add to that, helping Mama with the store and now Miss Marge's estate. Well, I'm having to shuffle a lot of things and I wanted to see if there is anything urgent you need from me before I get any more involved." Another bad habit due to nerves . . . rambling. I took a deep breath and reminded myself this was Olivia, who'd come to my defense earlier in the week.

"My goodness. I had no idea you had quite so many irons in the fire." Olivia stood and came around her desk. She leaned against it and crossed her ankles.

"Believe me, I had no intention of taking on so many things. I came here to help Mama with the store and wound up with your gracious offer at the historical society. The murder investigation and helping Miss Marge just grew from that." Her perplexed look caused me to add, "Oh, but you don't know about that. She's asked me to go through all the rooms at Rose Haven and provide her with an inventory of her possessions. I should have asked before I just said I'd do it." I paused. I'd learn much more if I listened more than I talked.

Olivia came and sat beside me. "That sounds like a splendid idea. I'm sure that old place could use a good cleaning. Imagine over two hundred years of family heirlooms. Rumor has it, they've not gotten rid of the first item even after all these years. And . . . well, I know I'd like to know what all is inside." She shifted on the sofa, then reached down, removed her right shoe, and rubbed her stocking-clad foot against the soft rug. "Unless someone from the society says they have an urgent need, I can't think of any reason for you to do anything other than what you're currently doing." Olivia touched her hair before tugging on the hem of her cream-colored jacket.

That was Olivia. Always dressed in creams or camels, which complemented her platinum hair. True to form, she wore her owl pin which, she informed me at our first meeting in her home, was representative of her initials, *OWL*, for Olivia Woodville Lawrence.

Olivia reminded me for all the world of Doris Day, one of the stars I loved.

"Charlotte?" She touched my arm. "Did you hear me?"

"Oh, I'm so sorry." My hands flew to my mouth. "I was thinking about what you said."

"I inquired about your mother and the investigation."

"Oh, Mama's fine. Busy. She's helping me get the store ready to sell. And the investigation is going okay, I guess. I've learned a few things. Not much. Some people are hesitant to talk. Others are quick to point a finger." I didn't want to say too much. Who knew what would leak and from whom? Best to keep discoveries between Fee and me.

"Well," Olivia slipped her shoe onto her foot, then stood. "I think you just need to keep investigating. Don't worry about the society. We can always put the meeting off until the next month if we need to. People here are pretty laid back and most are flexible. I would think that doing all you can to aid in finding Boopsie's killer is your primary concern for now." She walked toward the door. "But let me know if you find any buried treasures at Rose Haven. I'm dying to see what all Marge has."

I rose and followed, running back to grab my tote as quickly as I could in those heels. I'd been crazy to listen to Fee when she insisted these were the perfect shoes for the sapphire dress. These things may be the latest fashion, but they left a lot to be desired in the comfort arena.

Olivia opened the heavy mahogany door. "Thank you for coming by, dear. Do keep in touch."

"I will. Let me know if you need me to do anything for the society. Thanks for your time." I took a step before having a second thought. I stopped and turned back to Olivia. "Oh, I almost forgot. I met Mr. Lawrence at Rose Haven the other day. I've never really talked to him before. He . . . seems like a very charming man."

The look that fleetingly passed over Olivia's face said she wasn't pleased with hearing this. "Oh, he is that. A real charmer, my Max."

***

Never had I been so relieved to be out of shoes and a dress. It was much too hot for such. Fall couldn't get here fast enough. I wiggled my toes, all of which smiled with approval. Jeans were too hot, too. I pulled on a pair of cut-off jean shorts, knowing Mama would complain the minute she saw me in them.

Mama looked up from the sink when she heard me enter the kitchen. "Hey. Lord have mercy, child. What do you have on your body?" She grabbed a dish towel, dried her hands, and turned to stare at her only child, hands on her hips, a frown on her face.

"Shorts." I grabbed an apple from the bowl in the center of the kitchen table and took a big bite from it. Juice slid down my chin. I swiped at it with the back of my hand. "I bought them in Savannah," I said around the food. "Cheap, too."

"Bargain or not, I do not agree with my daughter parading around in them. You go right back upstairs and change." She pointed toward the entry hall and stairs.

"Can't."

"What did you say?"

"I said, I can't. And I won't. It's too hot to wear jeans and this is all I have that's cool enough. I have work to do in the cemetery and I'm not going to faint from heat prostration while doing it." I rarely talked back to Mama. Well, at least not now. When I was in my teens I had. A fact I wasn't proud of. There were many things I needed to apologize to Mama for. That was one of them.

Add it to your growing list, Charlotte. And quit talking to yourself while you're at it. With that, I grabbed my bag and headed toward the family plot.

***

Two hours later, I had most of the headstones done. I did a few rubbings, and I'd snapped a few photos with my little camera. I'd save the paper and charcoal in case Miss Marge wanted rubbings of any special gravestones. Perhaps of her parents. And I could always return to the hardware store for more sheets of copper. That would make a lovely gift for Miss Marge. A thank-you for her hospitality. I needed to get this roll of film developed, and put the photos in order by birthdates, match them to the names in the family Bible, then approach Miss Marge with what I knew.

This one should be fairly easy. At least I was going to tell myself that. Some of the pieces seemed to be coming together. Maybe Fee would be out tonight.

I had much to tell her.

Chapter Twenty-seven

Fee's countenance revealed just how shocked she was. "There's no way all those people could be related."

"I'm telling you, it's the truth. And we know what our mamas always say, 'The truth will set us free.'"

"But this doesn't make any sense whatsoever." Fee pointed to a name in the family tree I'd hastily compiled. "How could he be our cousin?"

"You can see it right there in black and white." I leaned against the squished pillows on the bed.

"I don't have to like it, do I? Or him?" Fee shuddered and frowned. "So, what are you going to do with all this information?"

"For now, nothing. I have to figure out a lot more stuff before I can tell any of this."

Fee shifted on the bed. "How can I help?"

"Just help me finish those outbuildings. It should be an all-day task for a couple of days to get the others cleaned and then we can begin inventorying what we keep." I stroked the ever-present Oreo, who responded with one of her deep purrs. "Think you could get Ned to come help us again?"

Fee blushed at the mention of his name. "I think I could talk him into it." She bowed her head and bit her bottom lip, then shifted and rose from the foot of the bed where she had perched, a telling sparkle now in her eyes. "I think I'll just go on and give Ned that call." She eased her way to the door and blew me a goodnight kiss.

I rubbed behind Oreo's ears. "Tell me. What do we do with all this, Miss Oreo?" The degree to which I'd become attached to this creature was shocking. When this investigation was over and I had to go back home, Oreo was one of the things I'd miss the most.

***

"That's the last load for today." Ned Cecil slammed the gate of his pickup. "I'll get these things on over to the thrift store. Lots of folks out of work right now." He reached into his pocket, pulled out his keys, then entered the cab of his seen-cleaner-days pickup. "Miss Marge is one kind lady to donate this. I'll be back to help you move the other things around just as soon as I get my truck unloaded. Ladies." He tipped his hat to us, allowing his gaze to settle on Fee. He gave her a wink, then drove away.

Fee feigned a Vivien Leigh move. "Doesn't he just make you swoon?"

"Swoon?" Had Fee had lost her mind? "Since when have you used that word?"

"Since I met Ned Cecil. He is such a gentleman." She sighed and smiled. "A true Southern gentleman."

"You are smitten, for sure."

"Smitten?"

"If you can *swoon*, I can *smitten*." I stepped into the third building we'd emptied. "Come on. If we hurry, we can have these two cleaned out and ready for Ned to move the things back when he returns. It'll be dark soon."

"Sounds good. That will give me more time to just sit on the porch and look at the moon while I talk to him." Fee grabbed the broom and began sweeping.

I got the long-handled duster and went to work on the cobwebs. "I'm beginning to hate spiders. I don't know why they have to exist."

"To rid the world of a whole bunch of bugs is why, but I don't like them either." Fee stirred up a cloud of dust with her sweeping. "Did you know that Ned and Roan are good buddies?"

"Now how would I know that? I don't talk to Roan and I don't really know Ned."

"Well, we wondered if the two of you would . . ."

"Wait, wait." I stopped and held up the hand that wasn't holding the duster. "There is no *two of you*." I resumed my work and whacked at a stubborn cobweb with a vengeance. "How many times do I have to tell you? Roan and I are no more. It's in the past. It's done. Over. Ended."

"I think you're protesting too much, if you ask me."

Duster still in hand, I turned on my cousin. "That's just it. No one asked you. Not Roan and certainly not me." I swung the duster at a cobweb in the corner, whacking the resident spider with all I had.

Fee stopped sweeping in mid-stroke. "Well, actually, Roan did ask."

I spun around. "Fiona Campbell. What are you doing talking to Roan Steele about me? You have no business bringing my name up to him. Ever." I stomped out of Building Three and headed to Building Four, muttering along the way.

Fee took off after me. "Charlotte Graves. I'm just about over your attitude. Number one, Roan did nothing wrong. Nothing. You're the one who hightailed it out of here without hearing him out. You spent eight years, *eight years*, Charlotte, away from the people who love you the most. And all because you believed a lie. Now, it's time for you to grow up, go find Roan, talk this out, and get the truth out there once and for all."

This was unbelievable. Fee. *My* Fee had been talking to Roan. About *me*. About the past. About heaven only knew what else. I threw down the duster, stomped even harder than before and made my way to the edge of the woods.

Once past the tree line, I took off, running as hard as I could within the sea of pines. I didn't even bother to follow the trail. I just ran, saplings slapping me as I went, dodging fallen logs, zigzagging left and right around the thick, tall pines. Fee called in the distance, but I didn't stop.

Out of breath and sides aching, I dropped to the ground and leaned against the nearest tree. What had Fee meant? I'd believed a lie?

"No, no, noooo." I laid my head on bent knees and rocked, trying to soothe my broken heart. Boopsie's diary. It wasn't true even then. I'd intuitively known, and yet, I'd run. Why? What was wrong with me? Why couldn't I have stayed and faced up to Boopsie? To Mama? To everybody thinking I was a loser? I wasn't. I'm *not*. I'm strong and capable and . . . "Oh, no," I moaned again. Realization hit me as soundly as the saplings had. "I still love Roan." I leaned my head back, closed my eyes and fell into a deep slumber with that awful realization dogging me.

When I woke it was to one thought: would Roan ever be able to forgive me for acting so foolishly? So childishly? Fee was right. I did need to talk to him. First, I had to get out of these woods. Get back to Rose Haven and a phone. I pushed up from the ground and brushed the pine needles from the seat of my jeans, then turned in a circle and tried to get my bearings. Darkness shrouded the world around me, everything much darker than when I'd entered the woods.

How much time had passed? I went to check my watch, then realized I hadn't put it on that morning. Well, wasn't that just peachy-keen ...

And where was the trail?

Confused, I looked left and right, down and up. Scant light came through the thick forest. Evening had fallen and here I was. In yet another predicament. "Will you ever learn, Charlotte? Running away always lands you in trouble."

Another issue: I was talking to myself . . . again.

***

An hour later, I remained lost. Finding a way out of the deep woods eluded me. Animals scurried about. An owl hooted in the distance. Forward movement was all I could manage. I kept making mistakes, but mostly, I hadn't learned from repeated ones. Somewhere along the way, I'd forgotten who I was. More importantly, Whose I was. "God, if you still listen to me, I could use some help. A little light would be nice." Tears pooled in the corners of my eyes as I stumbled along singing a tune I'd learned one summer at Vacation Bible School: "This

Little Light of Mine." As tears trickled down my face, I put one foot in front of the other, step after step, sobs coming between the words as I did my best to sing.

How much time had passed, I had no way of knowing. I was tired, hungry, and cold. And I couldn't stop shaking . . . from fear or the cool night air, I couldn't say.

A movement in front of me made me stop.

I sniffled and wiped my nose on the bottom of my shirt. Was that . . . *smoke?*

It was … and if I could follow it, it might lead to a way out. These woods belonged to Miss Marge, but old country roads ran all through them. There were scattered homesteads. They could have a cook-stove. Or maybe I was near the little cabin.

Please, no.

A twig snapped behind me.

I froze.

I strained, listening. Animal? Human? No clue.

I took two more steps, stopping when another twig snapped.

Whatever it was, it was big.

Stand still. Don't panic.

The need to run was overwhelming, but how could I with the trees so thick and not one tiny beam of light to be had? Realization hit me— no one was coming to my aid. No one and nothing. Not the dirt which had lain for tens of thousands of years on the forest floor. The trees which stood like a million-man army would not come to my defense. The most I could hope for was to be shrouded within their shadows.

I took another step, then another . . . until "Umph!" Down I went.

A bright light shone directly into my eyes. "Well, lookie here, Doo. What you reckon we done caught tonight?" A man snickered.

I raised one hand in an effort to block the light. "Who's there?" No one answered. "I'm lost and I need help to get back home." I reached out with my left hand and shielded my eyes with the right. I waved around.

A hand clamped down on my arm and I screamed.

The hand released and went over my mouth. Then an arm went around my waist, lifting me off the ground. I kicked for all I was worth, thankful I wore heavy boots.

"Ouch. Dabnabit. Stop that," the man who held me yelled, "Doo, get over here and help me."

"Okay, Hal." Doo put down the light and took a step toward his friend.

"Not like that. Now go get the light. How you 'spect us to get outta here if we ain't got no light?"

"Sorry." Doo picked up the light as the beam shone directly onto his face.

Oh, no. It *was* one of the men with Cam at the cabin that day. Did he have a gun? *Please don't have a gun. Please, please.* I kicked with all my might, hoping one would take purchase in a painful spot.

The grip on me tightened. "Now stop that infernal kicking. Ya don't want me to haul off and knock some sense into ya, now, do ya?"

"Whatcha want, Hal? Should I grab her legs or her arms?"

"Get her feet."

So, the one barking orders was Hal? Well, Hal, too bad for you. I kept kicking.

"Stop that. I done told you twicet."

No way was I going to obey these hooligans. I continued wriggling and kicking.

"Owww." Hal yelled. "You done went an' done it now."

I continued to kick when suddenly, Hal rolled to the ground and pinned me down.

"Shoulda done that to begin with."

"Woooeee, Hal. We gonna have some fun now?" Doo chortled above.

I could barely breathe as the one called Hal sat on my back, pressing my chest into the limbs and rocks beneath me. My face bore into the pine needles which poked like a thousand hypodermics. I wiggled and kicked to the best of my abilities, trying to buck him off, but to no avail. How could such a scrawny little guy keep me pinned down like this?

"Run get Cam, Doo. And hurry."

"Sure thing."

From the sound of it, he ran off to the right. Was that where the cabin was? How had I gotten so turned around? But now that there was only one of them, maybe I could try again. I lay still for a couple of minutes trying to lull Hal into thinking I'd given up the fight. His grip felt looser.

This was it.

I heaved with all my might and threw him off me. If the cabin was to the right—the direction Doo ran— I needed to go left, hopefully toward the path. I was on my feet in less than a second.

But Hal was just as quick.

He grabbed my leg throwing me off balance. Down I went with a thud like one of the pines, felled for its lumber.

***

A moan escaped my lips as I rubbed my head. How had I gotten such a big knot? Events came rushing back and I opened my eyes. The light and the knot on my head made it ache. I blinked, then narrowed my eyes to slits. The little cabin again. And that awful odor, too. The one Fee and I had smelled the first time we'd come upon it. Was that urine? Rotted animals? From these nasty men or wild animals? Whatever it was—it overpowered.

"What we gon' do with her, Cam?" Doo again. Sadly, I now knew their names and the voices that went with them. And Cam was here, too? Focus—eyes and mind.

"We aren't going to do anything. But I'm gonna have some fun with this little trouble-maker." Ah. So, Cam was here. He pulled my hair . . . again.

Why did he keep doing that? Every time Cam showed up he pulled my hair. But he didn't really pull it. He only made it seem that he was doing so. Even though it wasn't painful, I still pulled back and winced.

"When you're done, can we have a turn?" Doo asked then chuckled in that awful way he had. He reminded me of one of the bad guys captured by Sheriff Taylor on *The Andy Griffith Show*. On second thought, the guys Sheriff Andy captured weren't anywhere near this bad. They weren't evil, just dim-witted. Apparently, Cam's goons were both.

Cam pulled me to my feet. "You guys clean up here and go back out there and clean up the mess you made. We don't need folks looking for her and finding anything to lead them back here." He tied my hands behind me with an old rope which hung from a nail driven into one of the logs. "I'm going to go take care of this one. I'll call the boss to relay our little find here. Y'all lay low." He pointed to the fireplace. "And put out that fire. I should be back before morning." He shoved me toward the door. I stumbled but righted myself. Once outside, Cam threw me into the back of his old, uncovered Jeep Wrangler and, again, pulled my hair as he turned and waved to his goons.

What on earth had I gotten into? And all because I was running away.

Again.

Chapter Twenty-eight

Something didn't add up. This was, what? Three, four times Cam had acted as if he was pulling my hair when he really hadn't. Maybe I should just wait and see how this played out. On the other hand, what if he really was about to take me some place to do heaven-only-knew-what?

I wriggled my way up in the back of the Jeep, the wind knocking around me. Man, did my head ache. "Where you taking me?" I all but hollered.

Cam stared straight ahead but remained silent.

"I know you heard me," I shouted toward the front. "*Where* are you taking me?" I sounded frantic. Not good. Fear would only goad anyone who wanted to harm me. But did Cam intend to hurt me? Or worse? I couldn't, wouldn't, let my mind go there.

Silence.

So that was how it was going to be? Well, two could play that game. I fixed myself into a safe position, then tried to untie the knot from my wrists. The rope rubbed against my skin each time I moved. I'd be raw from that for sure. Still, raw was better than dead.

Paved road sounds. Out here, that could only be one or two. Could I figure out where we were if I listened and paid close attention? Cam turned off onto another dirt road, the long branches of the foliage on both sides of the road slapping his Jeep. I ducked to keep from getting hit as I jostled about, still making attempts to untie the rope more difficult. Nothing shook one like the ruts and rocks and holes in a dirt road. But where were we? I recognized nothing. This was South Alabama where dirt roads existed in abundance. We could be anywhere. Still in Alabama? Thus far there'd been no sign indicating the Florida state line. But then, not all these back roads would have such a sign. Would they even be visible if they existed?

The old Jeep bounced as we roared down the road. Every time Cam hit a hole, I fell against the back's metal and had to right myself. I was like a fish in a tin can. If only I could get the rope off my wrists.

"We're almost ..." Cam said, his last words lost in the night air.

I looked out the windows for signs of . . . anything, really. Street signs didn't exist wherever we were. Just trees. Miles and miles of dark pine forest and ribbons of hard dirt road. Were we still on Miss Marge's land? We hadn't been in the car for long, so we very likely were.

Cam slowed and turned left down a road so narrow I assumed it to be a driveway. Another couple of minutes and he stopped, cut off the engine, and climbed out of the Jeep.

"Come on," he said, grabbing my arm to pull me toward another cabin, this one bigger. Nicer.

And vaguely familiar.

"Come on, hurry." Cam pulled me up the stone steps to the door. When it opened, I sucked in my breath.

Roan.

He took a step toward me and, instinctively, I backed away.

He held out his hands. "Hey. I'm not going to hurt you." He glared at Cam, his eyes cold and hard. His jaw tensed. "Turn around and I'll untie you."

Roan pulled out a knife and cut the rope from my wrists. I rubbed at them just as I'd done in the jail when he'd removed the handcuffs, only this time, my wrists were rubbed almost raw. This was becoming a habit. One I needed to break.

"So." I looked from Roan to Cam and back again. "Either of you want to tell me what's going on?" I studied the surroundings. Roan's dad's fishing cabin. No wonder it had seemed so familiar. I'd spent many happy days here with Roan and his dad before . . . well, before.

"May as well tell her," Cam said.

Roan broke the silence. "You walked into a drug sting." He pointed to Cam. "Cam here's been working undercover for the past year or so to help us find the leader ... or leaders ... of our local drug syndicate."

My mouth flew open. I looked back and forth between the two men again. "Sorry, but I'm not buying that. There's no way the Cam Lawrence I knew would do anything on your side of the law." I shook my head and winced at the pain.

"It's true. Cam's reputation as town-bad-boy came in handy when we needed someone to help from the inside." Roan took my hand. "You're hurt. That rope rubbed your skin raw." He glared at Cam, this time far more than the first time.

I nodded and pulled my hand away. "I'm bruised, I'm sure, and my head is throbbing, but I'll be okay." I rubbed my forehead. "So how long has this been going on?" I indicated Cam. "Him ... helping you?"

Cam answered this time. "Almost a year. We're close, but we can't quite get this figured out."

"So, what are you planning to do with me? How do I fit into this?" The familiar green-and-red plaid sofa where Roan and I had snuggled back in high school beckoned me. I didn't need those memories. Not here and certainly not now. Pushing aside the past, I sauntered over and sat. Dizziness and nausea overtook me. I leaned onto the arm of the sofa and moaned.

Roan rushed to my side. "Cam, get some water, quick."

Cam went into the kitchen and brought a glass of water then handed it to Roan who held my head. "Here, drink this." He held the glass near my mouth.

I opened my eyes and took a sip. "I don't feel so good." My hand automatically went to my head. "Ohh. Stop the pounding."

"So, what happened?" Roan looked at Cam. "Cam?"

"Hal and Doo got hold of her. One of them tackled her. She hit her head pretty hard from what I could tell. I got her out of there as fast as I could. Told them I was going to get rid of her." He paced in the big room and ran his fingers through his long, greasy blond hair.

"Well, we can't keep her here for days. You can bet her mother already has the sheriff looking for her." He placed the water glass on an end table, picked up a sofa pillow, and eased my head down. "We need to think about how to get her back to Rose Haven without Hal and Doo asking too many questions." He went to the wall phone in the nearby kitchen. "I'd better call Tank. See what's going on. He'll have a good idea of what our next step should be." He pointed to me, then made the call.

With his broad shoulders turned, I could only catch a phrase or two of his side of the conversation, even with my eyes closed. I opened them again only when he'd ended the call and re-entered the room. "Well?" Cam looked eagerly at Roan.

"Says it's up to us to figure this out, but folks are out looking for Charlotte. Woods are full of volunteers. This is going to be tricky."

"I can escape," I said.

"From two armed men? And one of them a deputy?" Roan scowled.

"No … from Cam." I kept my voice low. "I got out of the ropes and ran through the woods. He couldn't find me." I winced when I tried to sit up. "Ohhh. Got any aspirin? Or, better yet, morphine?" I eased my head back down.

Roan went into the kitchen area, opened a cabinet, and returned with a bottle of Bayer. He touched my shoulder. "Here." He shook out two pills and handed them to me. "That's all good, but what on earth do you plan to tell them once you do get back? No. I don't like it. We have to think this through."

I raised up on my elbow and swallowed the two pills with a shudder. Nothing worse that swallowing Bayer aspirin. "Look, I need to go to the doctor. I could have a concussion. I can't stay here. I can't go to sleep. You can drop me near Rose Haven, and I can make my way back to the house."

"Look, Roan, she's making a lot of sense. I can say I didn't tie the rope well. It was hard to do. I was in a hurry, you know. To have some alone time with her. Just didn't do a good job. She got her hands loose and hit me over the head and got away."

"It all works except for the hitting on the head. Where's the evidence of that?" Roan rubbed the back of his neck.

"Well," Cam said, "you'll just have to hit me, that's all."

"Oh, good. Just what I need. Two concussion victims in the same night."

"I didn't say knock me senseless. Just a little whack will do."

"For Pete's sake. What's the matter with y'all?" I said as loudly as comfort allowed. "You just put a little ketchup or something on his head and muss his hair. Those guys are as dumb as dirt and won't even notice."

Cam looked at Roan. "She's right about that. They're about as dumb as they come."

Roan returned his attention to me, his gaze all seriousness. "This is all fine, but I'm taking you to the door of Rose Haven. I'll say that after I learned about you being missing, I went out looking for you and ran across you staggering down one of the back roads."

I eased my feet to the floor. "Works for me."

Chapter Twenty-nine

All the lights were on at Rose Haven and a crowd had gathered with hound dogs. From the looks of it, the sheriff had called in a lot of favors.

Roan pulled up in front of the main entrance and the crowd hurried to his cruiser when they realized he had a passenger. He exited the car and motioned for everyone to step back. "Come on, now. Give us some room and some privacy. I'm sure the sheriff will make a statement soon." He came around to my side and helped me out. I stumbled and Roan put his arm around my waist.

I looked up at him as old feelings came to the surface. This wasn't happening. Not now. I ducked my head and took a step toward the front door. Before we reached the top step, Mama ran out to greet us. Miss Marge, George, Aunt Becky, Uncle Angus, Fee, and even Ned Cecil gathered behind her.

"Baby, oh, my baby." Mama swept me into her arms. She stood arms-length away, looked me up and down, then turned to help me inside.

Roan walked closely behind. The sea of spectators parted to let us pass.

"I'm okay, Mama. I just got lost in the woods. I couldn't find my way out. I'm fine."

Mama looked up at Roan. He nodded toward the door.

The next few hours went by in a blur.

***

I awoke in my room at Mama's. I glanced at the bedside alarm clock ticking softly nearby. Three o'clock. Surely, three in the morning. But, wait. A glance around told me the sun was shining beyond the window. Had I slept all day? That couldn't be right.

I threw back the covers and tried to sit up. Well, that didn't work. Why did my head hurt so much? Oh, yeah. I returned my head back to the imprint in my pillow, then slowly put one foot on the floor. This couldn't be good. Where was Mama? Last I remembered, doctors were looking me over in the ER, Mama at my side.

I pulled the quilt around me, taking in the comfort it gave. I'd missed this room during the past few days at Miss Marge's, but I knew my days here were coming to an end. At least, they needed to. A grown woman didn't—couldn't—live with her mother forever. Mama seemed to be doing better in dealing with Papa's death. She'd never get over it, but her heart would heal.

I pushed those thoughts to the back burner. Right now, I had to find the person who'd killed Boopsie. My instincts were on high alert with Cam and those two men, Hal and Doo. But if Cam was one of the good guys, who was the ringleader? More importantly, did I need to get involved in this in order to find Boopsie's killer?

Fear wrapped its cold, probing fingers around my heart. I didn't like the answer to that question. Not one little bit.

Horrific headache or not, I still had work to do. I sat up . . . slowly this time. My head still spun, but if I moved with ease, it wasn't unbearable. Where was Mama? Aromas told me she was cooking, lured me toward the pleasant smell. Sure enough, Mama was taking something out of the oven.

Mama looked up at the sound of my footsteps. "Charlotte, what are you doing out of bed?" She put the pan on the stove top, laid a couple potholders on the countertop, and appeared at my side. "Here, let me help you." She wrapped her arm about my waist and guided me to a chair at the table.

"It's okay, Mama. My head aches like crazy and I'm a bit dizzy, but other than that, I'm just sore from being tackled so hard."

Mama's mouth flew open. "What are you talking about? You said you tripped and fell. I knew it. Charlotte Isabelle Graves, you'd best come clean right now. No more skirting around the truth."

"Me and my big mouth." I rested my head in my hands, elbows propped on the table. "I figured Roan had told you. I don't mean to upset you. I shouldn't have said anything."

"But you did. So now, out with it." Mama pulled out a chair opposite me and waited for me to tell her the sordid story of last evening's events.

Twenty minutes later, I'd revealed all I could remember. "Have mercy. If I'd known that, I would've been twice as worried when you didn't come back last night."

"It's my fault. It always is. I got mad and ran away . . . again. Just as I've done all my life." I laid my head on my arms and closed my eyes. Seconds ticked by without Mama saying anything. "What? You aren't going to argue with me? Tell me I'm wrong?"

"No. I think I've done enough of that. If I'd told you long ago that you had to face up to your shortcomings and disappointments when you always ran away, maybe none of these things would have happened. You would've stayed and talked to Roan. You would've been here to help your daddy. You would've known Fiona was right and you wouldn't have run off."

I raised my head to look at Mama. "Mmm. So, she told you?"

"Did you think she wouldn't after you didn't come home? Somebody around here has to be an adult and face things even when they aren't pleasant." Mama looked squarely into my eyes. "Yes, she told me you'd had words."

"It seems like I've spent more of my time apologizing than anything else here lately. I'm sorry, Mama. For everything. I'm going to try to do better. Really, I am. I thought I'd made some improvements, but maybe I was just fooling myself." I lowered my head to my arms. "Do I have a concussion? My head is killing me."

"No. No concussion, but the doctor says you'll have a heck of a headache for a couple of days. Need some aspirin?" She glanced at the stove's clock. "It's been long enough. You can have a couple more." Mama got a glass of water and shook two white pills from the bottle.

More Bayer. Yuck. "Here. This should ease it in just a few minutes."

"Thanks, Mama." I swallowed the pills and placed the glass on the table. "I have work to do on this murder case."

"You need to get better first. How can you reason with your head pounding like that?"

"I can work through it. I need to work fast before anyone else is hurt. Or worse . . . killed."

"I don't like it, but I know you're going to do it anyway. Please promise me you won't take any unnecessary chances." Mama paused as if to collect her thoughts. "And, Charlotte? Ask Roan for help before you get yourself into something you can't get out of."

"As a matter of fact, talking to Roan is first on my agenda. I realize you were right about that." I eased from the chair and went into my bathroom. The first order of business was to clean up.

***

Mama dropped me on the corner at the park. I arrived at the bench ahead of time. I glanced at my Timex. Too early. Better than late. I could at least prove that some things did change. In the past, Roan had to wait every time we did anything, from going to church together, to a movie, to the fateful grad-night party.

Church. Mama hadn't said much since I'd come back home, but I know she wished I'd go with her on Sunday mornings. I'd gotten out of the habit in Savannah. Linden hadn't been raised in the church as I had. We spent Sundays like any other day, catching up on work stuff. I *did* miss the music—*the Gospel in song* as Nana used to say. Hmm. Nana and Grandpop. I had to shove that thought away for now.

I looked at my watch again. Only two minutes had passed. I tapped my feet on the brick pathway. Gazing around, I marveled at how cool it was beneath the spread of the oak trees. Until recently, it had been a mild summer. We'd had a couple of unseasonably hot days, but fall was closing in. Soon, these leaves would turn, not as vivid as those in the mountains, but they did put on a subtle show. Then fireplaces would send the smell of smoke through the neighborhood. Nothing like a crisp fall day with the aroma of smoke in the air.

I glanced at my watch a final time. With Roan still not there, I was about to pick up my tote and leave until I spotted him walking toward me.

"Hey," he said as he slid onto the bench.

"Hey." I scooted away just enough. "Thanks for taking me home last night. Well, back to Rose Haven."

"No problem." He nodded and rocked a bit. "You doing okay? Concussion?"

"Nope. No concussion." Why did things always have to be so uncomfortable with Roan? Once upon a time, they'd been so easy. But we were different people now. A lot had changed during the past eight years, including Roan . . . and me.

He leaned forward, rested his elbows on his knees, then rubbed his hands together and glanced sideways at me. "Listen, we need to talk. I think you have—"

"Wait. I know we do, but I have things I have to do first and I need your help. I have to find Boopsie's killer, unless you and Tank have already found him. Or her." That the killer might be a female hadn't occurred to me before. But, surely, they'd let me know if they had arrested or even guessed at who may have killed Boopsie.

Roan sat back and laid his arm along the back of the bench. "No, I'm sorry to say, we aren't any closer than the day we found you hovering over her body."

"Y'all don't still think I did it, do you?" My hand went to my chest when Roan hesitated a second too long. "Well, maybe I don't need your help after all." I stood and started to walk away.

"Wait." Roan was quick. He grabbed my arm before I ventured far. "I didn't say we do. Come back and sit down and tell me what you need." He urged me back with a nod of his head toward the bench.

I paused long enough to decide that I really did need his help. Anything else could wait. I sat next to him.

"I think I've made some connections."

"What kinds of connections?"

"Between Boopsie and some of the people in this town." I looked at Roan, trying to read his face. He gestured with his hand, urging me onward with the story. "I've found some things. Things I should have told you before, but I wasn't sure if they were connected to Boopsie's murder or not. But now, after last night, I'm almost positive they are."

"Do I need to see the things you've found? Are they physical, or just thoughts?"

"A little of both."

"Okay. I guess this is as good a place as any to talk. No prying eyes. No eavesdropping diner patrons. So . . . talk."

We settled on the bench and I shared my thoughts about the things I'd learned in the past few days. I answered Roan's questions to the best of my ability and at the end of an hour or so, we'd formulated a plan.

But would it work?

Only time would tell.

Chapter Thirty

I had my part of the plan well in hand. If Mama would stay at Rose Haven for a few days without me, I could stay home and do what needed to be done with no one being the wiser. But, could I convince Mama to stay? That was the $64,000 question.

We returned to Rose Haven that afternoon because I wasn't about to leave Miss Marge way out in the boonies alone, especially not with the knowledge I'd recently gained. Thank goodness Mama had readily agreed to accompany me. I think it was more that she didn't want me out of her sight these days, but especially after the events of last night. I may have been nearing my thirties, but I was still Mama's only baby.

My bags—packed and ready to go back to our home—waited inside. With luck on my side, I'd leave with them in just a little while. I made my way to the kitchen for supper. The plan Roan and I had cooked up had to work. Otherwise, well . . . there was no otherwise. *Act casual. Laid back. Natural.*

Mama and Miss Marge bustled in the kitchen putting the last touches on the evening meal. They'd insisted I do nothing but rest once Mama and I got back to Rose Haven. They enjoyed these little get-togethers at the end of the day. Almost like a real family. With Fee staying in town for the past few days and nights, Aunt Becky had taken that time to catch up with Uncle Angus and decided to stay at her home, too. So, it was just Miss Marge, George, Mama and me, gathered at Rose Haven for dinner.

Fried chicken, fresh field peas, juicy sliced red-ripe tomatoes from the garden, and my favorite, fried corn, were the night's offerings. Mama and Miss Marge had gotten to be quite a team in the kitchen, leaving me to wonder if they were trying to out-do each another. Maybe so. I was just thankful for the delicious meals I'd eaten.

"I'm going to be as big as your old barn, Miss Marge, if you and Mama don't quit feeding me so well." I probably said that at every meal. I spooned a heaping serving of the fried corn onto my plate, followed by a couple slices of the tomatoes. "I'll need to double up on my exercise. I haven't trekked through many cemeteries lately."

"Well, thank goodness for that," Mama said. "You spend more than enough time in those overgrown graveyards. I can't for the life of me figure out why you love it so much." Mama looked across the table at me. "And you don't have a good sense of direction, either. I think that worries me the most."

"Aw. Leave her be, Mary. She's young and learning the history of some interesting people while she works." Miss Marge laid her fork on her plate, lifted a napkin and wiped her mouth. "I think it's grand that you are taking a shine to the past, dear. Who will preserve it for the next generation if someone like you doesn't step up?"

"Thanks, Miss Marge. It may seem a bit macabre to some ..." I looked pointedly at Mama. "... but I love what I do. If I can help a family find a long-lost ancestor, then I've done my job well." I took a sip of sweet tea then returned the glass to the table. I smiled across the space at my mother. "And I don't really spend that much time in cemeteries, Mama. It's just a small portion of what I do." I waved my fork in the air. "Speaking of other parts of my job. I thought I'd spend a few days at home." I looked at Mama again. "Alone, if you don't mind."

"Alone? Whatever for? After what you've just been through?" Mama laid down her own fork and grasped the edge of the table. "You don't want me to go back with you . . . do you?"

"It isn't that I don't *want* you to, it's just that . . . I *need* some quiet time for paperwork on a couple of genealogical lines." I looked from Mama to Miss Marge and back to Mama. "And I can see how much you and Miss Marge have enjoyed one another's company. This will give y'all some girl time and *me* some work time."

Miss Marge brought her hands up to her face in a prayer-like pose. "Oh, I think that's a splendid idea. Don't you, Mary?" She appeared pleased.

Mama hesitated just a second. "I suppose it's okay. I mean, I love being here. It's so peaceful and . . . and I can help with the inventory of Miss Marge's things."

"Good. Then I'll leave right after I help with the dishes."

An argument over whether or not I'd stay and help was put to rest by George. "No need for that, Miss Charlotte. That's my job since I'm not much of a cook."

We all laughed at that one. Our George was old school. He didn't cook. Period.

***

Home felt good. I loved my time at Rose Haven, but truly, there was— cliché though it may be—no place like home. I was quite aware that my time in my childhood room was coming to a real close. I could feel it. "May as well enjoy it while I'm here." I looked around the room and at my feet. Goodness. I'd gotten so used to talking to Oreo, I was doing it when she was nowhere around. "Get a grip, Charlotte. You've got work to do."

I pulled out the notes I'd taken in the courthouse and library, and the envelopes of the photos I'd taken, thankful that the local camera shop got them developed for me as quickly as they did. Then I pulled out the papers from the back of the hymnal. I stacked them according to family. This one here, that one there. These two here. But where did they all cross? I located my working ancestry charts and began with the pile on my right. I began with the youngest generation and worked my way back, pleased at the lack of brick walls. A question or two in this line. Now, to start this one. I looked at a newspaper article I'd found in the stacks at the library.

I read over the article, making note of the dates and the names of the cities. Nevada was the last place I would have considered looking, which meant I would have to make a phone call for confirmation. Did I know anyone in the historical or genealogical society there? Or perhaps even the courthouse? I pondered for a moment. No, but I recalled that Linden did. Dare I place a call to him? After a few minutes spent arguing the merits, I gave in. This was far too important not to talk to him if he could help in any way.

I picked up the receiver from the bedside table, smiling at the memory of talking to Fee on this old Princess phone during our senior year in high school. As soon as we'd seen them advertised in *Glamour* magazine—the one with Tony Dow on the cover—we started begging for a matching set. But Fee wanted pink, of course, while I insisted that mine should be powder blue.

I took a deep breath then dialed the number, noting that I still had it memorized. It was time I forgot it.

Linden picked up on the tail-end of the third ring.

"Hey, Linden."

"Charlotte?" His voice was familiar, but this time, it didn't call to my heart as it once had. "Is everything okay?"

"Yes, of course. And this is not a personal call, this is business."

"Oh, I see. I thought . . . well, never mind. What can I help you with?"

Had that been disappointment in his voice? Well, too bad, Mister Two-timer. "I recall a case we worked that led us to Nevada. I need the name of your contact out there if you still have it available."

"Ah. Genealogy, I suppose?"

"Yep."

Five minutes later, Linden had supplied the name of his contact in Nevada's archives with the detail that if anyone knew how to find the information I was looking for, it would be Amelia Hernandez. I thanked him, then hung up with a polite good-bye, then returned the receiver to the phone, but not before hearing Linden say, "Charlotte, wai—"

A glance at the clock told me, even though it was earlier in Nevada than Alabama, the courthouse would be closed by this hour. I'd have to make that call tomorrow.

***

By the next day, as the hour neared noon, I'd called Amelia and we'd talked for a good half hour. Linden had been right; there was no way I would ever have conjured the information Amelia shared with me. My hand flew to my mouth. "Are . . . are you sure?"

"Of course, I am. I have the records right in front of me."

"I-I'm so sorry. I don't mean to doubt you. It's just . . . this was not what I expected at all."

"Believe me, I understand." Amelia let out a little laugh. "I get this kind of reaction all the time."

"I can't thank you enough for your help. I'll have our local sheriff request those records."

"That's good, since many of the parties are still living. That will make everything easier for both of us if there is ever a question. I'll send you certified copies if you need them."

"Oh, that would be great. Thank you so much."

Amelia told me the total cost for the four documents then added, "Jot down my extension in case you need me again and give it to your sheriff. Your calls will come directly to me."

I scribbled down that number and we ended the call.

The information from Amelia was surprising—in fact, life-altering. Stunned was the only word to describe my reaction to the revelations. I thought I was prepared for anything she might say, but this certainly hadn't been a part of it. A birth certificate, plus a certificate of divorce, and two marriage certificates? I wouldn't let this new information keep me from the task at hand. I'd worry about the fallout later. A quick call to Tank relayed the latest along with a request for his help in procuring the records in question.

***

I sat at the kitchen table with the information I'd gathered spread out in front of me. From across the room, Mama's Westinghouse clock radio played a soft country and western hit, "There Goes My Everything," a song Linden had crooned on more than one occasion.

I frowned at the memory—and the occasion—and wondered at what he might have said the night before had I not hung up on him, as I stared at the records Amelia had shared. Unbelievable, but before I told anyone else, I'd need the certified copies. I hoped they'd arrive soon, but I knew that was only a remote possibility. Things like this usually took at least a week or more.

Armed with the explosive information, my hand shook as I wrote my name in the proper space on the ancestral chart. Next, I entered Papa's name and then Mama's. Then I entered my grandparents. As I wrote the names in the blank spaces, tears trickled down my cheeks. How was I ever going to explain this? Should I even?

Truth, Charlotte. The truth will set you free.

Hours later, I laid down the pencil. I glanced at the Westinghouse clock that continued to play the latest country hits and yawned. No wonder. It was after midnight. As much as I wanted to finish this tonight, my energy reserves were depleted. Truth may set one free, but it didn't mean that it was easy or pleasant. Were some truths supposed to remain in the past? I made a final entry in my notebook and headed to bed. Like Scarlett, I'd think about it tomorrow.

**

The weeks flew by and I'd pored over every single detail on the ancestral charts making sure they were all correct. If I counted the facts once, I checked them twice, some even more than half a dozen times. I was beyond exhausted, and that morning had reared its ugly head in the middle of the night. I glanced at the bedside clock. It seemed all I did these days was watch a clock. Five a.m. Could be worse. At least I'd finally dozed . . . somewhere between midnight and three.

In the kitchen I made one last attempt at making decent coffee. I couldn't make a drinkable pot if my life depended on it, but what perked would have to do. My cup filled, I added a generous amount of sugar and even more cream. Mama, who drank hers black, was forever asking me why I even bothered.

Mama.

After eating rice cereal and half a banana, I moseyed to my bedroom and picked up the charts I'd checked again last night. Nothing had changed while I slept. There were those names, right where I'd written them. I ran fingers through my hair. "I need to talk to Fee," I said to the room around me. "I can't do this without hashing it out first." I gathered the papers and placed them into my tote bag. "And here I go talking to myself again."

***

"You're never up this early." Fee sat behind her desk in the office area of Soilse, a spreadsheet visible on top of her desk. "Turn Around, Look at Me" played from her radio.

I pointed toward it and said, "Love that song."

"Me, too," she said. "Now, what gives?"

"Well, I've been up since five. Awake, at least. Didn't get up 'til after six." I fiddled with my keychain.

"Aunt Polly didn't have you up and working early?" She looked across at me. "That isn't normal."

"I've stayed at home for the past few nights. Mama's been at Rose Haven." I twisted around on the little sofa, threw my legs over the arm of one end, and leaned against the other.

Fee stopped her work and rested on her elbows, propped on her desk. "Okay. Again, what gives? You at home without Aunt Polly definitely isn't normal. Especially without telling me about it. Spill it, Cuz."

"I don't even know where or how to begin, Fee. It's all so complicated." I swung my feet back to the floor before chewing at a fingernail.

"Stop that. Just talk to me. So, life is complicated. When is it not complicated?"

"This isn't normal complicated. This is complicated, complicated." I looked at Fee and eased back onto the sofa. We sat in silence for a few seconds as my heart raced. If I couldn't tell Fee, how could I possibly reveal what I knew to the others involved?

I stared at my clasped hands and spoke barely above a whisper. "I-I found out some stuff that's going to be life-altering for a lot of people—our mothers included. Maybe even *us*." At least I 'd begun to tell it. That was good. But how would I reveal the worst of it?

I took a deep breath and related what I now knew . . .

The truth.

Chapter Thirty-one

Fiona sat in silence, staring at me. Her brow furrowed as she chewed her bottom lip. "That couldn't be true. It just couldn't. No. Unh-unh. No way. I'm sorry, but I just don't believe it."

"I was in denial at first, too, but we have the paper trail as proof." I reached down and pulled a manila folder from my bag. I opened it and thumbed through the tabs until I got to the one marked *Vital Records*. I held the top document, staring at it for a second before handing it across the desk to Fiona. "See for yourself." I slid a second one, and a third to my cousin. "Here. May as well see this one, too. Further proof."

Fee held the first document with a trembling hand and reached for the second one. "This is . . . well, it's unbelievable, that's all. Can't these things be faked? They have to be fakes." She looked at me, hope in her eyes.

"Not fakes. They're the real thing. Copies, sure, but certified by the states."

Fee threw them back at me. "Well, I just don't believe it. I don't care what you or anyone else says, it's just not true. Nana would have told us. Our mothers would have told us."

"Our mothers didn't know, Fee. They still don't know. And Nana? Well, I can't even think about that right now. I just can't."

"Well, I don't know who you think is going to tell them this, but you need not look at *me*, because I want no part of it." Fee stood and came around her desk, her long legs clad in pink stockings that accentuated a flattering pink-and-mint green minidress. She opened the door to her office and looked at me. "You need to leave." She returned to her desk and grabbed the offending papers, then thrust them at me. "And take these lies with you."

"Fiona Campbell. What is wrong with you? I didn't do anything but uncover the truth."

"Sometimes it's best to just let sleeping dogs lie. Just like Miss Sarah said. She told you. You should have listened for once instead of going off on Lord knows what kind of wild-goose chase." Fee flailed her hands through the air. "You haven't done anything but open up a Pandora's box. How many lives do you think this will affect? For good?" She pointed to the door. "You need to leave . . . now."

The hum of the flourescent bulbs in the fixture above Fee's desk hung between us like a blanket. I stood with the papers in my hands, shaking as I stared at Fee. Tears pooled in the corners of my eyes, and try as I might, I couldn't stop them from spilling. I turned and rushed through Soilse, wondering if I'd ever step foot inside again.

***

I exited Fee's store and walked past the dime store where Miss Ludie had practically accused me of killing Boopsie. I hurried past the hardware store where George had been working. I lost no time in moving past the bakery and the shoe store, the bank, and on toward the park.

I settled on a bench near the fountain whose gurgling waters offered no amount of their usual comfort. Here I was again, running. Is that all I was ever going to do with my life? I wasn't the one who created this mess. That was Grandpa. And *her*. I needed answers. I couldn't fix any of this without them. But would she talk to me? And right now, I wasn't sure how I felt about *her*.

Please. Help me.

I sat for what seemed like hours. I wiped at the tears that refused to cease. How could this ever be told to those involved? I clutched the crumpled certificates. How to resolve this in an acceptable manner? Everyone was going to hate me. "I was right. I should have stayed in Savannah."

"I'm glad you didn't."

I looked up and saw those deep gray eyes shining down on me. I swiped again at my tear-streaked face.

I stood. "Roan. I didn't hear you. I . . . I have to go." I took a step.

"You can't run forever, you know."

I stopped, my back to him.

"We still need to talk."

I turned and saw the concern in those gray eyes.

"But right now, I need to know if you're okay." He sat on the bench and rested his arm across its back. "Bad day?"

I nodded, then returned to the bench and sat next to my old boyfriend. "The worst. Ever."

"Need a shoulder? I happen to have a couple. And, if I remember correctly, you used to think that was a good thing."

I cocked my head and looked at him with a half-smile. "Funny. Seems like a lifetime ago." I shoved the papers into my tote bag, then sat back, crossing my feet at the ankles. I tossed the bag to the ground.

"Whoa. This must have really been the worst day."

I looked at Roan, then off into the distance. "Fee hates me. She threw me out of her office."

"What?" He put his finger beneath my chin and turned me to face him. "Why did she do that?"

I tried to pull away, but Roan wouldn't let me. I closed my eyes then opened them to find concern written all over his face.

After a few moments of staring, he blew out a deep breath, then finally let go.

"I learned some things." I shook my head. "She doesn't believe me." I clasped my hands rather than wringing them. "Told me I was giving her fake documents." I looked up at Roan. "As if I'd do that."

"There's one thing I know about you, Charlie . . . you're an honest woman. If you say something, you can bank on it being the truth."

There was that name again. *Charlie*. This time I didn't light into him for it. In fact, it sounded comforting. I dared a sideways glance at Roan. "Thank you for that. But I still have to figure out how I'm going to fix this. How I'm going to make all the people involved understand that I did what I *had* to do."

"So, how can I help?" Roan reached for my hand, gave it a quick squeeze and let go.

"Well, I can let you and the sheriff handle the bad guys. I'm not into violence and I've been through enough already. But I do have charts that I think will explain why some of the people involved did what they did."

"Charts?" He looked at me, clearly confused.

"Genealogical charts. You know, you, your parents, and on back in time. I do those all the time when I'm helping someone trace their family." I reached for my bag and drew out the crumpled papers and the manila folder.

He laid the papers on one thigh and pressed the wrinkles from the pages with the palm of his hand. After a quick perusal, Roan handed them back to me. "Whoa. I think we'd better do this down at the jail. We don't want the wrong people to see this."

"I can't help but wonder who the wrong people are. I have an idea about a couple, but I haven't been able to figure out who in all this mess killed Boopsie."

"But you will. You've always had a mind that could solve any puzzle. The way I see it, you've only missed one thing in your whole life, and that was something right in front of you." He looked at me for a moment too long. "Come on. Let's get on over to the sheriff's office."

***

Sheriff Turner rubbed his chin. "Are you sure about this, Charlotte?" He picked up the documents in front of him and studied them one more time. "These are the ones I okayed that lady to send to you?"

"Amelia Hernandez. Yes, they are." I shrugged. "And I'm about as sure as I can be about *any* of this."

"There's gonna be some mighty upset folks in this little town of ours, I can tell you right now." He pushed out of his chair and walked to the window. He stood for a good minute, his hands clasped behind his back, before he turned around. "Where do you want to start with this?"

"I'm not sure. I gather facts. You and Roan catch the bad guys . . .

or gals. I'm not sure which it is in this case."

"Thanks to our helper you met the other night, we have our end of things covered. We'll be making an arrest or two soon." He looked at Roan. "Anything new out there today?"

"No, sir. They seem to have bought the idea that Charlotte escaped, and I found her wandering down the road." Roan shifted in his chair and leaned on one arm. "Old news now that a couple weeks have passed."

Tank crossed to his desk and sat in the worn-out swivel chair. "We aren't any closer to arresting anybody for Boopsie's murder, then. I'd hoped to have that figured out by now."

I leaned forward. "Me, too. I so wanted to prove to you I didn't do this."

"You've gotta stay out of this now, you hear me? Things have gotten too far gone and are too dangerous for you to be snooping around." The sheriff riffled through a drawer. He pulled out a bottle of Rolaids and offered them to Roan and me. We declined, and he put it back in the drawer without taking one for himself. "I know you want to be telling what all you've discovered, but I'd appreciate it if you wait on us a bit. Let us hash out a plan."

"I wouldn't do it without you, Sheriff. I'm not sure I could do this without backup of some kind. Seems like having a couple of able-bodied, armed men with me might keep things a bit calmer."

"Let us get this set up then. Likely take about a week, give or take a day or two. Roan and I'll fill you in on the details." He got out the Rolaids again, this time, he opened the cap and tossed three or four into his cupped palm. "I think we just may flush out a murderer."

***

I wasn't sure I could pull off a poker face around Mama and Miss Marge. But I had to try. Telling them my discoveries in private would be better. I was thankful Tank had agreed to let me be the one to do that. My biggest challenge was coordinating the meeting with all the people involved. And that was most of Loblolly. But first, I had to confirm a couple of things with Miss Marge. I couldn't share what I knew without running this by her. With any luck, I'd find Miss Marge without Mama by her side. After that . . . well, it would be the most difficult conversation I'd ever had with Mama.

I wondered if Fee would show up at the meeting. All I could do was send out word and hope for the best. If all else failed, I could call on the sheriff. No one would dare ignore his edict. With a sigh, I exited my little Chevy with its shiny new windows and walked to the back door of Rose Haven.

The screen door slammed behind me as I entered the kitchen. Since it was nearing dinner time, I figured Mama and Miss Marge, and maybe even George, would be in there.

"Hey, y'all. Smells good." I went to the stove and lifted a lid from a pot. Green beans with new potatoes. I replaced the lid and gave Mama a kiss on the cheek. "Y'all miss me?"

"Charlotte Graves, what's going on? And don't tell me 'nothing' because I know you better than that." She wiped her hands on the apron tied about her waist and turned to me. "Long as you're here, you may as well help," she said, not waiting for the answer. "You can set the table. For seven."

"Oh? Who's coming to dinner?" A quick wash of my hands and I got out plates and silverware.

"Angus, Becky, and Fee. And the four of us."

I winced as I looked at Mama.

"And what's that look for?"

"Just, well . . . Fee and I had words and we're not exactly on speaking terms right now."

Miss Marge pulled salads from the refrigerator and set them on the counter. "Lands sake, child. Why would you and your best friend not be on speaking terms?"

"It's a long story. Just silly stuff, really." I couldn't get into this now. Not yet. The timing had to be right, and I had to coordinate with Sheriff Turner and Roan.

"Mama, may I borrow Miss Marge for a minute? I need to make

sure I'm doing things in the out-buildings as she'd like me to."

Mama lifted the lid and stirred the beans and potatoes. "Of course. I'll put the finishing touches on this meal before the family gets here. The meatloaf is about ready to come out of the oven." Mama waved her hand in a shooing motion.

I held the back door then led the way to the fourth outbuilding, noting that we still had six more to inventory. It was going to be a hard task, but one I loved doing. But would I have Fee and Ned to help? Who knew? Only time would tell. Once inside the building, I pulled out a chair from a small stack against one side wall.

"I'm sure you've been on your feet all day, as usual. Here." I indicated the chair. "Have a seat."

Miss Marge eased her aging body into the spindle chair. "It does feel good to sit for a little while." She looked around at the cleared space. "My goodness. You young people have done such a good job of clearing out and cleaning these old buildings."

"Am I keeping things you'd like to have? Have we overstepped our bounds in some of the things we've donated?" I leaned in the doorway.

"I told you from the beginning, I trust your judgment. I haven't changed my mind about that." Miss Marge smiled up at me.

I maneuvered myself to sit on the steps at the entry of the building. With my back on the doorframe and a deep breath, I began. "Miss Marge." I looked across at my companion. "I have some questions that aren't going to be easy to ask, so answering is going to be difficult on your part. Do you think you're up for that?"

Miss Marge played with the edge of her apron, picking it up, putting it down. She looked at me. "I wondered when you were going to get around to asking." She nodded. "Go ahead, dear. I've been ready to answer for almost fifty years."

***

We returned to the house just as Aunt Becky, Uncle Angus, and Fee entered the kitchen. I looked up at my cousin with a tentative smile.

"I brought dessert." Aunt Becky lifted the glass dish with pudding, bananas, and vanilla wafers arranged artfully. "Guess what it is."

"Here, let me take that, Aunt Becky." I placed a quick kiss on my aunt's cheek then took the dish, still warm from the oven, and placed it next to the stove. I took a deep breath before turning around to face my family, a smile plastered on my face.

Uncle Angus broke the silence. "You had any leads in your investigation, Charlie-girl?"

I smiled at his use of my old nickname. Only Uncle Angus could still get away with that. "A few, yes, sir. Trying to put together all the pieces of the puzzle." I looked over at Fee who wouldn't look me in the eye. Oh, well. Let her act like that. She'd find out. They'd all find out. And it wasn't going to be a picnic.

After dinner, our little group gathered in the rockers on the front porch to eat the banana pudding.

"This is so good, Aunt Becky. Did you use a family recipe?" I rolled the creamy goodness over my tongue.

"Mmmm. Thanks, sweetie. Yes, it was our mother's. Remember when we put leftover pudding in a butter dish and Aunt Merle put it on her baked potato?" The two sisters burst out laughing.

"I don't think I'll ever forget that. Mother was so mad. She was trying extra hard to impress Aunt Merle."

"She definitely made an impression."

We ate in silence for a few minutes, savoring every bite of our dessert.

Uncle Angus placed his empty bowl on the wicker table between him and Aunt Becky. "You ever find that grave you said was missing?"

"No, sir. I have an idea of where it could be, but I haven't had a chance to look for it lately. Besides, getting lost in those woods really scared me." I didn't mind admitting how much those crazy men with Cam had frightened me. What if Cam hadn't been there? I shuddered at the thought.

Finding that grave was the last thing on my mind right now. Proving the genealogy hadn't required the grave once I had the letters, documents from the local courthouse, and those the sheriff had gotten for me. Of course, finding Josie's resting place and righting a wrong was important. I felt that Miss Marge would agree.

But how I dreaded the forthcoming meeting.

Chapter Thirty-two

The group gathered in the main parlor at Rose Haven was quite large. Thank goodness Sheriff Turner and Roan—who looked better in his uniform than I preferred—stood close to the door. Miss Marge seemed in her element surrounded by so many of the citizens of Loblolly. She sat like a regent at court in her Queen Anne chair. Others sat on sofas and side chairs, and chairs pulled in from the dining room. Still others sat in the old ladderback chairs from the kitchen. Not one more soul could squeeze in.

I looked across the sea of faces. Mama was here, of course. The late-night conversation I'd had with her had been difficult, but as usual, Mama accepted the truth with southern grace, even though it had been painful. She was a lot stronger than I had ever given her credit for being. Aunt Becky, Fee, and Uncle Angus sat near Mama. Olivia and Max were there, with Cam who leaned against a wall, his eyes never leaving me for long. Sarah Harkins came and even Boopsie's mother and brother had come.

Miss Ludie sat next to Sarah. Serena from the diner sat in the back of the room, near Cam. Lanie Kellogg sat next to Serena. George stood near Miss Marge, ever her protective sentinel. Thankfully absent were the two guys, Doo and Hal, who had been with Cam at the cabin. Various other people had come, likely from curiosity rather than anything else. Even Oreo didn't want to miss the events of the evening. She sat curled at the feet of Miss Marge.

You can do this. The truth will set you free, just like the Bible says. As I moved to the podium borrowed from Rose Haven's library, I sent up a silent prayer. A table to my left held stacks of papers. Each pile was covered with a piece of construction paper, each a different color, on which I'd written a note giving me a clue as to what lay beneath.

I rapped my knuckles on the podium. "Welcome to the second meeting of the Woodville County Historical Society. We have quite a large crowd tonight. The library just wouldn't hold all of us and when Miss Marge offered Rose Haven, I gladly accepted." I looked at Miss Marge, then across at all the faces looking back at me. "Thank you all for coming. I know this has been a stressful few weeks, living with a killer in our midst." I cast a quick smile toward Tank. "I believe our sheriff will tell you that I did not kill Boopsie. Though it looked as if I had done so, evidence has proven otherwise." I turned to the sheriff who nodded acknowledgement. "Sheriff Turner will share more details with you later, but we believe that Boopsie was killed because … well, because she knew too much."

The group grumbled, looking from one person to another to see if one appeared as perplexed as the next.

"Mrs. Sweets," I said, now looking directly at Boopsie's mother. "I have to thank you for planting Boopsie's diary in her room. You knew that no one would know what it meant except for someone who understands genealogy and its ramifications to the people in this community."

An audible gasp sucked half the air from the already seemingly airless room. They whispered amongst themselves. Heads shook. Perspiration gathered on my upper lip and I wondered if I should have asked Miss Marge to bring in a few oscillating fans.

"You see . . . Boopsie was forever underfoot here at Rose Haven. First when her grandmother, Norah, worked here, and later when her mother came to work for Miss Marge." I looked at the faces staring back. "To fill her time, Boopsie began writing stories about things she overheard here at Rose Haven. One conversation here, one there. When she was a child, none of it made sense. But as she aged, so did her powers of reasoning. She was able to piece together the whispers and tie all the secrets into a story that many didn't want to become known. Certainly, not those who had the most to lose." I looked at Max who squirmed in his seat.

"Rose Haven's story is a love story. More than one love story, truth be told. Unrequited, unfulfilled love stories. Nonetheless, passionate, true love stories." I looked at Miss Marge. "Shall I go on, or would you prefer to tell it?" I didn't really want to reveal all of this publicly, but Miss Marge had insisted that I share what I'd learned when the two of us had met in the outbuilding earlier in the week.

The elderly woman wiped at her eyes with a handkerchief. She shook her head and waved at me in a manner indicating I was to continue.

Mama was as stoic as possible, knowing what was to come. I hated that our family secrets were about to be revealed. A quick smile at Mama, a deep breath, and I continued. "Many years ago, back in the 1800s, two young people married and began their family. The young woman was Josephine Jones. The young man was Daniel Lanier. They were my three-times-great-grandparents." I let the information sink in as the old grandfather clock broke in and chimed the quarter hour.

I looked at Fee and Aunt Becky, who wore puzzled looks on their faces. I knew they didn't understand. Not now. But they would soon enough.

"After the birth of their son, Evan Lanier, Daniel, the father, was killed during the Civil War. With no one to care for them, Josie, as she was called by her family, and her young son, Evan, moved in with Daniel's brother, Richard Parker Bray Lanier, and his wife, Margaret Lowell. Richard and Margaret had a son, Parker Bray Lanier, who was about nine at this time. Josie and Evan remained in the home of Richard and Margaret for a few years, with Josie helping out with the little children and the household duties each time her sister-in-law gave birth One of her duties was to tutor the older children, one of whom was Parker Bray Lanier, the eldest son of Richard and his wife. All was well within the household ... until Parker and Josie fell in love." I paused as the group gasped and chattered.

"You mean, the young man who was, what? Eighteen, twenty years her junior?" Sarah Harkins sat up straight, her mouth gaped open and her eyes wide. "How do you know it was a love match? Could she not have taken advantage of his tender years and ... well ... you know?"

"Miss Harkins, that is a very good question, one which I'll answer once I've laid out the entire story." I looked around the room to see if anyone else wanted to interject a comment or ask a question. Satisfied none was coming, I began again.

"Yes, you're right in thinking there was a considerable age difference. But apparently, love has no age limits." I looked at Miss Sarah. "Perhaps the time they spent together as student and teacher brought them together. Who knows? All I know is that it *was* a love match. And please remember, this is after the war years. Times were tough in the South. There could be many reasons for such a match." I reached toward a side table for a glass of water, took a sip, then returned the glass. "Against the protests of his parents, Parker married Josie and she gave birth to their son, Bray Jones Lanier. But all didn't go well with the birth. Josie was very ill afterward, and, on her deathbed, she asked her dear friend, Anna Mayhew, to marry her husband, Parker, and to raise the baby as her own."

"*Mayhew?*" Someone in the back of the room called out. "As in Miss Marge?"

"Yes, as in Miss Marge's *family*." I looked at the sheriff. "Shall I continue?"

His nod urged me on.

"Anna protested, saying that Josie would be fine and would raise her own baby. But that didn't happen. Parker and Anna were married within mere hours of Josie's death. True to her word, Anna did raise and love Bray as her own."

Silence gripped those gathered in the large parlor. Miss Marge sniffed and wiped at her eyes with her handkerchief. Mama sat, jaw flexing at the revelations coming from my mouth. Without a doubt, Mama longed to rearrange something in this room. All she could do was clench and unclench her hands while shredding the tissue she clutched.

"Parker and Anna didn't wait for Josie's funeral. They left right away. Because Parker's parents had come to resent Josie and the relationship she had with their son, they refused to allow Josie to be buried in the family plot. Instead, they had her taken deep into the woods and buried there. But when Anna returned to Rose Haven, she promised to find her friend's grave and make sure she had a marker and a decent burial."

At the mention of Rose Haven, the people looked at one another and at Miss Marge, who sat with tears coursing down her cheeks.

"Wait a minute." Olivia jumped up and placed her hands on her hips. "What on earth are you talking about? And what does any of this have to do with Rose Haven or the rest of us gathered here?"

Max stood beside Olivia. "Olivia's right. This was supposed to be a WHS meeting, not some hash-the-dirty-laundry-of-our-ancestors meeting."

Clearly, Olivia and Max sounded a bit put out with my presentation. But there was no way I could have forewarned Olivia. If this upset her, what was going to happen as the meeting progressed? And Max's presence only made matters worse.

"It's a long story. A story that involves many of our ancestors." I waved my hand indicating those in attendance. "When I finish, you will find that many in this room are more closely related than you may have thought. And some aren't as close. Some of you will be thrilled. Others . . . well, just bear with me ... please." A sea of puzzled faces glared at me. No way did I blame them. I'd wanted to do this quietly. Privately. But Tank wanted it to be public.

I shifted my weight from foot to foot. I didn't like this at all. By the time this night was over, *everyone* would hate me. How would I ever mend my relationship with Mama or with Miss Marge? Or Aunt Becky and Fee? *Papa, it's a good thing you aren't here to see this. I think you would be heartbroken, at the very least . . .disappointed.*

"Boopsie figured all of this out a long time ago. Truthfully, Boopsie could have and should have been the genealogist and the head of the WHS. She understood the relationships and had even made family trees for some of you." Even more confused faces stared back at me. They looked at one another, questions in their eyes. In denial of their knowledge of Boopsie's handiwork? Maybe.

Sarah Harkins spoke up again. "Well, I'm wondering if you knew all that, what's to make the sheriff or any of us believe that you aren't the one who killed my poor great-niece? After all, *you* were the one caught leaning over her body and that iron skillet right there." She stood defiantly, hands on hips, chin in the air.

Tank spoke up. "I'll get to that in a bit, Miss Sarah." He nodded again for me to continue.

I retrieved a pile of papers from the nearby table. "I'll hand these out. Let you see them." My gaze swept across the room. "Before you ask questions, I want to assure you that the majority of the people involved most closely in this line are aware of the relationships." I stood at the end of the first row. "You may be confused, but I believe, as does the sheriff, that among other things, this knowledge is what got Boopsie killed. Someone wanted to silence her or protect someone else, or maybe a bit of both."

"What is this I'm looking at?" One of the older members of the group stood and waved a sheet. "Just a bunch of names and dates? What's this got to do with anything else, especially a murder? And, what do *we* have to do with that? We sure as shootin' didn't all kill that girl."

"It's the genealogy of Miss Marge Mayhew . . . and my mother." I looked at Mama knowing how much she was hurting. The conversation we'd had had been so difficult . . . for both of us. But I'd had to tell her. A public forum wasn't the place for this to come to light. After a long, long night of answering Mama's myriad questions, she was finally at peace with the information I conveyed to her. Her soft, sweet smile made me want to run to her and wrap her in my arms.

The crowd sat in silence. The gentleman sat down. Heads bowed as they all took time to read.

If only Papa were here. Mama and I were both going to need him tonight. Thank goodness Uncle Angus had come. But would he be supportive since these revelations would be so upsetting to Aunt Becky and Fee? Only time would tell. Right now, my job was to lay out the facts.

"Charlotte?" Olivia called out again. "Did you check your facts?

You've documented all of this? You have proof?"

"Yes, ma'am. I would never submit any line that I couldn't back up with a paper trail." I took another sip of water. The temperature in the room was rising in more than one way. "Plus, we have the validation of Miss Marge." I breathed deeply. "If I can bring your attention back to the paper ... I'll read it out loud." I looked out at the crowd.

Puzzled faces looked at one another. Aunt Becky and Fee, even Uncle Angus looked up at me. I picked up my glass and took another sip of water then set the glass down, almost knocking it over with my shaking hands.

I took a deep breath. "Are there any questions?" What a silly thing to ask. Of course there were. The looks on their faces said all I needed to know. "Just follow as I read, please."

Would any of this make sense to them? A list of names and dates which meant nothing to most of them would be confusing at best. But they had to see it; otherwise, they would never take my word for it. With this, I at least had proof of the people, the ancestors and how they all fit together. I got to the last line.

Aunt Becky sprang from her chair and waved the paper. "Wait a minute. This has my father's name on it as being married to Miss Marge. That can't be right." Aunt Becky was as pale as the wispy white curtains blowing in the open windows.

"Aunt Becky, I'm so sorry, but it's the truth. Miss Marge and Grandpop were married before he married Nana."

"But . . . Polly and I are still sisters, aren't we?"

Mama jumped up at that. "Of course we are. We just have different mothers, that's all."

Aunt Becky fell into her chair. She looked at me then at Mama, finally settling on Miss Marge with a shake of her head.

Mama eased into her seat as the group looked around at one another, heads shaking as they glanced from sheet to sheet to see if they all read the same way. I could assure them they did. At least a couple more faces went pale. Maxwell Lawrence was one of those. Lanie Kellogg, who sat next to Serena, looked up at me, daggers coming from her eyes as she crossed one leg over the other and began to frantically pump her foot, which was clad in the most shocking red-patent stiletto I'd ever seen. I'd warned them that some wouldn't be happy at all. Several people squirmed in their seats. I noticed a look exchanged between Sarah Harkins and Max.

I picked up another stack of papers. "Please note that I've included Parker Woodville Lanier and Caroline Simmons, our founding family, about whom I spoke at our first meeting. I didn't want to get too confusing and complicated, so I decided to explain the relationships to you." I shuffled the pages then continued.

"Caroline and Parker are the five-times-great grandparents of Cam and me. They are the four-times-great grandparents of our mothers, Olivia and Polly." I looked out at a sea of puzzled faces. I wasn't surprised. It took me a whole week to figure out all of this and to put the proper names in the blanks. Heads nodded. Some were looking at others' papers. Did they think I gave out different ones? I couldn't say. "Shall I continue?"

When there were no protests, I began again. "Daniel Lanier, born in 1828, first husband of Josephine Jones, and his elder brother, Richard Parker Bray Lanier, had a sister, Elizabeth Lanier, born in 1833. She married her second cousin, Samuel Woodville, and it is this line that branches off to Olivia and Cam." More odd looks and shaking heads. "Some of you won't be happy. I'm sorry, but truth is truth. No one wants laundry hung out in public. And you must remember the times in which they lived. And this is the only way to unravel a genealogical mystery."

Miss Sarah slid to the end of her seat. "How much more of this— this *farce* are we to endure? This must be trumped-up. Just bold-faced lies."

While the people grumbled and nodded and seemed to all agree with Miss Sarah, I passed out the second paper.

"Let me assure you that every single piece of information within these papers has been certified by the state archives. If the event took place outside of Alabama, then the state in question certified the proofs." I picked up another set of papers while the group studied my latest handout.

Sarah Harkins pushed back her chair, picked up her papers and made to leave. "Lies. All lies, Charlotte Graves. Your mother always was one to tell lies and I see it was passed down to the next generation." She turned to Roan. "You can be thankful that she ran away all those years ago and you didn't get stuck in a lie of a marriage with the likes of her." She turned away from Roan and pointed to me, pure hatred on her face.

Miss Marge was on her feet quick as a flash. George put his hand on her arm and guided her back to her chair. George looked at Roan.

Roan came up behind Sarah and placed his hand on her shoulder. "You'd best sit down, Miss Sarah. You really don't want to miss the rest of this." He flashed me his warmest smile, then nodded at George and Miss Marge.

The woman jerked away from Roan, but he blocked her path and placed his hands on his hips, the leather of his gun belt squeaking in protest. He glared down at her. When Miss Sarah saw that he was that serious, she sat, arms hugging her pocketbook against her body.

Grumblings spread across the room. I took yet another deep breath, then gripped the sides of the podium while the people read the latest document. Olivia looked at Max. She shifted in her seat and adjusted the owl pin on her lapel. Max's eyes narrowed into slits. There it was, that look that could kill. Aimed directly at me.

Wasn't that how all this mess began?

How was it all going to end?

Chapter Thirty-three

Copies of the letters found in the back of the hymnal were my next handout. More grumblings and questions followed. With the table cleared of the stacks of paperwork, I ended the meeting. Trying to explain all of this would only cause tempers to flare worse than they already had. It was best just to end things and let them all go home to ruminate on the facts. And facts they were. Forget the questions they may have had. I was emotionally and physically exhausted and could take no more tonight.

"I think this is enough for now. There's so much information in here. Some of you will find you are related, mainly at the distant-cousin level, while others will learn that you aren't as close as you once thought, or even related at all." I looked at Aunt Becky and Fee. They were never going to speak to me again. And how could I blame them? But Mama was the one who had to come to grips with the life-altering information.

And Miss Marge. She'd known the truth all these years, but making it public was quite another matter. Her need to protect those she loved the most, including Mama, had ruled all her decisions since that fateful time so long ago.

"I know this isn't going to be easy to digest. But I've always been told by a very wise woman, that the truth will set us free." I looked up to see Mama smiling at me. "I hope that's what you take away from this evening's meeting. If you think of questions for me this week, jot them down and maybe we can have an extra meeting this month." I looked at Olivia for approval, but she was only staring back and forth between the documents and Max. I held out my hands, palms up, in a we-shall-see sort of motion.

"So, meeting dismissed." I gathered the leftovers from the stacks, opened my tote bag, and put the papers inside. At the close of the last WHS meeting, the group had gathered around me. This time, they just left, talking amongst themselves. What that meant, I had no clue. Confusion at the very least. But was anyone angry enough to kill again? There was still a killer amongst us.

***

Staying in town at Mama's felt strange, even with the days I'd already spent there these past weeks. But the sheriff thought that was where I should be. I didn't like leaving Mama and Miss Marge out at Rose Haven alone. Well, George was there, but he wouldn't be any help if someone tried to do harm to the women. And after the evening's revelations, Tank felt sure someone was going to make a play to rid the town of some of its finest citizens "before the cock crowed," as he put it.

I glanced at the time. Tank and Roan had decided the best course of action was to station deputies around the two houses—Mama's and Rose Haven—by eleven o'clock, which provided me only a modicum of comfort. I sighed. Twenty minutes until they arrived. It couldn't be soon enough.

Exhausted, I climbed into bed and turned off the lights, then settled onto the pillow. With all those dead people, and a few live ones, running around inside my head, I'd never get a good night's sleep. Too many secrets had been exposed. But one big one remained. Who was the leader of the county's drug ring? Whoever it was, Boopsie had gotten too close and the sheriff thought that was why she'd been killed. *Not* for any of the genealogy-related reasons. But telling the town about the drug ring in its midst wasn't my job. The culprit had no way of knowing that Boopsie hadn't divulged that bit of information. This trap had to work. Otherwise, the people of Loblolly and Woodville County would have to live with this scourge on their peaceful existence for heaven only knew how long.

I prayed for peaceful rest. Still, my mind refused to shut off and I doubted that Mama, or Miss Marge, or anyone else in that meeting was sleeping well tonight. Lanie Kellogg was bound to be doing a huge business at her drugstore, selling sleeping pills.

Sudden knowledge hit me like the proverbial ton of bricks. More like one of the tall pines in the forest toppling right on top of me. Could that be it? Without stopping to consider the sheriff's orders, the old impulsivity grabbed me. I pulled on jeans and a T-shirt, socks, and my Army boots. A quick look inside my bag told me I had all I'd need. Good. A glance out my bedroom window proved the deputies hadn't taken their post yet.

I headed out.

And this time, I remembered to bring a flashlight.

***

The deep woods loomed in front of me like silent watchmen, offering protection from the unknown inhabitants of its cover, be they animal or human. I expected to find the culprit at the little cabin. I managed to park where the deputies guarding Rose Haven couldn't see me.

At least some good had come out of that night lost in the woods. I had just about memorized all the back-country roads. But could I maneuver the path in the dark of night? Please let it be so. The voices inside my head longed to burst forth in song, my way of coping with fear. Admitting my fear wasn't hard but accepting what lay ahead of me ... was.

Dare I use the flashlight? No. Best to find my way with the limited amount of moonlight shining between the branches of the pines. The near-full moon was a blessing. I eased forward, one timid step at a time, careful of footfalls crunching upon the fallen pine needles. I jumped at scurrying to my right. A dog barked in the distance. From one of the homes I'd seen after I'd parked my car on a nearby dirt road? No clue.

Stopping momentarily to allow my eyes to adjust to the darkness surrounding me, I ventured farther. Was I still on the path that led to the cabin? No guess. *Man. If I could only turn on the flashlight.* Too dangerous, but if I tripped over an exposed root or fallen limb—big trouble. Go slowly, one foot in front of the other.

The heavy scent of pine was the only comfort afforded in this dark, unfamiliar place, never mind that I'd been lost here twice lately. It was still unfamiliar. That pine mingled with the smells of rotted wood and the musty odor of moss or mushrooms didn't escape my ever-aware sense of smell. Roan had always teased me about my ability to smell something before we were within a mile of it. Where had that come from? Thoughts of Roan were the last thing I needed right now. *Concentrate. Shoo, Roan.*

A root, or perhaps a fallen limb, caused me to stumble. I caught myself on the thick, rough bark of the nearest tree. Sticky pine tar clung to my fingers. *Oh, good. Just what I needed.* I took one more step and stumbled again. I put out my hand and grabbed . . . fabric.

I opened my mouth to scream, but the hand that covered it prevented that reaction. I began to kick, and a shushing sound blew across my right ear.

"Don't scream," he whispered. "Do you understand?"

I nodded.

Have mercy. Could I not stay out of harm's way for even one day? Right then and there, I made a vow to never enter these woods again. That is, if I got out of them . . . alive.

"Shhhh. Be very quiet and I'll let you go," he whispered against my ear.

I knew that voice. I nodded again. Faster this time.

He released his grip on me.

"Roan. What are you doing here?"

"The better question is, what are *you* doing here?"

"I think I know who the drug kingpin is. I came to see if I was right." My voice sounded too loud in the quiet of the forest.

"So do we. Believe it or not, we do know how to do our jobs, Charlie." He took my arm. "Come on. I'm taking you to one of my men down on the road." I jerked away from him, almost causing both of us to fall. He caught us by grabbing at a nearby tree. "Will you listen to reason? For once?"

"I'm the one who figured out all of this. I should be here to see it through to the end."

"You could get hurt. Or worse. You're lucky one of my men saw you sneaking away from your car back on the road there." He pointed toward my parked car. "Now let me take you to my man."

I stood my ground by crossing my arms and taking a firm stance. Roan's exasperation could be felt by his heavy breathing.

"I really don't have time for this." He looked heavenward, shook his head and blew out a heavy breath. "Okay, but you stay behind me. Do you hear me?" He grabbed me by my shoulders and turned me so that I was forced to follow him to the cabin.

"Yes. I promise."

We stood there for what seemed an eternity. Roan looked at me. I stared back, wishing . . . what? *Get a grip, Charlotte. This is a dangerous situation . . . in more ways than one.*

Roan turned toward the cabin then made some sort of signal to his crew. Soon, we were joined by four more officers, one the female deputy who'd been at Boopsie's on the night of my arrest. Roan gathered his troops around him and half-whispered and half-gestured his orders. At his signal, the group began advancing on the little cabin. Roan motioned for them to stop at the edge of the clearing before looking at me. "You stay put. Do not follow me. You hear me?"

I nodded and hunkered down behind a large pine.

Roan and three of his men made their way to the cabin, stopping beneath the windows on each side. Officer Travis, the lone female officer, remained with me.

How the people inside didn't know we were outside was a mystery. Every sound seemed amplified a thousand times over. Dried pine needles crunched beneath our feet. Twigs snapped. Animals scurried through the forest. The wind, gentle as it was, moved trees which creaked and moaned with each movement. And those dogs still barked in the distance.

Travis knelt beside me. "Stay here."

I nodded.

She made her way to the window on the right side of the cabin.

As soon as Travis joined her fellow officers, I moved as quietly as I could to the left, the side I'd seen Roan take. He was nothing but a lump within the shadows of a cluster of pines and a few bushes planted near the cabin. I inched up next to him, holding my breath for fear of being found out.

"I told you to stay put," he whispered.

I opened my eyes wide, shrugged, and held my hands, palms up.

Roan held his fingers to his lips when he thought I was going to speak again. He shook his head, then jerked his chin toward an open cabin window. If ever I should keep my big mouth shut—now was it.

A voice shouted from inside, "If you'd done your job and killed her when I told you to, none of this would have come out." A female voice. One I recognized. I took a slow breath.

Yep, I'd guessed right.

Lanie Kellogg kept talking in her trademark New England accent. "How many people are we going to have to take care of now? Huh? You want to tell me that?"

"Look, I had no way of knowing she'd find all this." Another familiar voice. "I took records from the courthouse long ago. Tore pages from old books. I did that for us. If I ever get rid of my wife, I told you, no one will know, and we can be together."

"And what about him?"

"We can take him out, too. He's not my kid. I never could stand the brat."

Well, that answered that. Max, for sure. And he was willing to kill Cam, the boy he'd raised as his own, his namesake. Heartless—that's what he was.

"So, how are we going to get out of the murder of that nosey girl?" Lanie asked.

Footsteps—the kind made by red patent stilettos—on the wooden floors within the cabin followed her question. "Boopsie?"

"Of course, Boopsie. Who'd you think I was talking about?"

"I told you, I didn't do it. My mother came in and hit her with the iron skillet when she heard Boopsie threaten me."

Lanie paused before saying, "Well, I guess I believe that. Crazy old bat. You should have taken that skillet and hit *her* with it." More walking.

Roan shifted his weight, a twig snapped, and he cringed.

"What was that?" Lanie asked.

"Forest sounds," Max practically yelled. "You hear them out here all the time. Trees creak, branches snap, pine needles crunch, animals run about. Forest sounds."

"Well, we have this one last batch of acid ready to hit the streets," Lanie said, her voice now a provocative melody. "Sometimes it pays to have friends in the know."

Man, she was evil.

"Let's get Hal and Doo out here tomorrow and get this in the hands of our dealers," she continued. "There's a lot of money to be made. The crop won't be ready until another month. That should net us at least another million. It's so deep in these woods, they'll never find it. After that, we can get out of this little nothing place, head back up north. Divorce or not. We can change our names. Get married up there. Live out our lives together in luxury."

"But what about all those people? There's too many to get rid of all of them."

"Accidents happen every day. And every single one must be an accident. Got it?"

"So, who's on your list this time?" Max sounded weary.

"You can start with that meddling genealogist," she said, and I swallowed hard. "And do us both a favor and make hers painful. Then you can move on to your crazy mother. I'd like to take care of your wife, but I'll let her live. She's too stupid to even guess at anything anyway. She never suspected our little affair. She won't figure this out, either. Cam here can have a night-time hunting accident. Tonight."

So, wait a minute. Cam was inside? With them. Roan and I exchanged a look of realization.

"What about Rose Haven and all this timberland? That was supposed to be mine one day. I've as much right to it as Marge Mayhew.

Jackson was my father, too."

"I know, Darling. But, you aren't going to need that old place. You'll have me and we can have homes all over the world."

I'd heard about all I could take. I stood, and when I did, my bag slipped from my shoulder and hit the ground with a *thunk*.

Max shot out the door and onto the porch. "Who's there?" His footsteps traveled to his right side and he looked into the darkness toward us. The porch light glinted off the blade of the knife he carried as he jumped to the ground.

I didn't wait for instructions. "Max? Is that you?" I asked as I came out of the shadows and casually walked toward him, even as my knees knocked together.

"Well, well," Max said as he ambled toward me. He stopped then and watched as I moved to stand mere feet from him. "Seems you keep getting lost in these old woods."

"Apparently, I can find my way in, but I can't find my way out. I was trying to get my compass to work, but it was so dark, I couldn't see it. Dropped my bag trying to get my flashlight out." *Just sound silly and incapable.* I forced a giggle. Would Max buy my story? Maybe. But before he could respond, Roan's officers stormed the cabin. Two in the back as he and the other two ran toward me and Max.

I attempted to duck and run, but Max grabbed me before Roan could push me out of the way.

Max pulled me against his chest, hard against my back.

"Let her go, Max," Tank's voice, powerful and strong, came from behind, inside the cabin. "There's no way for you to get out of here. We've got you surrounded."

More officers stepped out from the edge of the forest, firearms aimed at Max ... and me.

Roan moved closer to Max, who still held the knife against my throat. My height, or lack of it, caused me to struggle to keep my feet on the ground. "You heard the sheriff. Let her go. You've got no way out of this."

Max's grip tightened and he chuckled. "You wouldn't shoot me. I've got your precious *Charlie*." The cold blade of the knife rested against my neck, forcing my chin up. The smell of Max's after shave didn't agree with my nose at all. Then again, Aqua Velva never did. It would be so like me to sneeze while Max held that knife to my throat.

"Haven't you heard?" Roan said, his eyes never leaving Max's. "She's not been *my Charlie* for quite a while now. And precious? He chuckled. "Only in her own mind, believe me."

What was Roan saying? Was he faking his dislike for me? Or had the words he'd spoken to me before been the lies? He could have been using me for what I might learn... or ...

I jerked, rammed an elbow into Max's side, then brought my heavy boot down hard on his foot. He stumbled and, as he tried to catch his footing, I kicked him in the exact spot my daddy had always told me to if I ever found myself in such situations. The knife dropped to the ground as he went down for the count.

Roan rushed forward, kicked the knife toward one of the other officers, then grabbed Max who lay in a fetal position. "Maxwell Lawrence, you're under arrest for . . ."

"*Precious*? In my *own* mind?" I stormed.

Time stopped, even as the racket of officers dragging Lanie out of the cabin, her hands cuffed behind her, reverberated on the front porch.

With all eyes now on me, I squared my shoulders, chin lifted toward Roan. "Well, Mr. Roan Steele ... I'll show you precious!"

And with that, I marched out of the woods—not losing my way even once.

Chapter Thirty-four

By mid-morning, I sat in the conservatory in Rose Haven, surrounded by Mama and Miss Marge. Aunt Becky, Uncle Angus, and Fee were on their way over. A phone call to Mama relaying the middle-of-the-night happenings had apparently softened any hard feelings between the family.

"I'm so thankful all of this is over. I don't ever want to live through anything like this again." Mama sat next to me, holding my hand.

"It's okay, Mama. I doubt I'll want to get involved in such. Ever … again."

"I think I'll go make us some sweet tea and bring in some teacakes as a little mid-morning snack." Until now, Miss Marge had been unusually quiet. "I don't know about the rest of you, but I'm a little hungry."

I got to my feet to follow and realized that eating when nervous was definitely genetic. "Let me help you, Miss Marge." For once, Mama didn't have to prompt me by clearing her throat or using one of her looks.

"I really don't need any help, dear, but if you just want to, then that's okay. It is a long way to carry a heavy tray."

Mama left her seat to join us, but we stopped in the grand entry hall when a knock came at the door.

"I'll get it," Mama said. "It's probably Becky and her family." As Miss Marge and I continued toward the kitchen, Mama opened the door to Aunt Becky, Uncle Angus, and Fee with Ned, followed by Serena, Cam, and Roan. Behind them, Olivia and Tank. "My." I heard my mother say. "This will be quite the surprise for Miss Marge. Come on in, all of you."

I'd expected my family, but not Serena and Cam, the sheriff and Olivia, and certainly not Ned or Roan. I scurried around the kitchen with Mama and Miss Marge.

"Oh, my," Miss Marge clucked. "This is quite the gathering, isn't it? Shall we just sit here and enjoy our tea and cookies?" She indicated the long kitchen farm table.

"That sounds perfect." Aunt Becky bustled at taking glasses from the cupboards, just like before. She turned and smiled at her sister who took her hand and squeezed.

I arranged the teacakes on a platter, then searched for other goodies and found Mama's Aunt Vada's famous coconut pound cake. It was a little early in the day, but with everything we'd been through in the last twenty-four hours, we deserved all the sweetness life had to offer.

As I sliced it, I stole a glance at Mama, who looked at Miss Marge. The two women smiled at one another, an obvious mother-daughter moment. I knew that look. It was one of the nicest moments of my life, getting to see my mother share that look with her own mother.

"Sit, sit," Miss Marge ordered. "Everyone. Just grab a chair. I'll go call George."

"No need, Margie-girl. George is right here." He came in and placed a light kiss on Miss Marge's cheek. She blushed like a proverbial schoolgirl.

Gathered around the table, with her friends and family, Miss Marge couldn't hold her emotions in any longer. Tears sprang from her eyes. "You have no idea how good it is to be sitting at this table in this big old house, surrounded by *my* family, getting to claim you all as my family for the first time in my long, long life. You all have warmed the heart of this old woman."

George smiled at her. "You're not as old as you make out to be, Margie-girl."

"So, tell us how you all figured out this puzzle." Uncle Angus, always one to cut to the chase, just like Aunt Becky. "Who's the one who put all the pieces together?"

"That would be Charlotte," Tank said around a bite of cake.

"I don't know about that. I just put pieces where they needed to be. Anyone who does genealogy could have done it. It's simple stuff. I'm not a pro, really."

Miss Marge patted my hand. "Well, you are to us . . . your family."

"Charlie has always been good with puzzles and details," Roan said. And just like him, too. Always was one for adding his opinion.

Olivia smiled as she squared her shoulders with pride. "That is why I had the good sense and good luck to hire her to head up the WHS."

Uncle Angus raised his glass. "Hear, hear." He took a sip of sweet tea.

The group followed suit.

Mama was next. "Go on, Charlotte. Tell them how you put all those pieces together."

"It wasn't all me. I couldn't have done it without each of you. Tank sent off for papers I needed. I doubt they would have sent some of them had they not been requested by the sheriff. Records aren't released to just anyone when the subjects are still alive. Even if you are family. And I couldn't prove I am family at that time. As a matter of fact, I was a bit surprised. Not totally, mind you, but a bit. When I did my genealogy, I discovered things we'd never thought of before. Like the fact that Mama isn't fourteen months older than Aunt Becky, but closer to nine."

"Now, that isn't possible, Charlotte Graves," Serena said. "I may be a diner owner and know a lot more about food than genealogy, but I know that isn't possible."

"Well, I knew that, too, Serena. When I got the divorce papers from Nevada along with the marriage license for Nana and our grandfather, combined with Mama's *real* birth certificate and then Aunt Becky's so soon thereafter, I knew something very weird was going on. At first, I thought they had written the date wrong. I've seen that done before, but this time, they were both right. When I dug further, I learned that Miss Marge was Mama's birth mother and that Sophia—Nana—had only raised her as her own. She gave birth to Aunt Becky when Mama was a little over nine months old."

"But how were you able to determine that Miss Marge was her birth mother in the first place?" Olivia asked.

"Simple. I asked. If you want to know something, sometimes it's best just to go to the source. I was pretty sure, but I didn't want to embarrass Miss Marge or Mama. Or even Aunt Becky and her family. But I had to know. All the problems with Boopsie hinged on finding out the truth."

Fee cleared her throat. "When Charlotte and I stumbled upon a secret room upstairs, we found a photograph of a woman holding a baby. The woman was wearing a Huguenot necklace like the one Charlotte often wears." Fee smiled at me.

"Oh . . . the little nursery. You girls found it." Miss Marge looked from me to Fee, back to me as I fingered the Huguenot cross. "That necklace you're wearing, Charlotte, was a gift from Father to me when I was a girl. I gave it to Mary for Christmas many years ago. I suppose you gifted it to our Charlotte?"

Mama simply nodded.

"Charlotte's right about needing to know the truth.," Tank said. "We do feel that Boopsie was ultimately killed because she knew family dynamics that certain people didn't want the town to know."

Aunt Becky looked at me. "But, I still can't imagine wanting to protect my reputation by killing my niece. Miss Sarah had a much darker heart than we could have ever imagined."

"Well, she did it for two reasons," I clarified. "One was to protect her reputation, the other was to protect her son." I glanced around the room. "Tank just told me that as they were arresting her, she yelled out that Boopsie deserved it for threatening her son's reputation."

"Oh," Tank added, "that isn't all of it. She was so mad she yelled out, *'Just like Constance deserved it for taking my place at Rose Haven. It should have been mine. Jackson, the land, the position, should all have been mine.'*"

Miss Marge's face fell. "Wait a minute. What are you saying, Sheriff? That she *killed* my mother?"

"I'm afraid so, Miss Marge."

"So . . . she didn't just *trip* and fall down the stairs?"

Tank shook his head. "No, ma'am. We will reopen the case, of course. Take it from an accidental fall to a homicide."

Miss Marge worked her fingers for a moment before adding, "Well, I—I just—I can't believe she *killed* my mother. How could my father have had any feelings for such a person as Sarah? She certainly had us all fooled."

Olivia shook her head. "I still can't believe that Jackson Mayhew was Max's father and Sarah Harkins was his mother. He never *once* told me that. In almost thirty years of marriage." She paused as if to allow it to sink in one more time. "Furthermore, how on earth did that frail-looking woman manage to lift a skillet and hit Boopsie hard enough to kill her?"

"Oh." I placed my iced tea on the table and wiped my mouth with a napkin. "When Fee and I were at her home a few weeks ago, I noticed she had hand weights and an exercise bike in a front room. Who would have thought that Miss Sarah was the exercise type?"

"Yes. That was quite a surprise to us, too. But as for Max?" Tank's eyes found Olivia's and I couldn't help but notice that Olivia's had begun to brim with fresh tears. "He was keeping all manner of secrets from you, Olivia. The least of them being his relationship with Lanie Kellogg."

"They say the wife is always last to know." Olivia swiped a tear before it escaped to trail down her cheek and ruin what I supposed was a fresh coat of makeup. "I guess that's true. I didn't even suspect. Shows you how bad our relationship had gotten."

"Well, I'm glad you found out, Mama." Cam reached over and kissed his mother's cheek. "I never did like that man, and now I know why. I was never anything like Max. I always guessed my father was someone else." Thankfully, the fake southern accent was no more. Cam sounded like any other of Loblolly's fine men.

"You did?" Olivia asked, clearly surprised.

"I did. Mainly because I just couldn't stand the thought of that man being my father." He nodded once.

"Cam Lawrence, you never told me." Olivia looked at her son, her hand clutching her owl pin.

"No. I didn't. There was no sense in both of us being miserable. And I knew you would be if you knew that I knew."

Olivia turned to Tank. "But you knew all along, didn't you? That Cam was your son?"

The sheriff blew out a breath as a pained look crossed his face. "I suspected. Especially since Cam has so many of my old characteristics. The way he holds his mouth when he's thinking hard. Even the way he walks. Or in his case, struts."

The group broke out in laughter.

"That is so true, Tank." Serena turned to Cam sitting beside her. "You both strut when you walk into my diner."

Cam picked up Serena's hand and kissed it. "That's because I'm trying to impress the prettiest girl in town."

Serena blushed, matching the pink daisies dangling from her ears.

"Uncle Angus, what's going to happen to Max and Lanie and all the others involved in this drug ring?" I asked.

"Well, they'll get a fair trial, but I suspect they'll all be convicted. The evidence against them is overwhelming. Lanie and Max will be dealt with the harshest." He looked around the room. "We don't cotton to things like that around here, so I'm betting the judge will give them twenty-five to life. The others, a few years. They weren't involved in the murder and the threats of murder. All depends on the jury and the judge."

We all sat in silence for a while.

"So, Charlotte, you and I are still cousins, right?" Fee asked.

"Yep. Even though our mothers are half-sisters, we're still cousins because Alexander Jones fathered both our mothers. He was married to both Miss Marge and to Nana."

Fee cocked her head and rubbed her cheek. "I still don't understand the relationships. Can you explain it a bit better?"

I took in and released a deep breath, then looked at all the other faces. Each one seeming to agree with Fee. "When Constance died, no one expected foul play. They thought it was a fall, pure and simple. But Sarah hung around Rose Haven so much due to her friendship with Miss Marge."

"That's right. She was a constant companion to me before and after my mother's untimely death. It was sudden, but none of us ever suspected that she'd been deliberately killed. It just looked like she'd tripped on the stairs." Miss Marge dabbed at her eyes. "Sarah pretended to be my friend when all she wanted was my father and to be mistress of Rose Haven. After Mama died, I couldn't cope with the loss. But life had to go on. Papa was too important to the community. Sarah was here and she just naturally moved into that position since I was not capable of doing so."

Fee looked across at me. "But what about Nana and Alex? I still don't understand how——."

I looked at Miss Marge who urged me on with a nod of her head. "Jackson wasn't fond of any of the young men who showed an interest in his only daughter. He found every one of them unworthy. Considered all of them gold diggers." I took a sip of my sweet tea and placed my glass on the tabletop. "But Miss Marge and Alex refused to cow-tow to his demands that they not see each another." I smiled at her. "So, they eloped. Their few days together before they returned to Loblolly produced my mother."

Aunt Becky couldn't contain herself. "I still don't get what happened. *Exactly* what happened."

Miss Marge lowered her head for a couple of seconds to gain her composure. She then looked up and sighed. "My father could be a very harsh man. Cruel, even. When we returned, I didn't know I was pregnant, of course. I'm not sure if it would have made a difference or not, but that's no matter. Papa threatened to ruin Alex if I didn't agree to all his demands."

"Which were?"

"Papa had some business connections in Nevada. He fixed it so that Alex would have a job out there. He'd go and then, after the appropriate time, he would file for divorce. All very hush-hush, of course." She smiled weakly at Mama and Aunt Becky. "Sophia and I were friends, but I had no idea she was in love with Alex and had been for some time. And I suppose I was as surprised as anyone that, as soon as she learned of Alex's leaving, she took off after him."

"I don't believe—" Aunt Becky started, then stopped when Miss Marge raised a hand.

"We were all so young. So carefree. What did we know? You remember your mother as a *mama*, but I knew the often-impetuous young girl and woman. By the time I realized I was pregnant with Mary, three-almost-four months had passed. Alex had gained the divorce and Sophia had gained Alex.

"When Daddy found out that I was pregnant, he knew that to admit to such a thing would be to admit to forcing Alex to leave. And, of course, with Alex and Sophia now married . . . I knew the best thing, in the end, for our child was to be brought up with *two* parents, no matter how much I loved her. And no matter how much Papa loved Mary, he knew it, too. So, when Alex and Sophia returned—and Sophia newly pregnant—I handed over Mary." She raised a finger. "*But*, with a condition, which worked out okay for a while. But I suppose you can all figure out . . . what . . . Oh, dear Mary, if only I had had your and Charlotte's strength back then. Things would have turned out so differently."

Mama laid her hand on top of her mother's. "You did what you had to do, Miss Marge. None of us knows what we would have done in such a circumstance." She looked at Aunt Becky. "And Becky, if they hadn't done as Jackson wished, you wouldn't be here. And neither would Fee."

Fee spoke up at that. "Well, I can say that I'm very happy things turned out as they did." She turned to me. "And Cam is your cousin, but not mine?" Fee asked, a smile registering with a wink.

"That's true, too. Distant cousins. It's complicated."

"It always is when you're involved," Mama said.

The group laughed again.

"So," I continued, "the bottom line is that poor Boopsie knew every bit of this all along. When we were kids, she thought it was cute to tease me. I think she meant well by the time we were adults. I'd like to think that if I'd stayed in Loblolly rather than running away from the truth all those years ago, she and I might have become friends. Her mother planted her diary after the police searched her home. She knew me well enough to know I'd not let it be."

Mama placed her hands flat against the kitchen table. "Well, to think that Sarah killed her great-niece is more than I can bear."

"No one deserves that," I said. "But I plan to clear Boopsie's name and reputation at our next meeting. If that's okay with you, Olivia."

"By all means, Charlotte. It's the least we all could do to remember her."

"Well, let's get this kitchen cleaned up and get on home," Aunt Becky said. "I don't know about y'all, but I'm ready for a nap and it's not even time for lunch."

***

Later that afternoon, after naps in the conservatory and a late lunch, I sat on the front porch of Rose Haven with Roan. We rocked in unison as I stroked Oreo, who sat curled in my lap.

"This has been an unbelievable few weeks." Roan rested his head against the high back of the rocker. He gazed into the distance where the sun made a slow descent. The ducks out on the pond quacked. A few remaining fireflies flitted about, blinking private messages to one another.

"Mm-hmm. It has." I looked out over the beautiful land that was Rose Haven. "They won't have to exhume Miss Marge's mother, will they?" I rocked, too, and breathed in the lingering scent of honeysuckle and roses as Oreo purred.

"No. Sarah's confession is enough. And it's been such a long time." He stopped his rocker and turned to me. "Still mad at me?"

"Maybe," I teased. At some point, I'd figured Roan out ... but it didn't hurt to let him squirm a little.

"So, can we talk now?" he asked.

I stopped the rocker and gazed over at Roan who looked at me, hope shining in his eyes. I set the rocker in motion again. "You haven't talked enough for one day?"

"I barely said anything."

"Mmm. I noticed. Other than *stay here. Do not move. Do you understand? Do as I say.*"

"Ouch," he said with a smile. "Do I sound like that?"

"Not exactly, but you may as well have."

"Well, I was just trying to take care of you, keep you out of harm's way."

"I know that. Just as I know that you weren't kissing Boopsie all those years ago."

"You do?" His rocking stopped as he shifted to face me better. "Well, it's about time you told me."

"Truth is, I knew it then. It was just easier to run away than it was to admit I was wrong about you and then to have to make a commitment I wasn't ready for."

"Is that why you left? Commitment?"

I nodded.

"I wish you'd stayed and talked it out with me." He ran his hand through his hair. "Look, I wasn't ready for a commitment, either. We were kids. The only thing I wanted was a promise that we'd have a future. One day. Nothing else."

I looked at Roan. "I really messed up, didn't I?"

He grinned. "Nothing that can't be fixed."

"You think so?"

"I know so. How 'bout if we start over? Maybe as friends this time. No commitments for the moment. Just dinner every now and then. A Friday night game during football season. Maybe an Alabama game."

"What?" I feigned shock. "No way. Auburn or no go."

He laughed. "How about if we take turns? One week, Auburn, the next Alabama?"

"Sounds . . . workable."

"And Charlie, if you feel compelled to go digging up dirt, promise you'll let me help."

"Hmmm. I'll have to think about that. I kind of like having Fee as my sidekick."

Roan stood, then tugged me out of my rocker, causing Oreo to jump to the porch. He pulled me to him and gave me a quick hug.

"So, friends, then?"

I held out my hand which Roan took in his. "Yep. Friends. And one more thing. I think I can promise to at least let you know if I'm about to go digging up dirt."

We stood at the porch rail, looking out at one of the best sunsets ever, as Oreo meowed her approval of our new-found friendship.

Years ago, I had run away from Loblolly. Then, a few months ago, I had run back. No. I had come home. And coming home to Loblolly was proving to be a blessing ... in many ways.

A Few Recipes & Notes from the Author

Wouldn't you love to pull up one of the ladderback chairs in Miss Marge's kitchen and have a homecooked meal with her and the family? You may not be able to do that, but here's the next best thing—recipes for a few of the mouthwatering meals served in that warm, inviting kitchen.

I grew up in South Alabama, at my granny's heels, watching her cook. And my daddy was a mess sergeant in the Army. He attended baking school at Ft. Benning in Georgia during WWII and cooked for over three thousand soldiers each day while at Camp Hood, as Ft. Hood was called in those days. He taught my sister and me how to cook many things. Mostly, he just pointed to the kitchen and told us to clean up our mess afterward. He believed in learning by doing and making mistakes.

I've always been surrounded by wonderful cooks. My four sons have followed in some mighty big footsteps. They are all great cooks who prepare amazing homecooked meals. Son number two even makes his own breads.

I admit, I don't normally use recipes. I cook by intuition, I guess you'd call it. A bit of this, a pinch of that. The five men in our household, husband included, haven't complained about much, although none of them liked my batter-dipped, fried cauliflower.

I hope you enjoy making these recipes. Southern food at its finest.

Blessings,
Debbie

Chicken and Dumplings . . . Southern-Style
(Slick dumplings like my granny made!)

Ingredients
1 5-pound hen or chicken pieces of your choice
Cook chicken in boiling, salted water until tender
2 cups self-rising flour
¼ cup vegetable shortening (I can tell you, my granny used lard)
¾ cup boiling water
Salt and pepper to taste

Directions
Cook hen or chicken pieces in boiling water until tender; remove chicken from broth. Let the chicken cool, then remove it from the bone and set aside.

Measure one quart of the broth into a large saucepan. (I use my big soup pot.)

Bring to a boil and add chicken.

Put flour into a large mixing bowl. With a pastry blender or two forks, cut in the shortening. Add the boiling water, a bit at a time. Shape the flour mixture into a ball and roll out on a floured surface to a 1/8-inch thickness. Cut into strips, then cut strips into smaller squares.

Drop the strips into the boiling broth, a few at a time, cover after all are in the pot, cook for 8 to 10 minutes. Add salt and pepper to taste. Yields 6-8 servings.

Aunt Coty's Lemon Cheese Layer Cake
(One of my fondest childhood memories of food was my Aunt
Cleolua Draghon Dupree's Lemon Cheese Layer Cake.
It takes a bit of time, but the result is so worth it.
Definitely a South Alabama delight.)

Ingredients (for the cake)
1 cup shortening (Crisco)
2 cups sugar
3 ½ cups plain flour
1 Tbs. baking powder
1 tsp. salt
1 cup milk
5 egg whites, stiffly beaten (add last)

Directions
Cream shortening. Gradually add sugar and continue to cream until light and fluffy.

In separate bowl, mix dry ingredients.

Add dry ingredients alternately with milk.

Fold in the beaten egg whites.

Pour batter into three or more greased and parchment paper lined 8-inch layer pans.

Bake layers at 350 degrees for 25-30 minutes or until toothpick inserted in center comes out clean. (You may make a few thin layers if you wish. Adjust cooking times for this.)

Ingredients (for the lemon cheese filling)
2 sticks butter
1 cup sugar
5 egg yolks, beaten
Juice and grated rind of two lemons

Directions
Combine the ingredients in top of a double boiler. Cook over hot water, stirring until it becomes thick. Cool, then spread between the layers, on the sides, and top of the cake.

So tangy! This icing is like a lemon curd.

Don't be confused. This is a layer cake, *not* a cheesecake. In fact, its name is pronounced thusly: LemonCheese (without a pause between those two words, but a light pause before "cake." Or as I have it, a layer cake. Not one bit of any type of cheese in sight.

I hope you enjoy this truly Southern cake.

Merle Smith Williams's Famous Southern Meatloaf

(For the basic meatloaf, I mostly use my mother-in-law's recipe. I do add a bit of seasoning and the topping is my own creation.)

Ingredients

1½ pounds ground beef (use more if you have a big family)

1 cup cracker crumbs or stale bread broken into pieces (these days, I use canned breadcrumbs)

1 onion, chopped

½ bell pepper, chopped (I use red ones but you may use any or all colors)

½-cup shredded carrots

1 egg, slightly beaten

1½ tsp salt

¼ tsp pepper

½ can condensed tomato soup

Water if mixture seems too dry (add slowly, no more than ¼ cup at most)

(Here's a trick my daddy taught me: add 1 teaspoon baking powder to your meat mixture. It keeps it from drying out so much. I also do this when I make hamburger patties).

Directions

Combine all ingredients and form into a loaf, then put into a loaf pan.

Ingredients (for the topping)

½ cup ketchup
¼ cup dark brown sugar
1 tsp prepared mustard (the bright yellow kind)

Directions

Combine the above and spread over top of meatloaf.
Bake at 350 degrees for 45 minutes. Yields 8-10 servings.

Alternative Ingredients

I can change the way this tastes by the seasonings. For Italian, I use Italian breadcrumbs and I add about ½ cup grated Parmesan cheese to the meat mixture. For the topping, pizza sauce is delicious. You may sprinkle this with a bit of the Parmesan or another cheese of your choice.

For Greek, I add Feta cheese and my own Greek seasonings to the meat mixture. I top with Feta cheese during the last 10 minutes of baking time and leave off the above topping. Combine:

Dried onion flakes
Dried lemon peel
Dried oregano
Dried mint

The mint has a strong flavor, so don't use as much of that as the other ingredients. I go by look and smell. Start with a teaspoon of each, ½ teaspoon mint. Or simply used any brand Greek seasoning. No more than 1 tsp.

Mama Vada's Coconut Pound Cake
(For this recipe, do NOT preheat your oven!)

Ingredients
1 cup butter (2 sticks)
2/3 cup shortening (Crisco, solid)
3 cups sugar
5 eggs
3 cups flour (regular)
1 tsp. baking powder
1 cup whole milk
1½ tsp. coconut flavoring
1 cup flaked coconut

Directions
Cream together the sugar, butter, and shortening. Add the eggs, one at a time.

Sift together the flour and baking powder. Add this to the creamed mixture, alternately with the milk and the coconut flavoring. Stir by hand the flaked coconut. Bake in a tube pan at 325 degrees for 1 ½ hours. (I bake mine in a bundt cake pan. Take out about a cup or so of the batter if you choose to use the bundt pan, as this will be too much batter for that pan. Bake yourself a little cake as a treat for being so good to your family.)

PUT IN COLD OVEN.

This is such a good and gorgeous cake. You will not believe how good your house will smell while this is cooking.

This recipe was given to our family by my sister's mother-in-love, Vada Cross Foshee Grissett. I can't begin to tell you how many times we have made this. My husband hates coconut, but he loves this cake.

It's no wonder "Mama," also known as Polly Graves, whipped up one of these for dessert at Miss Marge's.

Granny's Tea Cakes

(My sister asked me not too long ago if I remember eating our Granny's tea cakes. I do, but it isn't a memory that stands out. Granny made so many delectable dishes, tea cakes seem to pale in comparison to others. Sis and I lamented that we don't have any of our granny's recipes. I doubt she wrote down anything. They were all stored inside her mind and her heart. This recipe is from my husband's grandmother, Alice Thames Findley Smith. She was born and grew up in South Alabama. She is buried in the cemetery with at least five or six generations of her family. Her great-grandmother was Emily Katherine Travis Brantley, sister of Lt. Col. William Barret Travis, commander of the American troops at The Alamo. WBT's uncle, The Reverend Alexander Travis, founded the little church, now known as Brooklyn Baptist Church, which sits at the side of the cemetery in which Granny is buried.)

Ingredients

    1stick butter
    1 cup sugar
    2 eggs
    1 Tbs. buttermilk
    ¼ tsp baking soda
    *Flour (Note: she didn't include the quantity. See below.)

Directions

Cream butter and sugar. Add eggs, buttermilk, then soda. Add flour and beat until it is of a consistency that can be rolled out. Roll out on floured board and cut into small cakes. Bake at 350 degrees until golden brown.